"OUR SHIP IS NEAR AMERICA AND CAN LAUNCH ITS MISSILE."

McCarter laughed mockingly, not wanting to believe the terrorist leader, but deep down knowing that the man spoke the truth.

"Oh, yes, you know it's true," al-Warraq said. "I would say that in approximately ten minutes there will be widespread death in the city called Dallas. Yes, I would think many people will die."

Manning appeared at the door to the bridge. "What's he talking about?"

"He's claiming they got the missile off and it's going to hit Dallas."

"I can't believe it," Manning stated. "Ironman wouldn't let that happen."

"Believe it," Encizo said, holding a headset to his ear. "I've just checked a secure channel. They've scrambled a response team. God help them all."

DON PENDLETON'S

STONY

AMERICA'S ULTRA-COVERT INTELLIGENCE AGENCY

MAN®

SENSOR SWEEP

A GOLD EAGLE BOOK FROM

WORLDWIDE®

TORONTO • NEW YORK • LONDON
AMSTERDAM • PARIS • SYDNEY • HAMBURG
STOCKHOLM • ATHENS • TOKYO • MILAN
MADRID • WARSAW • BUDAPEST • AUCKLAND

First edition August 2006

ISBN-13: 978-0-373-61968-9
ISBN-10:   0-373-61968-5

SENSOR SWEEP

Special thanks and acknowledgment to
Jon Guenther for his contribution to this work.

Printed in U.S.A.

SENSOR SWEEP

To the men and women of the United States Coast Guard

PROLOGUE

South African coastline

The caves were dark and damp, the perfect place to hide a small army.

That was just one of the many things Major Kern Rensberg had learned about his surroundings. A native of Cape Town, which was less than an hour drive from his current position, Rensberg had never considered someone might use the lower hills and caves of Table Mountain for such a purpose.

At first, Rensberg's superiors in the Intelligence Division of the South African National Defense Force had chosen to avoid matters of national security, since that kind of work was left primarily to the South African Secret Service. Rensberg's branch focused on domestic intelligence or with matters that threatened military stability. But at Rensberg's insistence, his superiors finally let him pursue his theory that a new terror cell was operating in the country with strict orders to return in thirty days or less with tangible proof.

Below his observation point, a massive ledge that overlooked the cavern, teams of men were busily unloading trucks stored with a variety of sensitive electronic equipment and materials that Rensberg's experience told him could only be used for building portable launching pads. In the midst of the busy group stood a tall, bearded man in a scarlet kaffiyeh and wearing on his arm an emblem of the Kaabar, the symbol of the Qibla organization.

Rensberg had become quite familiar with this man over the past several weeks. His name was Jabir al-Warraq, and while he claimed to be a peaceful member of the Qibla organization—appearing quite often at their demonstrations across Cape Town and other South African cities—Rensberg knew an entirely different man. Al-Warraq was anything but peaceful. The major had it on good authority that this particular man was responsible for the deaths of at least a dozen innocent citizens.

Over the past three weeks Rensberg had based his entire theory of a potential terrorist plot on the comings and goings of al-Warraq. He knew everything about the man, including his background, his associates, his habits and even the number of women with whom he kept company. In fact, Rensberg had a diary with him and detailed everything regarding one Jabir al-Warraq, and it now seemed he would see a return on his diligence.

Despite the activity, Rensberg kept his eye on al-Warraq, and the arrival of a new man—one that Rensberg had never seen before—commanded his attention. It surprised the South African to see the two men embrace in a very warm and traditional fashion, but the noise generated by the men working in the seaside cavern drowned the details of their conversation. Rensberg knew they were speaking in Arabic, a language in which he was fluent, but he could only catch a word here and there. Rensberg shifted slightly on the ledge, moving just enough to get his digital camera into position. He snapped several shots, hopeful that the portable lamps they had set up below illuminated the camera enough to adequately light the exposures. Rensberg took about ten shots—three of al-Warraq and the new arrival, and the remainder of the operation. When he'd completed that task, he returned the digital camera to the deep, well-padded hip pocket of his fall parka and then withdrew a notebook. After making several notations, he replaced the notebook.

But in that moment he also dislodged a rock and some loose gravel that spilled over the side of the ledge. Rensberg turned to watch the rock fall, involuntarily grinding his teeth and sucking in his breath. In spite of the noises in the cavern, there was no question he'd given away his position even as he listened to the rock bounce and clatter down the face of the ledge. Al-Warraq and his visitor turned and locked eyes with Rensberg.

Time to move.

The South African scrambled to his feet and raced for the tiny opening in the cavern through which water had once flowed. Fortunately the ledge wasn't accessible from the central part of the cavern, so the terrorists had apparently been unaware of the existence of the hole. Rensberg could feel the thumping in his chest and the blood rushing in his ears as adrenaline kicked his heart into high gear. He practically slid through the narrow hole, cutting his hands on the smooth, razor sharp sandstone. He squeezed his tall, lithe frame through and nearly continued over the side of the ledge. That led to a drop that ended on boulder-size outcroppings, worn smooth by years of crashing waves in Table Bay.

Rensberg continued carefully but with due haste along the ledge and soon reached where it branched off to an incline that led onto a wide, flat ledge. His hard rubber soles slipped on the sandstone slick with an earlier sprinkle. As he topped a rise he was surprised to see a half dozen or so Qibla hardmen rushing toward him armed with wicked-looking machine pistols. Rensberg quickly scanned the area for cover but discovered the terrorists had cut off his escape route.

The South African wheeled and headed back toward the ledge, hopeful that he could find another way out of this situation.

The major slipped and slid down the ledge, suffering abrasions to his hands as he worked to steady himself and prevent complete loss of footing. The ledge appeared and he jumped onto it, then headed in the direction of the hole. Perhaps it would buy him additional time. He knew the terrorists could put only one man on the ledge at a time, which would slow them as a group.

The South African stopped short when he saw the man al-Warraq had been talking to emerge from the hole. It was startling, this predicament in which he now found himself. He couldn't understand how the man could have possibly climbed the sheer wall of a twenty-foot cliff. Even more disconcerting was that the short, swarthy man with the long beard reached to the scabbard on his left side and withdrew a slender knife. Rensberg estimated the blade was a foot to eighteen inches in length, curved, and it appeared to be razor-sharp.

Rensberg reached behind him and lifted the tail of the parka to grasp the butt of his Vektor SP-1 sidearm. The grip felt comforting, and Rensberg couldn't resist a smile of relief.

The Arab shook his head in a barely perceptible fashion. "You smile at me to mask your true fear."

"I'm just wondering why a little chap like you would think it so easy to take me," Rensberg said as he drew his pistol. "I believe there is a saying, 'never bring a knife to a gunfight.'"

The man spit at Rensberg's feet. "A filthy, American saying. But it does not matter because you shall not live to see the sun set."

Rensberg reacted to the man's sudden movement by squeezing off a round. He missed. His adversary's reaction was lightning-swift. He'd never been much of a shot. He tossed a capsule at the South African, then ducked into the hole.

Rensberg looked down as the object struck his chest and exploded. Something splashed into his eyes, some kind of gritty liquid, and he immediately began to rub at them. The fluid burned his eyes, but not intensely; it had more the effect of salty or chlorinated water.

As his vision cleared and the world came back into focus, Rensberg's scalp began to tingle, then he started to sweat. His heart was still beating rapidly from the physical exertion, but his breathing seemed unaffected. The burning sensation had stopped, but Rensberg was beginning to feel odd. He was beginning to feel woozy, then his vision started to blur again. Rensberg shook his head and could feel something wet and warm leaking from his eyes. He reached his hand to clear them again and was shocked to see he'd come away with blood tinged with streaks of yellow.

The sweating increased and the warmth in his crotch caused him to realize he had suddenly relieved himself. A foul odor assailed his nostrils, then his extremities began to convulse uncontrollably, first his arms and then his legs. But through his still blurry and rapidly dimming vision he could see the man had emerged from the hole once more and he could hear the man begin to laugh.

BLOOD, SWEAT AND other bodily secretions began to ooze from the infidel dog, Mahmed Temez saw, and he couldn't resist the urge to laugh. God had guided his hand when he tossed the capsule filled with Jabir's latest triumph. The chemical, code-named "musrah," acted quickly and effectively. Musrah didn't know mercy or remorse, friend from foe.

This would be an abomination of desolation unlike any foretold in the Christian Bible. This would go beyond anything, any victory they had known before, and it would earn every member of his cousin's organization a rightful place in Paradise.

So Temez watched with satisfaction as the man convulsed and bled and sweat and soiled himself. And he danced too closely to the ledge, but before Temez could act, the man toppled over the side. Temez watched helplessly but not without some fatalistic interest as the body bounced off the cliff face several times before smashing into the rocks below.

"Mahmed!"

Temez looked up to see al-Warraq approach. The look in his cousin's eyes, the reddening of his face, told the entire story. Al-Warraq obviously wasn't happy with the circumstances. The Qibla leader looked over the ledge and then pinned Temez with a disgusted look.

"You were not supposed to kill him," he said quietly.

"My apologies, cousin, but he would have shot me if I hadn't done something. But it isn't without value. This man reacted just as expected to musrah. It works."

"Of course it works," al-Warraq replied, not without

a mocking hint of satisfaction in his voice. "And it shall also work when we complete our plans."

Temez nodded, excited by the thought that soon, they would embark on their journeys. He peered over the ledge and said, "What of the body?"

Al-Warraq shook his head. "The tide will come soon and wash it away. And even if it is discovered, the water will have washed away any evidence. It will look like a simple accident."

Temez nodded. "Then perhaps we should go. There is still much to do."

CHAPTER ONE

Stony Man Farm, Virginia

Once again Harold Brognola had gotten the go-ahead from the President of the United States to call together the toughest and bravest men on Earth to face down a major threat against the world.

Able Team assembled first, since Rosario Blancanales had already been at the Farm and was resting following minor injuries received in his last mission. It didn't take long for them to recall Carl Lyons and Hermann Schwarz, who were camping in the nearby Blue Ridge Mountains.

The men of Phoenix Force, on the other hand, were returning from a mission in Buenos Aires when Stony Man got the call to action, and even at top speed it still took nearly eighteen hours for them to arrive. The weariness was evident in their faces.

The lights in the War Room snapped out, everyone got quiet and then a flickering appeared at the doorway. Suddenly, Barbara Price's lilting voice broke into a rendition of "Happy Birthday," which was quickly joined by the rest of the team, some on key and others horrendously not. Still, the spirit of the moment surprised Brognola, particularly when he remembered the festivities were for him. He shook his head and smiled self-consciously.

By the time they finished singing, Price had walked forward and reached him with the very large cake topped with candles. Brognola stared at it a moment, then his eyes took in every face. He supposed he should say something based on the looks he was getting, but he wasn't sure he could find a voice to do so. As they continued to stare at him expectantly, the big Fed's heart softened so much that he had a difficult time choking back the unsteadiness in his voice.

He cleared his throat to cover and said, "They say that the difference between friends and family is that you get to pick your friends. Today, I realize that's not always true. I am a very fortunate man, not only because of my family and health but also because of you, my extended family. Each and every one of you are the best. Thanks for remembering my birthday." Most of the rapt expressions gave way to smiles as he gave the group another pass, and then concluded, "Now enough of this sentimental stuff. Let's have some cake!"

Everyone in the room broke into hoots and cheers. A moment later Lyons rose, purposefully strode to

Brognola, bent and kissed the Stony Man chief on top of the head. Uproarious laughter rippled through the room as Lyons returned to his seat, David McCarter and Gary Manning slapping him on the back as he passed by. Brognola just shook his head while shaking his fist at Lyons, but then he couldn't keep up the facade and joined in the laughter.

As it started to quiet with the consumption of cake, Price took a seat and put her hand on Brognola's forearm. Quietly she said, "Hal, Mack really wanted to be here, but he got logjammed on a personal mission and just couldn't make it in time. He said he hoped you'd understand—" she slid a small, plain box in front of him "—and he told me to make sure you got this."

Just a small, simple box, and yet Brognola couldn't imagine what was inside. Finally, after a nod and knowing smile from Price, Brognola lifted the lid, then gingerly lifted the brand-new pocket watch from the case. The spring mechanism of the cover jumped aside effortlessly with the press of an elegant release nestled into the top. Buried in the face beneath the precise gold hands was the image of an all too familiar symbol: an Army marksman's medal.

"There's something engraved on the back," Price told him.

Brognola turned it over and read the inscription, which was engraved in script lettering. It read, "To Him Who Lives Largest: Happy Birthday, Old Friend. MB."

Brognola was shocked, unable to speak for having received such a generous and classic gift from a man to whom he owed much more than was ever repayable. Still, Bolan never seemed to take that into account. In the Executioner's eyes there was no account, and this was his own unique way of saying so.

Brognola grinned. "Make sure after we're finished here that we find a way to contact him. If the poor guy can't be here for the festivities, the least I can do is to thank him personally."

Price nodded and then turned her attention to the teams. "Okay, we'd better get started. You can eat and listen at the same time."

"Calvin might have some trouble with that," T. J. Hawkins joked. "He's getting senile."

"I got your senile, puppy," James cracked as everyone started laughing.

"Big words from such an old fart," Hawkins shot back.

"All right, let's cut the banter and get to business," Brognola said. "We have a situation and not a whole lot of time, so we're only going to highlight the details. You can study the files in transit."

"Where we headed, Hal?" McCarter asked.

"South Africa," Price answered for Brognola. She nodded at Aaron Kurtzman, who dimmed the lights from a computer console, then a young, handsome face appeared on the wall screen. The man had graying hair and dark eyes, was middle-aged with a slightly ruddy complexion. He was dressed in a military uniform, and there was something pleasant behind the eyes.

"This is, or 'was,' I guess I should say, Major Kern Rensberg," Price began. "Two weeks ago, his body washed up on a beach in the Cape Town suburb of Sea Point. The local authorities estimated he'd been dead three days."

"He's South African military," Gary Manning stated.

Price nodded. "The South African National Defence Force's Intelligence Division, to be exact. As all of you probably know, the seventies and eighties were choppy water where intelligence services for South Africa were concerned. It wasn't until 1994 that they established the National Intelligence Coordinating Committee and reorganized their intelligence services."

"Rensberg was a career guy all the way, people," Brognola interjected helpfully. "Very dedicated, and well respected by superiors and subordinates alike."

"Well, I have to believe there's a little more to our being here than the death of an intelligence agent," Rafael Encizo said.

"You bet," Price said, nodding at Kurtzman, who tapped a key.

The next picture displayed two Arab men, one wearing traditional garb and the other dressed in military-style fatigues.

Price continued. "This is just one of the many pictures that were recovered by South African Secret Service officials. The SASS took over the investigation from the military once they realized the impact of these photographs, and rightfully so since foreign intelligence-gathering falls into their jurisdiction. Apparently, Rensberg was on some kind of special thirty-day assignment approved by his superiors. He strongly suspected that there was an international terrorist cell operating in South Africa, one financed by al Qaeda, coincidentally. Based on the evidence found on his body, the SASS now believes he was correct.

"The SASS intelligence liaison to the U.S. Embassy in Pretoria identified the man on the right in this picture as Jabir al-Warraq. He's practically a legend in Cape Town and a card-carrying member of Qibla."

Encizo looked puzzled by that one.

"Did you say Qibla? The anticrime protestors headquartered in Cape Town?"

Price nodded.

"That seems very strange to me, too," Gary Manning chimed in. The burly Canadian was familiar with nearly every terrorist group in the world, and was a sort of aficionado on terrorist activities. He had served as a member of the Royal Canadian Mounted Police force's antiterrorist unit, then as an explosives instructor with Germany's GSG-9 before his induction into Phoenix Force.

"Qibla is an offshoot of People Against Gangsterism and Drugs, an organization started in the sixties. It isn't large or politically powerful, its members keep pretty much to themselves and are only usually concerned with the domestic crime problems in South Africa."

"Agreed," Carl Lyons said. He turned his attention to

Price. "Phoenix Force has the bigger experts on matters of international terrorism, Barb, but I know enough to know that Gary's right. I can't see any credibility in the theory of a connection between the Qibla and al Qaeda."

"Maybe not," Brognola interjected, "but based on this information the South African government is taking that theory very seriously, and so is the Man."

They all knew to whom Brognola referred: the President of the United States. It was at his discretion and pleasure that both teams served, and all of Stony Man for that matter. If he was concerned about the situation, then Hal Brognola was concerned about it and that meant a mission, plain and simple.

"We haven't yet been able to identify the other man in this picture," Price said. "Aaron, please show them some of the others."

The cybernetics expert did as requested, cycling through the next few. There were images of men offloading equipment from trucks and views of sensitive electronics equipment, their padded cases being opened and inspected, as well as barrels upon barrels of fuel. The quality of the photographs made it very difficult to make out most of it, but they were clear enough to get the general idea.

"We've had to enhance many of these so that they're printed to near opacity," Kurtzman remarked. "Although the camera Rensberg carried was waterlogged, it wasn't internally damaged, so the digital images remained intact for the most part. Mostly we think it was just the poor lighting that affected image quality."

And if that was Kurtzman's assessment, everybody believed it. Affectionately known as "The Bear" for his gruff exterior and his warm, generous heart, the bullet that had paralyzed him for life had affected neither his brilliance nor his indomitable spirit. Kurtzman headed Stony Man's cybernetics team, which included Carmen Delahunt, Akira Tokaido and Huntington Wethers. His genius was surpassed only by his devotion to duty, both of which spoke volumes when it counted most. His improvements in information and intelligence-gathering, and his monitoring of operations, had saved the lives of every person in the room more times than any of them cared to count.

"These pictures are believed to have been taken in the same place," Price said. "What you're seeing in this picture, in fact, are the notes SASS analysts think Rensberg scribbled in reference to the photographs, and after some analysis of our own, we agree. You see, Rensberg had been smart enough to keep most of his information in this notebook, all of his case notes, the habits and such of this al-Warraq. But what's even smarter is he wrote in grease pencil."

Lyons understood what it meant. "Kept it waterproofed."

"Correct," Price said. "And according to his notes, these pictures were taken in some caverns near Table Mountain."

Calvin James whistled. "That's a big place."

"The problem is that Rensberg didn't say exactly where," Brognola replied. "That's where Phoenix Force comes in. You guys are going to South Africa to help in the search."

"My team is already working on ways to use recent improvements to the satellite to track clues that might point to their location," Kurtzman added. "We'll have everything on-line by the time you get to Cape Town."

"Your liaison will be the same one who worked with the Ambassador Volt's people in Pretoria," Price said. "Her name is Jeanne Marais. She's with the SASS and from everything we know, she's excellent. You shouldn't have any problems."

"We've already received assurances through the Oval Office that you'll get full cooperation," Brognola said. "Sky's the limit."

"Oh, goody, a female type," Hawkins said, rubbing his hands together as Price threw him a flat, unimpressed look. "I wonder if she's single."

"Down, boy," Manning said, patting the youngest member of the team on the head.

"Don't worry, mates," McCarter said, noticing Price and Brognola's expressions. "We'll make sure his shots are up to date before we leave."

"Ha!" Hawkins wagged his finger at McCarter. "None for you if she has friends."

"While I hate to break up social hour," Lyons said to

Price, "I imagine you didn't call us off vacation just for cake and punch."

"No, you have an equally important assignment," Price replied. "You're getting an all-expenses paid trip to Boston."

"Come again?" Lyons said.

"What gives with Boston?" Schwarz asked. "I'd rather go to South Africa. Maybe pick up my fishing where I left off."

"Two reasons," Price replied. "The first is that Qibla has a representative chapter here in the United States, which just so happens to be in Boston. The second, I'm afraid, is a bit more serious. Now while this information is sketchy, it does seem to have some merit. The SASS believes that the equipment you saw being off-loaded in those pictures may be used for a terrorist attack. They don't know on who or where, but they're convinced that this activity points to something very bad."

"Yeah, but an attack where?" McCarter asked. "They can't do much at the top of a mountain. And I don't think the South Africans believe that, either."

"We think that this equipment is designed for overseas use," Price replied. "Recent records show that a large number of start-up corporations have been buying and remodeling Merchant Marine vessels at South African ports. These corporations were recently investigated and it was determined they were dummies set up to protect someone. We just can't prove it beyond all reasonable doubt, and the South African government's not ready to move without proof."

"And you think the someone these dummy corporations are trying to protect is al-Warraq?" Encizo asked.

Price nodded. "Or one of his representatives. And we're especially concerned about this other man he met with, who as yet remains anonymous."

"It only makes sense," Brognola said. "It's entirely possible this unknown party could be an Iraqi arms dealer, in light of the fact we came up virtually empty in our search for weapons of mass destruction in Iraq."

"We certainly gave them enough warning," Blancanales interjected.

Rosario "The Politician" Blancanales had earned his nickname for two reasons. First, his ability to suppress a potentially hostile situation with a dose of good-natured diplomacy, and second, the plain fact that he was charming enough to sell an ice cube to an Eskimo. Simultaneously, he was a fierce and cunning ally in a firefight and a force to be reckoned with. Combined with Carl "Ironman" Lyons's nut-up-and-do-it attitude and Hermann "Gadgets" Schwarz's skill with electronics, Politician was the perfect complement to Able Team.

"So you think maybe they're going to launch these floating pillboxes and then disperse them to targets that could really be anywhere," Blancanales added. "Am I warm?"

"You're red hot," Price replied. "If Hal's theory about

this mystery man who met with al-Warraq is true, it's possible that Qibla acquired some of those missiles we've always believed were somehow moved by Hussein before the U.S. invasion. Even if we're wrong, and they have some other weapons source off the international arms black market, we can't allow them to just roam the oceans freely."

"And there's another possibility," Brognola added. "We could be dealing with some type of new chemical weapon."

Brognola could sense the mood change in the room. Without question, chemical and biological weapons were the most frightening to the Stony Man teams. With nuclear weapons the enemy just incinerated you, your body reaching ten million Kelvin in a millisecond. Bullets and bombs also usually did a quick number if applied correctly, but chemical or biological weapons were the equivalent of burning to death. It usually involved slow and painful suffering before sweet death claimed a person.

"Now it's only a theory, but it happens to fit some facts surrounding Rensberg's demise."

"What about Rensberg's demise?" Lyons demanded.

"Well, most of this will perhaps sound Greek to everyone except Calvin, but here it is," Price said. "The medical examiner has ruled out drowning, gunshot or stabbing as the cause of Rensberg's death. He deduced it was trauma from fall from a great height, but that the fall was secondary to the acute and rapid onset of hypovolemic shock."

"And in English, that means…?" Lyons replied.

"Sudden, severe fluid loss," James interjected. "And the only thing I know of that causes that kind of reaction is cholinesterase poisoning. The nerves in our body release a chemical called acetylcholine that stimulates the parasympathetic nervous system."

"As relates to the communication between cranial nerves and the nervous system?" Schwarz asked.

James nodded.

"Until about ten years ago, a number of pesticides containing cholinesterase were freely marketed because they're very effective in protecting crops," Price said. "Recently, however, and with the passing of the *Patriot Act,* there are very stringent controls on this kind of material. Anyone caught illegally possessing pesticides or other chemicals with cholinesterase faces a minimum of twenty years in a federal penitentiary."

"So what exactly is this stuff?" Hawkins asked.

"Cholinesterase is an enzyme," James explained. "It turns acetylcholine into choline and acetic acid and when the body is exposed to it in high quantities all muscle control and fluid regulation goes haywire. Victims will go into seizures and simultaneously urinate, defecate and sweat themselves dry. And when third-stage shock sets in, which can be anywhere from three seconds to three hours depending on type and length of exposure, they'll start bleeding from the eyes as the blood coagulates inside the veins, and soon after they're dead."

"Holy cripes," Hawkins mumbled, eyes widening at James's effective verbal imagery.

"Yeah, that pretty much sums it up," Brognola said matter-of-factly. "This is some bad stuff we're getting into, so you guys need to be careful and keep us in the loop. And that goes especially for you, Carl. No cowboy crap this time. I want to know each move, and that's not negotiable."

Lyons nodded his understanding.

"Are there any questions?" Price asked.

After a short silence Brognola said, "Good hunting, men."

CHAPTER TWO

Thomas Jackson Hawkins reviewed the mission information in the manila file folder with feigned interest. The Phoenix Force commando wasn't into much of its contents, which consisted of a lot of history of South African politics and jargon related to its intelligence agencies. Still, Hawkins knew it was a matter of discipline to review every scrap of intelligence provided, so he'd suffer through the information without complaint and try to make the best of it.

Rafael Encizo suddenly interrupted his reading by waving a cup of hot coffee in front of him. "Man, the expression on your face betrays almost too much enthusiasm. Why not try to tone it down some, eh?"

Hawkins laughed, taking the cup with gracious acknowledgment as Encizo took the chair next to him at the table. They were on their way to South Africa aboard a Gulfstream C-20D. The Gulfstream was a versatile aircraft, being large enough to carry a five-man crew plus fourteen passengers, and one of the first choices in most missions due to its range of more than 3,500 nautical miles.

The C-20D was powered by twin Rolls-Royce Spey MK511-8 turbofan jets. Its electronic suite included a surveillance package with a Westinghouse AN/APY-2 slotted, phased-array antenna and Eaton AN/APX-103 Identification Friend or Foe interrogator that could link directly to the Department of Defense's Joint Tactical Information Distribution System. These detection arrays were as powerful as anything in the current Air Force arsenal, and provided communications by digital satellite linkup as well as VLF, VHF and UHF channel monitoring and override.

Built into the aft compartment of the craft was a General Instruments ALR-66 threat warning system, and beneath the rather normal-looking nose cone there were tactical targeting systems hooked to a Synthetic Aperture Radar system that used an APY-3 SLAR antenna extending from the left rear of the cone. While the C-20D didn't have a full-strike military system complete with missiles or bombs, it could be outfitted with a pair of Sidewinder air-to-air missiles or an AGM-65 air-to-ground missile within a few hours. While it didn't have the speed and maneuverability of a jet fighter, at least it wasn't totally defenseless.

Perhaps the greatest weapon of all, however, was the

man flying the C-20. Stony Man pilot Jack Grimaldi's skills were second to none.

Encizo nodded toward the file folder. "Find anything useful in there?"

"Well, I decided to start reading a bit more on this cholinesterase," Hawkins said, deciding to change the subject. "It's nasty stuff, Rafe, make no bones about it."

"Chemical warfare usually is," the little Cuban replied.

"No, I mean it's bad and all, but also a little surprising."

Encizo expressed some interest now and leaned forward to look at the sheet of paper Hawkins was reading. "How so?"

"Well, you remember that Calvin said earlier today that this thing could take anywhere from three seconds to three hours to grab hold of you. But according to what I've read here, that's not exactly true. Normally this cholinergic effect, that's what they call it here, takes some time to spread through the bloodstream."

"Well, Cal did say it depended on the method of exposure."

"Okay, but that's what got me wondering about Rensberg."

Encizo studied Hawkins a moment and then shook his head. "Sorry. You just lost me."

"According to the reports we got from their intelligence people, the ME in S.A. ruled that Rensberg died of a fall from a significant height. The severe fluid loss was secondary. That means he was exposed to this cholinesterase poison before he fell, which also means that it was delivered in the form of either a liquid or gas, since he had no puncture marks and he hadn't been shot or stabbed."

"I see what you're saying now," Encizo said with a nod. "Yeah, that is kind of interesting."

"You bet," Hawkins drawled. "It means that this guy either ingested or inhaled this stuff."

"Maybe they used him for a guinea pig. Exposed him to the stuff and then after he died they tossed him over a cliff."

Hawkins shook his head. "With a digital camera full of pictures and a notebook detailing their operations?"

"You aren't suggesting we were supposed to find him," Encizo said.

"Nothing of the kind," Hawkins said. "In fact, I'm guessing whoever was behind his death was probably expecting we wouldn't find him. But if that's true, it means he was exposed to the stuff very quickly and it's probably what caused him to fall."

"So you think they've found a way to rapidly distribute this stuff into the body?"

"Why, I do believe you have it, Watson." Hawkins knew even as he attempted the British accent that it came out sounding corny. Still, he'd hammered his point home and now sensed he had Encizo in agreement. For some reason he felt he'd need that to convince the others of the potential danger they faced, while maybe it wouldn't take any convincing at all. It made sense to him, and now Hawkins had something else that concerned him. He didn't want to panic his teammates, not that such a thing was even possible, but he wanted them to be aware of the possibility. Phoenix Force had to protect itself, not only because of what was potentially at stake but also for them to remain an effective and cohesive unit. Now, not only would they have to worry about the terrorists dumping toxic missiles on an entire population center, they would also have to be concerned about personal exposure to the cholinesterase chemical.

The others were finally roused from their sleep with an announcement from Grimaldi that they would arrive in South Africa within the hour. As each man joined the pair, Hawkins would fill them in on what they had been discussing. McCarter was the last to join the group, and after firing some additional questions at James about the medical implications, he admitted he had to agree with Hawkins's assessment.

McCarter rubbed his face. "Whatever happened to the good old days of bullets and bombs?" he asked.

None of the other Phoenix Force warriors bothered to respond to the Briton's rhetoric, each choosing instead to visit his own somber thoughts on the subject.

Cape Town, South Africa

JEANNE MARAIS TRIED TO contain her excitement as she watched the plane taxi to a stop in front of the SASS private hangar at Cape Town International Airport. Marais had served with the SASS since its inception in

1994, the result of the established National Intelligence Coordinating Committee. The NICC was responsible for all four of the intelligence services in South Africa. Besides Marais's organization, South Africa had the National Intelligence Agency, which was responsible for investigating domestic matters, the military intelligence agencies and the Police Intelligence Unit. While each unit cooperated with the others fully, they were autonomous and generally restricted to investigating only those cases that fell into their jurisdiction.

Marais had been sorry to hear of the fall of a fellow intelligence officer, but as far as she was concerned Rensberg had been both smart and stupid. It was risky enough investigating areas for which one had no familiarity, but Rensberg had also chosen to go it alone. It was odd that his superiors had allowed him to proceed. The matter should have immediately been referred to the NIA, and if it involved security issues on an international level, which counselors to the NICC deputy minister now believed it had, the SASS would take over. Messy and inefficient were the only words Marais could find to describe the situation.

The engines began to wind down and Marais could see the pilot motion that it was okay to approach. Having a private hangar was one of the many privileges afforded the SASS. All nine commercial airports in South Africa were owned and operated by Airports Company South Africa, including the three international hubs in Cape Town, Johannesburg and Durban. Only because the SASS was a government agency, and because they did a considerable amount of flying in and out of Cape Town, were they able to procure a private hangar for their operations. In most cases, such ventures and luxuries were reserved only for the very rich or prestigious among South Africa's culturally and ethnically diverse population.

Marais watched the men with interest as they deplaned from the Gulfstream jet that, from where she stood, anyway, looked as if it was a bit more than the average executive transport. To the untrained eye, the plane would have probably looked quite normal, but to Marais the antennas and other equipment that bristled cactus-like from its fuselage provided the telltale clues that the aircraft was more than met the eye.

And, she knew, so were the five men that emerged from her. A man with a Coca-Cola can flashed a warm, genuine smile as Marais approached, and offered his hand. His grip was firm but considerate, and he spoke with an unquestionable British accent.

"You must be Marais," the Briton said. "My name is Brown, David Brown."

Cover name, Marais thought as she shook his hand. "It's a pleasure to meet you, Mr. Brown, and welcome to South Africa."

He nodded in way of acknowledgment, then gestured toward his comrades, introducing them by last name as Matthews, Gomez, Jackson and Smith. It was painfully obvious they were cover names, but that went without being said. During her briefing at the SASS headquarters in Pretoria, Marais's superiors had described the men as "specialists" in a variety of areas, and said that the U.S. government liaison at the embassy had made certain "guarantees" about the efficacy of their methods. Marais had hoped the entire intel hadn't been just a line, and, looking at them now, had the sense to believe every word.

She shook hands with each man, then led them to the Lincoln Navigator she'd signed out specifically for the mission. The men stowed their gear and climbed aboard as Marais got behind the wheel. Soon she was on the N2 and headed toward the downtown area.

"I have arranged accommodations for you at The Table Bay Hotel," Marais told them, directing her attention primarily to Brown, who had identified himself as the team leader.

"Sounds nice," Hawkins purred.

She looked at the youngest of the group in the rearview mirror and replied, "Very nice place… a five-star hotel. In fact, it's adjacent to the Victoria & Alfred Waterfront, where there's shopping and entertainment."

"Which we're not going to have any time for, mates," Brown interjected, directing his voice toward the other men, "so don't bother asking. So Ms. Marais," Brown continued, "what did you have in mind for our first move?"

"I was hoping you could tell me," the woman replied. "I understand that all of you are experts in terrorism, and right now I'm ready to take any help I can get. This assignment comes straight from the Deputy Intelligence minister, which means my job's riding on the line."

When the new arrivals remained silent, Marais realized her mistake and added quickly, "Don't worry, fellows, I'm not looking for any career moves. I'm happy where I'm at, and I take the threat of terrorism in or against my country very seriously. And by the way, I expect nothing less from all of you."

"Point taken," Gary Manning said.

"What can you tell us about this Jabir al-Warraq?" Rafael Encizo asked. "We're still a little fuzzy on his possible involvement, and we didn't seem to get a whole lot of information on him."

Marais nodded. "Which you find strange because he's a rather public figure in Cape Town. Am I correct?"

Encizo indicated she was correct with a curt nod.

"Gentlemen, you must understand something up front about my country. Despite our significantly shaky history, or maybe because of it, we take the privacy of citizens quite seriously. We also take the security of our citizens seriously, and unlike in most regions of your country, we generally do not permit citizens to own firearms."

"The right to keep and bear arms in our country is based on the citizen protecting itself from a government takeover," T. J. Hawkins replied. The man's accent betrayed his Southern United States upbringing, so Marais wasn't offended by his patriotic move to defend American laws.

"I'm not attempting to place aspersions on your culture," Marais replied. "I'm trying to help you understand that the citizens of the country rely on the protection of the police as their primary means of security. The right to peaceful protest and political views are just two of those freedoms, and aside from some radical ideas, we've never had any reason to consider al-Warraq a threat."

"Despite the fact he's an Arab with known ties to a domestic vigilante group here in your country?" Calvin James said with some surprise in his voice.

"He is also a citizen of South Africa. He was born in Cape Town, and has just as many rights as any other citizen. When he was first investigated following the 2001 attacks in your country, we didn't find any evidence whatsoever tying him to any terrorist activities with South Africa or abroad. He is politically motivating, yes, and has a number of close ties with local officials, but he has never been caught committing an act of violence, let alone being involved in any conspiracy to do the same."

"So what you're saying," McCarter interjected, "is that the bloke has been running around here doing whatever he bloody well felt like, while making fools out of local authorities as he secretly plans terrorist attacks behind their backs."

"I would say that's a fair assessment," Marais admitted. She knew Brown was right, but she hadn't been much for the way he presented it.

"Okay, so the key is to find this guy," McCarter said. "That means we'll have to get our man in the air while we conduct a ground search. Where do we start?"

"Don't you want to go to the hotel first?" Marais said.

McCarter checked his watch. "If we can do it in high gear, then I guess it won't hurt."

Hawkins leaned forward from the seat and said, "You'll have to forgive his lesser social graces, ma'am, but we got it from our higher-ups that this was sort of a matter of urgency."

"I understand," Marais said. "Frankly, I'm as anxious as the rest of you to get this operation moving forward. I was ordered to wait for your arrival, so we've already lost more time than I would care to imagine. We have actually arranged to take a boat to the area we believe Rensberg referenced in his notes. I'm afraid we'll have to hike the rest of the way in."

"That doesn't sound like it will be too much of a problem," Encizo said. "We've been there before. In fact, I'm sorry to say that we've probably grown a bit used to it."

"Yeah," Manning added. "It'll be like a Sunday stroll through the park."

CHAPTER THREE

Boston, Massachusetts

Thus far, Able Team's trip to Boston had been uneventful and Carl Lyons intended to keep it that way; at least until they were ready for a confrontation on their terms.

The Able Team commandos sat in a nondescript SUV on loan from the FBI, studying the massive harborside home intently. Gadgets Schwarz had parked the vehicle directly under a streetlight, somewhat strange under the circumstances, and yet it provided the desired effect. If there were sentries, and Able Team believed that was the constant here, they would be more paranoid of objects they couldn't see lurking in the shadows than those in plain view. The side windows of the SUV were darkened and designed to prevent its occupants from being seen.

Able Team had been fighting a war on America's mean streets for a long time, and those experiences had shaped them into veteran combatants. They knew what they were doing, although it might not have seemed that way to their liaison, Special Agent Nootau Hightree, a Native American of Algonquin heritage.

Lyons had read the dossier on Hightree during their military flight from Andrews Air Force Base to a rented DOD hangar at Logan International Airport. After graduating from a scholarship for statistical analysis at USC Berkeley, the agent had applied for training at the Federal Law Enforcement Training Center in hope of eventually winning a coveted spot as a U.S. Air Marshal. However, his talents for analytics didn't go unnoticed and Hightree apparently jumped at the chance to become an FBI agent. Hightree took his first assignment in Illinois, Chicago, Organized Crime Bureau, then moved on to Philadelphia for more of the same. Now in his eleventh year with the FBI, he was newly assigned to the Boston branch in the Counterterrorism Operations Unit.

"You know, guys," Hightree said, his buttery-smooth voice cutting through Lyons's train of thought, "I've met a lot of people in my years, but you're a serious bunch. The info I got was somewhat sketchy. Who exactly did you say you're with?"

"We didn't," Lyons replied as he looked through the night-vision binoculars.

"We're on that page of the book with the fine print," Blancanales added easily. "The one that says 'don't ask too many questions.'"

"More like the invisible ink, I'd say," Hightree replied.

It wasn't far from the truth. They had Hightree whisk them from the airport to the downtown office where they cleaned up and changed into blacksuits and and well-worn combat boots with rubber-lug soles. They had shrugged into harnesses from which dangled stun and smoke grenades and Ka-Bar fighting knives. Each man also wore a shoulder holster with his favored sidearm. Blancanales carried a Glock 26, Schwarz toted a Beretta 93-R and Lyons had his trusted .357 Magnum Colt Python revolver.

They had also arranged for John "Cowboy" Kissinger to add some heavier firepower, since they weren't sure what they'd come up against. Stowed in the rear of the SUV was an M-16 A-4/M-203 combo for Schwarz. Kissinger had added a satchel with preloaded, 30-round magazines of standard SS109 NATO ball ammunition and a number of 40 mm smoke and high-explosive grenades. As for Blancanales and Lyons, they had decided to go with Heckler & Kach MP-5/40s, which were chambered for the .40 S&W cartridge. The MP-5/40 had two additional features: a carbon-fiber magazine with a two-magazine clamp for rapid change-outs and a 2-shot mode.

However, they weren't planning on toting the heavy hardware for this part of their mission. If at all possible, Lyons wanted this to be a soft probe. Their primary mission in Boston was to get inside and collect information from the computer system. Homeland Security analysts had determined that cryptic messages were being exchanged between computers originating at this address and those companies in South Africa that were remodeling the ships. If it went hard, they'd have to be ready for it and make do with what they had.

To get the information, they'd have to know what they were looking for in the first place, and that wasn't obvious.

"So give us the lay of land, Ironman," Schwarz finally said with a tinge of impatience in his voice.

Lyons lowered the binoculars once more, scratched his chin and replied, "Looks like six sentries, all told. Four men on roving ground patrol and another pair on the roof."

"Sounds like more than just your average security detail," Blancanales said.

"Just what exactly are we planning to do?" Hightree asked.

Lyons showed him a wan smile. "Well, you aren't planning to do anything. I want you behind the wheel in case we need to make a quick exit."

"Or have to give chase," Schwarz said, looking in the rearview mirror with a wicked grin.

"Oh, come on," Hightree protested. "That's bull-shit, man."

"Maybe so, but you're a federal agent and required to obtain a warrant before entering private property," Lyons continued. "We have no such restrictions. We operate with autonomy."

"We're not trying to cut you out of the fun, Hightree,"

Blancanales said. "It's just that we've trained long and hard and we can read each other's moves. Unless you know exactly how we operate, you become a liability."

"I see," Hightree said quietly, looking away.

Lyons clamped a firm but friendly hand on Hightree's shoulder. "Look, you still have an important job, and that's to be ready to cover our hides if this thing goes south."

"Which always seems to be the way it happens," Schwarz added.

"So be ready," Lyons finished.

With a new expression of resolve and trust, Hightree nodded.

"Let's go, guys," Lyons told his crew.

Able Team went EVA and Hightree traded positions with Schwarz, climbing behind the driver's seat as the trio moved nonchalantly down the sidewalk away from the house. Their combat gear was covered by overcoats, which weren't out of line considering it was late November.

After crossing the street and moving parallel to the rear of the houses facing the waterfront, the team reached a four-foot stone wall that encircled the property line of the corner lot. Lyons was the first one over, drawing his pistol and tracking the area to cover the other two as they followed him. They continued through the yard of each house in similar fashion. They crawled the entire length of the backyard of the neighboring house.

It took a while to reach the privacy fence that bordered the target property. Lyons risked a glance over the fence and ducked back in time to avoid being seen by a sentry. He knelt next to his friends.

"There's one sentry visible," Lyons whispered.

"Did he see you?" Schwarz asked.

Lyons shook his head. "We should take him out now."

"Let's not jump the gun," Blancanales cautioned. "If he raises the alarm, this whole party will be for nothing."

Lyons looked to Schwarz for support, but Able Team's electronics wizard simply shook his head. "It's your call."

"All right," Lyons whispered, sighing. "We wait until it's clear."

Lyons began to feel along the fence line until he found a small, rotted area. He noiselessly dug away at it with his fingernails until he had enough of a gap to afford him a view of the yard. He watched the boots of the sentry he'd seen a moment earlier, waiting until the man rounded the far corner of the house and disappeared from view. He then gave his teammates a thumbs-up. The two men got to their feet, then Blancanales immediately went into a crouch with his hands cupped at his left knee. Schwarz was the smallest and lithest of the team. He took his cue and immediately shoved a boot in his teammate's waiting hands. He went over the fence in one smooth motion and landed quietly on the other side.

Blancanales was next, and after he touched down he followed suit with Schwarz, who had already produced his sidearm. The two men provided cover and swept the area with the muzzles of their weapons while Lyons followed effortlessly over the fence. Once all three were set, Lyons was the first to go for the house. Fortunately the grounds were massive and the four-man roving patrol was taking its time. Still, the Able Team leader knew he couldn't dawdle.

There was nothing in their intelligence information that led them to believe the house was wired. Perhaps the Qibla felt that human security was good enough, and perhaps the intelligence had simply been wrong. Either way, they would find out soon enough. Lyons gave the heavy double doors the once-over, looking for any wires or other security devices, and then went about the task of picking the locks with a set he pulled from a slit pocket in his blacksuit. Lock picking was a fine art. To do it successfully was the mark of a skilled burglar. To do it quickly with success—especially in the dark— demonstrated an even higher level of expertise. Lyons had the door open in under a minute.

His teammates made their way past him and into the house while he covered the exterior with his pistol. The three-story home was dark. As their eyes adjusted to the gloom, the room lit only by the streetlights, they could see it was some kind of large den. Blancanales led the way, careful to navigate around a coffee table and a pair of overstuffed recliners. Lyons secured the door and catfooted across the carpet to catch up with his friends.

The trio had memorized the house plans, acquired

from the builder's database through the technical machinations of Kurtzman's cybernetics team. The team knew where it was going and wasted no time getting there. The computer systems were on the third floor. It wasn't ideal, since it trapped them thirty feet above ground level if the probe went hard, but Able Team would cross that bridge if they came to it.

The interior was deserted. A few digital clocks along the way cast the only real light. The silence was deafening, but if the house was in fact unoccupied, they didn't have to worry about being detected. As long as the sentries remained where they were, they could get what they came for and get out in a timely fashion.

NOOTAU HIGHTREE SAT behind the wheel of the SUV and watched the action. Or maybe it was the lack of action. He was still miffed about being left behind, but he knew the leader of this mysterious team was right. He had no "real" authority to enter the premises without a warrant, and he wouldn't have dreamed of doing so. Hightree believed in operating within the code of ethics as proclaimed by the FBI. His organization had taken enough black eyes over the years without his actions adding another.

The legalities aside, he knew good and damn well he wouldn't have violated the code of conduct given his own personal values and morals. Hightree strongly believed that the FBI acronym—Fidelity, Bravery and Integrity—were at the very heart of what he did. As a

Native American, he'd been raised to be proud of his heritage and his country. Hightree had never heard his parents bad-mouth the American government like so many of their peers. His father had served as an infantryman in Vietnam, his grandfather in World War II and Korea. He couldn't think of anything that would have caused him to betray the sacrifices of his blood-brothers in those conflicts.

No, betrayal wasn't a word in either his vocabulary or his nature. He had served with honor and distinction in the FBI, and would continue to do so until he took his dying breath. Which was possibly coming much sooner than anticipated, he thought. A black Town Car cruised past the SUV and pulled to the curb in front of the house. Hightree watched with interest as the driver exited the vehicle, crossed around the back to the other side and opened the rear door.

The back seat occupant who emerged was short with dark hair, but Hightree couldn't make out more than that. However, there was no mistaking the other two men who climbed from the vehicle. They were big and dressed in loose-fitting suits; attire unquestionably designed to hide the bulges of firearms they probably wore beneath their jackets. Before Hightree could react to their appearance, a second Town Car stopped behind the first—parked almost parallel with the SUV—and five more gunners emerged.

Hightree's increased adrenaline caused his blood to

race, but he quickly regained his composure. He had to think about this. His three new friends had left him out here in the event they had to make a quick getaway, but they hadn't said a word about what to do if anyone arrived. Hightree looked at his watch and realized it had only been about fifteen minutes. Assuming that was enough time for the three men, they were now probably inside and searching for what they'd come for. If Hightree permitted the group to enter the house before the team could escape with their information, this entire trip would be nothing.

And Hightree knew he couldn't let that happen, no matter what the cost.

ABLE TEAM REACHED THE computer systems unmolested.

Lyons kept an eye on the door while Blancanales and Schwarz got to work on the computer system. The first step would be to bypass security, a daunting task in lesser hands, but Lyons knew the skill of his teammates. The pair had actually been doing this kind of work longer than Lyons.

"Okay, looks like we're in business," Schwarz told Blancanales. "The computer should boot to the CD-ROM, and then the hashing algorithm will take a few minutes to get the password."

Blancanales nodded as he withdrew the one-gigabyte memory stick from a hidden pocket. The stick utilized a universal serial bus interface, and most computers these days were configured with USB 2 capability. This one happened to have a USB front-side interface.

"We'll have to work fast once we're inside," Blancanales said as he handed the memory stick to his partner. "How long will it take us to download the entire contents?"

"Carmen and Akira swore it would take no more than five hundred megs a minute. Rather than the data actually being transferred, the application Akira created and burned into this stick will go out and create an image of the drive rather than copy it file for file."

"That's why so fast."

Schwarz nodded, then looked at his friend and winked. "We certainly don't have the luxury of spending hours burning files into a CD-ROM, as much fun as I know that sounds."

"Yeah, we never get the good assignments."

"Hey," Lyons whispered harshly. "You two want to keep it down over there? I'm trying to listen for bad guys."

"Sorry," Blancanales muttered.

"Just hurry up and get the inform—" Lyon's began, but he never finished the statement because the unmistakable echo of loud voices reached his ears.

The Able Team warrior gestured to his teammates to continue their work, then left the room and crossed the hallway to another door. It opened onto a bedroom. Lyons padded quickly across the carpet and reached a window.

He parted the sheer curtains enough to take in the scene below. Lyons immediately identified Hightree, who had obviously left the SUV and was now engaged in conversation with several beefy types in dark suits. Two vehicles that hadn't been there before were now parked in front of the house. He couldn't make out much more than that, but he watched long enough to see Hightree flash a badge. A few moments later the thugs had him surrounded. Hightree looked to his rear and obviously saw where the conversation was headed.

Then the group of hoods jumped him.

CHAPTER FOUR

"There's trouble," Lyons said as soon as he returned to the computer room. "Let's go, Pol."

"What about me?" Schwarz asked.

"You stay on that," Lyons said, checking his watch. "As soon as you've got the information, go out the back. We'll meet back at FBI headquarters in sixty minutes."

"Understood," the electronics wizard replied, although his expression said he hated missing out on the action.

The pair raced from the room and descended the stairs. They reached the first floor landing and on Lyons's signal Blancanales went for the door as the Able Team leader found a side window. They'd have to deal with the security team first.

Lyons could only hope they weren't heavily armed. Damn it! What the hell had gone wrong? Hightree's instructions were clear, and he should have kept out of sight. Then again, Lyons wondered if the guy hadn't simply reacted to the thought that Able Team might be discovered. Perhaps all he'd tried to do was to create a diversion, stall these new arrivals long enough for Lyons and the others to get the information and get out of the house. Well, he couldn't fault the FBI agent for that, and if that was the case then they owed Hightree enough to pull his ass out of the fire. He just hoped they weren't too late.

Lyons went through the side window and the first sign of trouble took the form of two of the sentries standing at the corner with their backs to him. They were obviously occupied by the action in front of the house. The Able Team leader knelt but it didn't do much good since he'd made enough noise to attract attention. The pair of guards whirled and peered into the darkness, but neither of them seemed to notice Lyons, who seized the advantage and charged with his KBD1 knife.

By the time the two pairs of eyes had adjusted, Lyons was practically on top of the sentries. He jumped into a flying sidekick and caught the guard on the right in the chest with his heel. The force of the kick cracked the man's sternum and air whooshed from his lungs as his diaphragm collapsed. The guard sailed about ten feet before landing headfirst and breaking his neck.

Lyons landed with the grace of a cat and turned to face his second opponent. The sentry clawed beneath his jacket for his pistol, but the Able Team leader never let him bring it to bear. He slashed downward, cutting a deep furrow in the guard's right forearm and catching sinew, cartilage and tendons, following up with a snap kick to the groin. As the man bent over in agony, the Ironman finished him by driving the knifepoint into the back of his neck. The man collapsed to the ground as Lyons yanked the knife from his neck.

The Able Team commando turned in time to see a sentry on the other side of the expansive lawn raise a pistol and aim it at him. The gunner never got a chance to take his shot, though. Blancanales emerged through the front door and fired twice on the run. The reports from the Glock 26 cracked through the chill night air as both 9 mm Parabellum rounds found their target. The first punched through the sentry's neck, and the second ripped away part of his right skull. The man's finger curled reflexively around the trigger as he went down, but the round slapped harmlessly into the dirt in front of him.

The shooting had drawn the attention of a number of the hardmen on the street who weren't immediately occupied in the assault on Hightree. Lyons started for them, sheathing his knife in and drawing the Colt Python. The .357 Magnum revolver had been his most trusted sidearm for many years. He'd first worn it as a duty pistol while serving with the L.A.P.D., and despite the much more advanced small arms of today, old habits died hard.

The Magnum revolver roared as Lyons took his first target. A 200-grain skull-buster slammed into the nearest thug and knocked him off his feet. Blood and brain matter sprayed the dead man's cohorts as his body hit the pavement. Pandemonium took over as the thugs realized they were now under fire.

Lyons dived for the cover of a large, decorative boulder and once there he keyed up his throat mike. "Ironman to Gadgets."

Schwarz's voice broke through immediately. "Go ahead."

"How much longer?"

"Wrapping it up now, boss."

"Step on it," Lyons said. "This party just went south."

"So I heard, but understood and acknowledged. Out, here."

Lyons and Blancanales laid down a suppressing fire designed more to keep heads down than to reduce numbers. Blancanales managed a lucky shot, catching one of the Qibla gunners with a 9 mm Parabellum round to the thigh. The man spun with the impact as the bullet shattered his hip and dumped him on the street. He screamed and writhed in pain, making it nearly impossible for one of his friends to try to staunch the blood spilling freely into the street. The amount of fluid seeping from the wound left no doubt Blancanales had hit a major vessel.

The remaining crew members took up positions behind the Town Cars and began to return fire, Hightree now obviously forgotten. Lyons hoped that was due to Able Team's intervention and not because the FBI agent was dead. If Hightree bought the farm, they'd have a lot to answer for back in Wonderland.

Lyons popped off another round from the Python, then checked Blancanales's position. He could no longer see his friend, but that didn't cause him worry as much as that he didn't have a sense for where their fields of fire interlocked. If he couldn't see Blancanales, then he couldn't be sure how much room he had on that side. He'd have to implement an extra dose of caution.

Hairs stood up on the Lyons's neck as his sixth sense kicked in. He jumped from his position just moments before the space he'd vacated filled with autofire. Lyons landed at a somewhat odd angle and immediately felt something pop in his shoulder. He bit back the sudden white-hot needles of pain that lanced down his left arm. The remaining sentry who had been roving charged toward him.

Lyons watched the muzzle-flashes and felt chunks of mud and grass pelt his face as the rounds from the sentry's SMG drew nearer. He raised his pistol even though he knew it might be too late.

JUST MOMENTS AFTER LYONS'S transmission, Schwarz finished imaging the computer system hard drive. He practically yanked the memory stick from the computer and stowed it in a pocket of his blacksuit. He thought at first about planting an HE grenade to erase any evidence of their work, but he opted to go ahead and let the algorithms designed by Kurtzman's team do that work.

In short, the program created by the cybernetics wizards at Stony Man would do what it had been designed to do. Right now, Schwarz knew his job was to get the information out of the house and back to the Farm.

But not before he helped his friends.

It wasn't often that Schwarz disobeyed Lyons's orders, but this would be one of those times. One thing his big, blond friend hadn't considered were the two sentries still on the roof. Even if his friends got off the grounds okay, and somehow managed to break through the line of defense forming outside, the enemy still held the advantage of higher ground. Unless Ironman and Pol got themselves under significant cover, they wouldn't just have the ground crew to worry about but they'd also have to contend with overhead fire. The odds weren't good, so Schwarz planned to do something about reducing them before just skipping out.

The electronics wizard slid his Beretta 93-R from shoulder leather as he made his way to the roof by a set of stairs recessed into a wall bordering the third-floor hallway. The house interior was still pitch-black and when Schwarz emerged on the roof the light that emanated from the streetlights was welcome.

The Able Team commando spotted his first mark kneeling at a far corner of the parapet encircling the roof. The terrorist gunner was leaning forward slightly, sweeping the area below with what looked like an assault rifle. No, there would be no murdering his friends from on high—that much was certain. Schwarz raised the Beretta 93-R and squeezed the trigger twice, the 115-grain 9 mm Parabellum rounds punching through the target's spine and neck. The impact flipped him over the parapet.

One down.

Schwarz knelt and swept the roofline with the muzzle of his Beretta. Lyons said he'd counted two. The echoes of gunfire reached his ears, an irritation that he tried to push from his mind—he couldn't allow it to distract him. Staying alive and keeping his friends that way, as well, took priority. The scuff of a soft-soled shoe alerted him to trouble from behind.

The Able Team warrior whirled in time to see the Qibla thug charge him, the point of a long knife glinting wickedly in the moonlight. Schwarz raised his right arm in time to block the overhead stabbing motion of his opponent, but the impact jarred the pistol from his grip as nerves in his forearm and hand went numb. He tried to sweep the terrorist's legs from under him, but the guy was faster. Sheer adrenaline saved Schwarz as the guy tried to distract him with an outside punch while attempting to penetrate his sternum with the knife.

His opponent might have been more agile, but he didn't have the experience of a battle-hardened veteran.

Schwarz blocked the knife attack first, then executed an elbow strike that caught his enemy under the chin. Warm blood sprayed their clothing as the Qibla thug bit his tongue. The electronics wizard followed up with a wraparound of the man's arm just above the elbow, then he yanked upward and snapped the elbow, causing the terrorist to let out a scream as his knife fell from sensory-deprived fingers. Schwarz put a knee in the man's groin, then ended the fight with a ridge hand strike to the throat. As the terrorist dropped to his knees and wheezed, Schwarz retrieved the Beretta and put a bullet between the man's eyes.

Checking his watch, then moving to a parapet near where the first terrorist had gone over, Schwarz took in the battlefield and almost immediately spotted Lyons in a standoff, and it seemed clear the Ironman was on the losing end. A Qibla terrorist was charging his friend, popping off rounds that were close to hitting the mark. Schwarz thumbed the selector to 3-round bursts, hoping the distance wasn't too great as he squeezed the trigger. A volley of 9 mm Parabellum rounds spit from the muzzle, followed by another trio. The terrorist stumbled in midstride, reeled forward and rolled to the dirt, coming to rest just a few feet from Lyons.

The Able Team leader began to look wildly for his benefactor, but Schwarz didn't wait for discovery. He left his position and headed for the rooftop entrance. He only had a few minutes to get to the first floor and make his escape. If the odds were with him, he could escape through the back and circle a neighboring house. That would put him in a flanking position, which might just buy his friends enough diversion that they could get better cover and catch the terrorists in a cross fire.

Yeah, all he needed was a plan.

ROSARIO BLANCANALES HAD earned his nickname for his ability to be diplomatic in almost any given situation.

But there were always scenarios where the other side understood only one type of diplomacy: justice by fire. And that was exactly the kind of foreign policy the Politician planned to implement in this situation. He was about to give some hell back to these Qibla hardmen, because it was high time they started taking some of what they were dishing out.

Blancanales opened those negotiations with a high-explosive Diehl DM51 grenade. The most recent addition to the Stony Man armory, the German-made hand grenade had both offensive and defensive applications. This particular feature was the chief reason for its growing popularity among the warriors of Stony Man.

The Able Team commando managed to circumvent the perimeter of the building and took up a position behind the tree-lined sidewalk of the neighboring house. He darted among the trees until getting within fifteen yards of the Town Car. A quick glance in Hightree's direction confirmed the FBI agent, while having taken a beating, was still moving. The big man would make it.

The same couldn't be said for his aggressors, however.

Blancanales removed the fragmentation sleeve from the DM51, then yanked the pin and lobbed it carefully so that it skittered to a halt beneath the closest war wagon. The concussion of a Diehl in offensive mode was definitely to be admired. The PETN-filled grenade exploded a few seconds later and lifted the heavy Town

Car off the ground. Flaming gasoline and metal fragments sailed in every direction, and the sudden intense heat melted the tires to the pavement. Some of the terrorists were ventilated by shrapnel and glass while others were simply bounced off their feet by the concussion.

"Gadgets to Pol," came a voice as the debris continued to fall.

"Go," Blancanales replied, smiling at the thought his friend had obviously made it out alive.

"I'd guess that was your handiwork."

"That's a roger," Blancanales stated.

"Copy." There was no mistaking the sound of victory in his tone. "I'm on the opposite side. Let's coordinate with Ironman and end this party," Schwarz suggested.

"Acknowledged," Blancanales replied. "Break. Politician to Ironman, where away?"

"I'm in the wind, somehow," Lyons said. "Don't know who or how, but someone's watching out."

"Maybe the man upstairs," Blancanales replied. "You in with us?"

"Yeah," he said. "You got the status on our number four man?"

"Alive and kicking. Just keep them high."

"Understood and acknowledged. We do this on three...."

As soon as Lyons had sounded off a three-count, the Able Team warriors opened up with their pistols simultaneously. The terrorists still on their feet began a grisly dance of death under the unerring accuracy of the gunfire. Blancanales took one of them with a clear head shot. The terrorist's skull exploded like a grape under the impact of a 158-grain 9 mm Parabellum round. From his vantage point, Blancanales could see Lyons begin to pick his way down the sloping yard, moving from one cover point to the next, picking each target carefully.

Blancanales did a quick change-out, then continued to pump out rounds as fast as he could manage. The terrorists were no match for such firepower placed with that kind of accuracy, and before he knew it he could hear Lyons calling for a cease-fire. As the ringing died in his ears, he detected the distant wail of approaching sirens.

The Able Team commando sprinted toward the carnage, arriving at Hightree's side first. He checked the guy's pulse: weak but regular. Lyons joined him a moment later and Schwarz arrived and immediately began to check the bodies for identification. The sirens were growing louder by the moment.

"Let's get Hightree to the car," Lyons ordered. "Quick! Gadgets, you help Rosario. I'll check these dudes."

Schwarz did as instructed.

Blancanales and Schwarz got Hightree up and carried him to the SUV as Lyons went quickly and efficiently through the pockets of the dead. He couldn't believe his luck when he discovered one of the terrorists was still alive.

Lyons holstered his pistol, then hauled the man to his

feet before slinging him smoothly into a fireman's carry. He trotted quickly with his burden to the SUV, tossed the guy into the back seat then slid in next to him. Blancanales had seat-belted Hightree in front and took the back seat while Schwarz got behind the wheel.

"Did you get it all?" Lyons asked Schwarz.

"Sure did. Every last scrap of information on those computers is now in my pocket."

"We'll need to get the information back to the Bear ASAP," Lyons said.

"Understood," Schwarz replied.

"Who's your friend here?" Blancanales asked Lyons.

"I don't know...yet. But he's the only survivor, and I figure that counts for something. I found him covered by the body of one of the others."

"Like the deceased had thrown himself on top of the guy?" Schwarz asked, sparing them a glance in the rear-view mirror.

Lyons nodded. "Exactly." He looked at Blancanales. "How's Hightree doing?"

"He'll pull through."

"Should we take him to a hospital?" Schwarz asked.

"Too early to tell," Blancanales replied. "We had to leave just a bit too hastily for me to conduct a thorough assessment. For now, I'd say the best bet would be to get him someplace where I can check him out better. "

"Agreed," Lyons said. "I'm not exactly big on returning him to FBI headquarters in this condition."

"Yes," Blancanales said with a nod, then gestured

with a thumb at their prisoner. "Not to mention the questions our new friend here will generate."

"Yeah," Lyons mumbled. "I can't wait to hear what he has to say. Sounds like we'd better get the Farm on the horn and see where we can lay low for a bit."

"Why do I get the feeling that the fun's just beginning?" Schwarz asked.

"I still wish we could have gone to South Africa," Blancanales remarked.

"Oh, come on," Lyons said. "And miss all this fun?"

Neither of them bothered to reply.

CHAPTER FIVE

South Africa

As soon as they had checked into their hotel, the men of Phoenix Force got to work.

A light, steady breeze blew in from Table Bay and cooled the sweat on David McCarter's brow. A lot had happened to the fox-faced Briton since taking over as leader of Phoenix Force. As he trudged along the rugged mountain terrain, his eyes roving the surrounding area and ears primed for any transmissions from Jack Grimaldi, McCarter briefly thought of his men. These were his friends and allies; he'd been through a lot with them. Despite such sentiments, McCarter counted himself as one of the most fortunate men on the planet. The men under his command were some of the best in the world.

Encizo and James were accompanying McCarter.

They were up against a critical time factor, so he had opted to leave Gary Manning and T. J. Hawkins in Cape Town. Jeanne Marais was with them along the wharves and docks of the city, looking for the ships that Stony Man intelligence had led them to believe might be somehow connected to the intent of the Qibla terrorists.

High above the trio Jack Grimaldi flew in a special helicopter on loan from one of Marais's contacts inside the SANDF. When the Intelligence Division had realized that they were going to get assistance investigating Rensberg's death from South Africa's Secret Service, they were more than happy to oblige. The chopper contained special scanning equipment, which Grimaldi had enhanced with some additional goodies they had brought from portable equipment stowed aboard the Gulfstream. Included was an infrared and motion detection systems array sensitive enough to detect heat signatures within a six-mile radius from a cruising altitude of up to eighty-three hundred feet. When attached to a forward-looking turret, the AN/APQ-174 radar developed by Texas Instruments provided superior tactical advantages in both targeting and clandestine operations. The chopper was a modified MH-60 Black Hawk, purchased specifically for special operations such as this one.

McCarter keyed up the transceiver. "Papa One to Eagle One."

Grimaldi's voice resounded immediately in his earpiece. "Papa One, go."

"What to report?" McCarter could hear the faint but

unmistakable sound of the blades chopping air far above them.

"Nothing so far," Grimaldi replied, but on after-thought added, "At least, nothing on two legs."

"You must be talking about Papa Three, mate," McCarter quipped, casting one eye in James's direction.

The black warrior flipped him the bird.

McCarter grinned into his microphone. "If the maps are correct, we're near the area where our intelligence thinks Rensberg bought it."

"Understood," Grimaldi replied. "We'll keep our eyes wide open."

"Acknowledged. Papa One out, here."

McCarter turned toward Encizo's position but didn't see the Cuban. He tapped the transceiver three times, the signal for James and Grimaldi that something was amiss.

James stopped immediately and turned in McCarter's direction. The Briton went to one knee and swung the muzzle of his Heckler & Koch G-36E into play. The G-36E was an export version of the German army's standard rifle, designed to conform to the NATO standard for 5.56 mm ammunition. It differed only in the fact it had a 1.5x optical sight, one half as powerful as the one issued with its sister model. In every other way, it was a superior weapon with a cyclic rate of 750 rounds per minute and a muzzle velocity exceeding 900 meters per second.

And David McCarter knew well how to use it.

The Briton studied the area where he'd last confirmed seeing Encizo, which happened to be just short of a small cluster of trees. He turned to look at James, who had taken up a similar posture, his M-16 A-4 assault rifle held at the ready. McCarter turned back and let his eyes sweep the expansive terrain. There wasn't a sound or movement, and now the veteran Phoenix Force soldier knew something was very wrong.

McCarter switched his handheld radio to the ground-team frequency and keyed the transceiver. "Papa One to Papa Two, where away?"

Only silence greeted him.

McCarter repeated the call, but still there was no reply. Finally he switched to their all-receive band and called Grimaldi. "Eagle One, I need you come in closer and do a full sensor sweep."

"Eagle One copies. What's up?"

"Papa Two's missing, mate."

GARY MANNING KNEW the six men were trouble when he first saw them.

They approached in two groups, three from the docks and the other three from the shopping district that bordered the waterfront. Such a public attack seemed bold, but obviously they weren't concerned with drawing attention—or who got in the way for that matter—and their micro-Uzi machine pistols left no question about intent. They were looking for a fight, plain and simple.

They'd come to the right place.

While Manning didn't react with quite the same speed of the younger T. J. Hawkins, he still performed like the veteran combatant he was. Simultaneously he saved Jeanne Marais's life. Manning whipped a .357 Magnum Desert Eagle autoloader from shoulder leather as he pushed Marais behind cover. He aimed toward the group coming from the docks, as Hawkins had already turned his attention on the trio trying to flank them on the side of the waterfront district.

Hawkins fired first, the SIG P-228 barking twice as the Phoenix Force warrior fired a double-tap. Both 9 mm Parabellum rounds caught one of the attackers in the face, the first ripping away part of his jaw as the second slammed through his forehead and blew out a better part of his posterior skull. Brain matter and blood washed over his two counterparts, and seeing that their quarry meant business, the pair dived for cover.

Manning triggered his own weapon twice, the first round missing but the second striking the terrorist's sternum. The guy continued in forward motion, propelled by his zeal, but the legs were rubbery and carried him right into a heavy wire-framed garbage can. The can was bolted to the sidewalk by a thick cable, but that didn't prevent its being upset. The terrorist landed face-first in a pile of refuse and one of his comrades had to jump over his body to avoid being tripped up by the sprawled corpse.

Sheer pandemonium erupted along the waterfront. A number of the Cape Town citizens grabbed their children and ran for cover, while others reacted simply by standing stock-still and screaming at the top of their lungs. Manning's chief concern was that the terrorists would try a different tactic, perhaps grabbing an innocent bystander as a shield. Worse yet, they could simply open up indiscriminately on the crowd with the micro-Uzis. Luck or something else seemed to be on their side, however, as the terrorists kept focus on him and Hawkins.

"What's the idea?" Marais hollered as she got behind a thick electric pole and drew her pistol. "I don't need saving…although you may be in need of some."

"Later!" Manning replied.

Hawkins changed positions, risking exposure to cross from where he'd grabbed original cover. Manning knew the play well. His friend was trying to draw fire away from the innocent targets and redirect it to where it would do the least harm. Manning returned to his own trouble, figuring Hawkins had everything under control on that end.

The big Canadian turned his attention to Marais. "You want to help out here, now's the time."

"What do you need?" she asked.

Manning nodded at her pistol. "You any good with that thing?"

A wicked smile was his answer.

"All right, then, when I go for that boat over there, you start shooting and don't stop until I'm out of the line of fire."

"You could have just asked me to cover you, Matthews," Marais shot back.

"Right," Manning replied, then he was off and running.

Marais moved with admirable skill and took up the firing position of a veteran shooter. She triggered her Glock 28, the compact model of the popular Austrian-made pistol chambered for 9 mm short. She fired a double-tap, her target crumpling to a heap on the ground.

Hawkins was busier, continuing to angle away from his comrades and innocent bystanders in an attempt to gain a better targeting advantage. The area around him came alive with 9 mm slugs from the Micro-Uzis, and the Phoenix Force commando shoved one young woman and her five-year-old daughter to the ground. The child cried out and the woman screamed at Hawkins, but keeping all three of them from being ventilated demanded his attention.

The Texan retaliated by triggering round after round toward the enemy's position. He managed to graze a gunner with one of the slugs, and the man reacted by ducking behind cover and grabbing at the wound. His shrill cry of pain drew his comrade's attention, and in so doing, also drew him into view for a few seconds. It was enough. Hawkins took the terrorist with a clean shot through the neck. Blood began spurting from the man's carotid artery and he grabbed at his neck even as he collapsed from blood loss.

The remaining terrorist fired a group of hasty rounds

at Hawkins, then burst from cover and raced toward the shopping district. Hawkins saw the terrorist drop a mag from the Micro-Uzi and insert a fresh one on the run. The Phoenix Force warrior cast one last glance at the woman and her daughter to make sure they were okay, then leaped to his feet and took off in pursuit.

Manning watched helplessly as his friend raced away. There was nothing he could do about it at the moment. The sole survivor on the dock had opened up with the micro-Uzi, trading shots with him and Marais and keeping both of their heads down. Manning risked moving to cover farther down the dock, eventually reaching a boat. The big Canadian leaped off the dock and caught hold of the stern deck railing of a small yacht. He vaulted it after gaining a foothold on the edge, then jumped over the railing on the opposite side and landed in a huge container filled with fish heads awaiting mass disposal at sea.

Any port in a storm, Manning thought.

The Phoenix Force warrior climbed from the rank container and hit the ground running. He flanked the surviving terrorist and drew a bead on him as soon as he came into view. The terrorist was occupied with Marais, now apparently content to believe that he'd either hit Manning with a lucky shot or the Canadian had simply turned tail and run. Manning shouted for the terrorist to surrender, but it did little good. The terrorist whirled, bringing his micro-Uzi with him.

Manning squeezed the trigger. The .357 Magnum

slug punched through the man's skull, entering just above his upper lip. The impact ripped through teeth, bone and flesh and continued out the back. Manning was in motion, sprinting after Hawkins. Marais could handle this mess here much easier than they could. Besides, he hoped to take at least one of them alive, and he stood a much better chance of doing that if he could catch up to Hawkins.

He ignored Marais's cry of protest as he continued after his friend.

DAVID MCCARTER CAUTIOUSLY approached the area where he'd last seen Rafael Encizo. Calvin James took rearguard. It wasn't like Encizo to just drop out of sight, but it especially puzzled McCarter that his teammate wasn't answering the radio—definitely not good. The Briton couldn't envision that the enemy had taken Encizo by surprise, although he couldn't entirely rule it out, either.

Still, McCarter wasn't buying that—not completely—and he figured there was no point in worrying until he had something to worry about.

Nearly fifteen minutes had elapsed in the search when Grimaldi's voice broke through. "I've got him, Papa One!"

"I'm listening, Eagle One."

"Heat signature directly ahead of your position, fifteen yards max. Signals from the heat source are ours."

McCarter looked at James at his rear, who shrugged,

and then shook his head as he looked ahead of him and squinted. "Check your instruments, Eagle One. I don't have anything directly ahead of me except dried grasslands and a few trees."

"I've already confirmed it, Papa One. Signature is directly ahead of you. I...well, this is odd."

That statement was followed by a very long silence. McCarter thought about doing a radio check with Grimaldi, just to make sure something hadn't gone wrong with the radio system, when suddenly Grimaldi's voice broke through the weighty silence.

"The heat reading I have isn't as intense, Papa One," Grimaldi said.

"Explain," McCarter demanded.

"Well, you're getting much closer to it, but, given the size, you should be able to see Papa Two by now."

McCarter stopped and thought about this a second. The air around them was clear with the exception of the chopper, which ruled out any likelihood that someone was jamming them or sending false signals. Besides, McCarter knew enough to know that it was very difficult to fake infrared readings on a remote sensor. Maybe if someone had programmed it ahead of time. McCarter wasn't buying that since Grimaldi kept the equipment close at hand when they were on missions to prevent sabotage, and the pilot would have thoroughly inspected anything the SANDF supplied on the loaner rotary.

So what did that leave? They couldn't see Encizo and he wasn't up a tree. That left only one explanation: The guy was "below" them. He'd either fallen into a trap, a well, or found some type of bunker. McCarter voiced his opinion to James and Grimaldi, and both agreed it was the most reasonable explanation. McCarter and James hastened forward and quickly found the hole. It wasn't that wide, and it looked natural.

McCarter got on his hands and knees, then snatched the minilight from one of the shoulder straps of his load-bearing equipment harness. He pushed aside some of the dried grass and clicked on the flashlight. A beam pierced the darkness and came to rest almost immediately on the motionless form of Rafael Encizo.

James stood behind McCarter, leaning over but staying a respectful distance from the hole. "What do you see?"

"It's Rafe, all right," McCarter said. "And it looks like he's out cold."

"We need to get him out of there."

"Working on that, mate," McCarter said as he reached to a thick pouch on his belt and withdrew a small, compact grappler. It was attached to one hundred feet of specially designed cord with a tensile strength of fifteen hundred pounds. McCarter handed the grappler to James, who immediately took it to the trunk of the nearest mature tree. McCarter had already played out the rope and was swinging his legs into the hole by the time James returned.

"Take it easy," James said, immediately taking up an anchor position on the rope.

McCarter went quickly and smoothly down the rope, advancing hand by hand, until he reached the bottom. He knelt next to Encizo and let out a sigh of relief when he located a strong, regular pulse. As his eyes adjusted to the gloomy surroundings, lit only by the light streaming through the hole, the Briton noticed a gash on Encizo's forehead. There were no rocks immediately visible; he had to have hit his head at the top or on the way down. McCarter quickly pulled a medical compress from his harness and a minute later had a makeshift bandage around Encizo's head.

"How is he?" James shouted.

McCarter looked up to the some thirty-foot span and grinned. "He's breathing and has a pulse. Looks like he hit his head, but I think he's going to be okay. We—"

Something hard and cold suddenly settled in the pit of McCarter's stomach as hairs stood up on the back of his neck. Sixth sense was kicking in, but not as McCarter would have experienced being in imminent danger. This was something else entirely; almost a sense that he hadn't paid as careful attention to his surroundings as he might have had he not been so concerned for Encizo.

McCarter rose slowly and turned to see that this was more than just a simple hole in the ground. The walls were too convex to be the product of natural design, and now he began to wonder what the hell might be on the other side of the waist-high tunnel, the entrance of which shone in his flashlight. The metal was shiny, indicating it was fairly new, and then McCarter suddenly understood.

He looked up at James. "Calvin, you better get Jack on the horn and see if he can raise Gary and T.J."

"What's up?"

The Briton shrugged. "I could be wrong, but I think Rafe here fell into an airshaft. There's some metal-framed ducting work that goes somewhere here."

James nodded, then keyed his radio. "Papa Three to Eagle One."

"Eagle One standing by."

"Papa One requests you raise the others and tell them to beat feet out here lickety-split. Also, be advised we found Papa Two and he's going to be all right."

"Copy, Papa Three, and that's good to hear. But I was just about to call you. I just spoke with Papa Four and he advised they were involved in something downtown. He couldn't talk, but I got something about they were chasing someone."

McCarter heard that and keyed the switch on his own radio. "What does that mean?"

"Like I said, Papa One, I didn't get more than that."

"Well, then, keep me posted," McCarter replied. "We'll just have to get Papa Two out of here, and we'll advise when ready for pickup."

"Understood. Eagle One is standing by."

CHAPTER SIX

Gary Manning sensed he was gaining on the enemy as he watched Hawkins round a corner fifteen yards dead ahead. He was just coming up on the turn when he heard the first shots ring out. The big Canadian took the corner and brought his pistol to bear, quickly realizing it wasn't necessary as Hawkins trotted nonchalantly to where their quarry lay facedown, and kicked the micro-Uzi out of reach.

Manning joined him thirty seconds later. "Is he dead?"

Hawkins shook his head and replied, "Playing possum." He reached down, grabbed a handful of the man's shirt and rolled him over.

The guy was breathing very heavily and immediately threw up his hands and began to speak to them in Arabic. It took the two Phoenix Force warriors a full minute to quiet him. After Manning caught his breath he knelt and checked the guy's wound. It was just a graze on the right side just below the ribs.

Manning rose and dusted his hands. "Good shot. A little more to the right and it would have been curtains."

"So do you think he really doesn't speak English?"

"I don't know," Manning replied, "and my Arabic's sketchy. But I think we ought to get him back to the hotel and just see how much English he knows."

Manning felt a vibration at his belt and realized from the expression on Hawkins's face that he was also getting it. It was the radio. The two men had switched to vibration mode and tucked the units on their belts beneath light jackets.

Manning switched over to their secured channel. "Papa Four, here. Go."

"Eagle One, here. You copy?"

"Loud and clear, ace. What's up?"

"Papa One needs your support at their location. We've got a class-one situation on our hands. I'll pick you up at the airport and fill you in."

"Acknowledged. We'll be there in about thirty minutes. Out, here." Manning didn't wait for Grimaldi's reply.

"We better get this guy to Marais," Hawkins said. "She can arrange to have him taken to our hotel and held there until we can interrogate him more thoroughly."

Manning nodded his agreement. They had been in the country less than four hours and already things were falling apart. That wasn't a good way to start off the mission. Terrorists had tried to kill them, and now McCarter was calling for support up on Table Mountain. A class-one situation, Grimaldi had said. That meant either a compromise in security or one of their own was down. In either case, it really meant the shit was hitting the fan and McCarter wanted everybody to form on him.

Yeah, it was turning out to be one hell of a day.

BY THE TIME MANNING and Hawkins reached the rest of Phoenix Force, McCarter and James had Rafael Encizo out of the pit. He lay on the ground. Manning felt some sense of relief when he saw the Cuban had regained consciousness.

"How's the patient, Doc?" Hawkins asked James as soon as they stepped off the chopper.

"I'll live," Encizo grumbled. "No need to go all mushy on me."

Hawkins shook his head in mock sadness. "Damn. And here I thought maybe you'd left me something in your will."

"It'll take more than a shallow hole like that to finish me," Encizo said, jerking his thumb to the left.

Manning looked in the direction Encizo had gestured, didn't see a thing then shot a questioning gaze at McCarter.

"He fell into a pit over there, but the blooming thing was hardly shallow," the Phoenix Force leader replied. "It's a good ten meter drop, so he's damn lucky he didn't break something. And he'd be in bloody worse shape if it weren't for that thick skull of his."

"All right," Manning said, "what's this about an air-shaft? Jack mentioned it on the ride out."

McCarter nodded. "The hole is actually a return air vent. There's some wire and metal ductwork that leads from the pit to who knows where. I wanted all of us together before taking a closer look."

Encizo sat up suddenly. "Well, we're all together now, so let's get cracking."

"Uh-uh, Rafe," Calvin James insisted. "You need that bump checked out before I can clear you."

"That's bullshit, Calvin."

"It may be bullshit, but that's the way it is," McCarter interjected.

"I feel fine," Encizo snapped. "I was only out—"

"At least twenty minutes," James finished. "Which means you could have a mild concussion, which also means you pose a risk to the rest of the team until you can be thoroughly assessed. Yeah, right now you seem fine, but that doesn't mean you are fine. Not at least until we get you to the hospital where they can take some pics of your head."

"But I feel fine," Encizo insisted.

"Sorry, Rafe, but I won't risk you or the mission," McCarter said. "I have to defer to Calvin's judgment, and that's the end of it."

Encizo looked just a moment at Manning for support, but the big Canadian shook his head. "You know he's right, Rafe."

Encizo finally nodded and they helped him to his feet

and got him to the chopper. The little Cuban was tough and fierce, but common sense told him that it was better to get a clean bill of health. Not only would it put his teammates at ease, but it would get him back in action all that much sooner. Grimaldi promised James to take him straight to one of the main trauma centers in Cape Town and make sure he got checked out.

Once the chopper departed, the four remaining teammates headed for the pit. It was time to find out just exactly what lay beneath Table Mountain.

IT TOOK JEANNE MARAIS a few hours to get things sorted out with the half-dozen or so local agencies that responded to the events on the wharf. She would have loved to just tell them to all mind their own business, but that wasn't going to work in this case. The South African government had a very strict hands-off policy when it came to local issues, and right now this fell into their jurisdiction. It wouldn't come under the authority of the South African Secret Service until she could provide proof of a threat to national security and get an order from the director to take charge of the investigation.

Fortunately, two of Rensberg's superiors made an appearance, so it comforted her to know that the military was standing behind its promise to support the investigation of Kern Rensberg's death in any way possible. They had acted with considerable unity, sticking close by while the Cape Town police questioned her. She had left the scene with her prisoner, quickly transporting him to the basement of a nearby government building, and leaving him secured under guard until she could retrieve him. She then returned to the scene and immediately reported her presence to the lead police inspector.

"We have witnesses that state you were accompanied by two men when the shooting started, ma'am," the inspector advised in a respectful but brusque fashion. "Where are they now?"

"I'm sorry, Inspector, but I'm not at liberty to disclose that information to you."

"And under what pretext do you not wish to answer my question?"

"Not under pretext, I can assure you, Inspector," she replied, forcing a grin. "I refuse to answer under Act 66."

She watched as the inspector nodded; he knew what she referenced. The *General Intelligence Law Amendment Act 66* of 2000 had been enacted by the President to amend the *National Strategic Intelligence Act* of 1994. One of the provisions in the act stipulated under certain conditions a local agency couldn't compel a member of any federal intelligence service to disclose the identities of contacts or informants if the agent reasonably suspected it would compromise national security. In this case, Marais felt she had evidence to justify her response to this man.

Following the questioning, Marais spoke briefly with Rensberg's superiors before returning to the basement, where she found her prisoner waiting. She nodded her thanks to the two men who had watched him in her absence, then dismissed them with orders they weren't to discuss his existence with anyone, or even acknowledge they had seen or spoken to her. They agreed, and Marais knew these men could be trusted, so she was satisfied with their word.

Marais took a seat across from the prisoner. Slowly and purposefully, she fished a silver cigarette case from her coat pocket, withdrew one, lit it with a matching lighter, took a drag then sat back as she studied the Arab in front of her through curling tendrils of smoke. She finally offered him one, but he declined with only a gesture. She shrugged, returned the case to her pocket and sat forward with her arms on the table—cigarette held carefully out of his reach—and stared into his eyes.

"What is your name?" she asked in Afrikaans.

He didn't answer, but instead looked confused.

In Arabic, she continued, "I know that you can understand me now, so let's stop pretending."

"You speak my language?" he asked, surprised.

"Yes, and you undoubtedly speak mine, but I'm in need of the practice speaking Arabic, so for now I will play your game."

"I do not speak your language."

"Shut up."

The man fell silent.

"Now, I ask you again, what is your name?"

"Fadil Shunnar," he replied, raising his chin some.

"Very well, Shunnar, let me explain your situation. You are charged with the attempted murder of an intelligence agent—me—of the South African State. Because you were in possession of an automatic weapon, and you acted without regard for the life and property of South African citizenry, this crime and all other crimes with which you are subsequently charged will fall under acts of terrorism. As such, you aren't entitled to standard representation, although you will be afforded an opportunity to retain private counsel and plea your case to a magistrate in Pretoria."

Marais sat back, looked at her cigarette and absently flicked the ashes onto the floor as she continued. "If, however, it is determined you are in this country illegally, then these acts will be considered an attack from the sovereignty of foreign soil. This makes your crimes, in effect, acts of war that fall to military and not civil authority, and is thusly punishable by summary execution."

"If this is some tactic to frighten me, it will not work. I am prepared to die for my cause."

"Maybe," Marais replied, "and then again, maybe not. Don't assume that I'm going to just turn you over to my government. They would be too lenient on you, I think. No, I believe that the Americans are much more anxious to speak with you."

That got a reaction—Marais had struck a nerve. Something like fear entered Shunnar's eyes, and his expression became downcast. This wasn't what he had expected. He'd probably hoped for a nice, comfortable cell in some jail in Pretoria where he could await trial or firing squad. But the idea of being turned over to the mysterious Americans seemed much less appealing to him, and Marais couldn't help but wonder if there was something behind that, some key aspect of which she could wield to solicit the terrorist's cooperation.

"Of course, if you choose to talk to me, it's entirely possible you could avoid any unpleasant confrontations. Perhaps, if you tell me of Qibla's plans, I can arrange for your protection."

Shunnar sneered. "Do you think that I am stupid? If I reveal the plans of my people, my life will be forfeit. I am not afraid to die for the cause, but I do fear the curses that will befall me if I die betraying it."

Marais took one last drag and exhaled forcefully as she dropped the cigarette and crushed it under the heel of her boot. She studied Shunnar carefully, looking for any sign of deceit, but she found only fanatical determination—and something else. Something like respect, but not quite that. Maybe the fear she sensed was one of loyalty. Yes, that was it—he was protecting someone. Marais thought she knew who it was and decided to see if Shunnar would play into her hand.

"Why are you trying so hard to protect him?"

"I don't know who you speak of," Shunnar replied quickly.

"Yes, you do," Marais replied. "You know exactly who I'm talking about. We know all about Jabir al-Warraq and his conspiring with known terrorists. We also believe he is responsible for the death of a military intelligence agent. I do not suppose you would know anything about that, either, hmm?"

Shunnar sat in stony silence for a long moment, then asked her for a cigarette. She gave him one, lit it and sat back and folded her arms. She wouldn't leave until she'd extracted all of the information from him she felt he possessed. Somehow, she planned to make sure that Kern Rensberg's death was avenged, but that in the future her country couldn't be used as a terrorist haven.

"I cannot tell you where he is," Shunnar finally said, smoking nearly half of the cigarette in the full minute of silence that had passed. "But you are right in that he's involved."

Marais nodded. "And what is he planning to do?"

"I do not know," Shunnar replied.

Marais let out a scornful laugh. "Sure you don't."

"I do not!" More quietly, he added, "I was not part of the final operation. I was ordered to stay behind and make certain that no one pursued those who would actually participate in Qibla's ultimate plan."

"How did you know we were investigating your operation?"

"From Jabir."

Marais knew it was the truth. "And how did he know?"

"He said it came from our spies inside your government."

"Who?"

"I do not know."

Marais stood and slammed her fist on the metal table. Shunnar jumped.

The sound it produced, like that of a gong being struck, echoed throughout the room. Marais felt the blood rush to her cheeks. "You are trying my patience with your pretended ignorance!"

"It…it is true," Shunnar stammered. "Every member in Qibla is specialized in a particular area. We do not know the operations of each other. This is for security."

Marais sat now, convinced he told the truth. "Continue, please."

"Jabir never discusses such matters with those below him. He confides in no one. He is a very secretive man, and is popular with those that have money or hold prestigious office. He is a difficult man to get close to, and even more difficult to find. I believe he has probably already left the country."

Marais thought about this for a moment. Shunnar wasn't really telling her anything she didn't already know about Jabir al-Warraq, or that she couldn't have surmised from the intelligence profiles they had on him. His activities in the Qibla were well publicized, but it was very true that one couldn't easily gain an audience with him. He was well guarded whenever he made a public appearance, and his social activities were said to be limited to only private homes of the rich and famous, which were quite often well guarded. No written records were ever kept of his movements previous to Rensberg's thorough notes.

Marais pulled a picture from her pocket—a copy of one of the photos found in Rensberg's camera—and set it in front of Shunnar. "Who is this man talking to al-Warraq?"

The terrorist leaned forward and studied the photograph for a minute.

Marais studied his face for any sign of recognition, but she didn't see it. Part of her recruit training into the SASS had been detecting telltale signs in body language or behavior that betrayed nearly any individual during interrogation. Sometimes these were designed to assess if someone was lying, and other times to note particular emotional responses such as love, hate, nostalgia or guilt. Mostly, though, these were techniques designed to assist interrogators in asking specific questions that would guide the interviewee down a particular path.

Shunnar finally sat back and shook his head. "I do not know this man."

"Have you ever seen him before now?"

"Yes," Shunnar said, nodding. "I do remember seeing him once before, but I do not know his name."

"What about this picture? Do you recognize where they are at, or where this picture might have been taken?"

"I do not."

Marais started to become angry again, but kept her temper in check. She had to remain calm and to keep Shunnar that way. For all she knew, he could be lying to her about everything. It might have been a stall tactic or a way to throw her off Qibla's scent. In either case, she couldn't lose control with him. She had to be the one who maintained control.

And, sadly, she would have to keep Shunnar away from the Americans. At least until she had finished with her mission. There were those powerful factions inside the South African government that had their own special interests and concerns about the Qibla threat going public. It couldn't get out, and it was her job to make sure it didn't. This was an election year. It wouldn't do anyone a spot of good if even the hint of this kind of thing were leaked to the public. Shootings like the kind that had occurred at the wharf today could be minimized in the sense of damage control. Press could be bribed and local officials could be told to keep their noses out of where they didn't belong.

And Marais was also responsible for insuring the Americans were kept on a short leash, as well. Let them chase their ghosts in Table Mountain. Even her own people, with advanced equipment, couldn't find any evidence of terrorists hiding or operating anywhere near that area. She didn't give a damn what Rensberg's notes said.

Marais didn't want to do this to her American colleagues, but she didn't see that she had a choice. She'd already kept her word to Shunnar, made him think she could keep them at arm's length, and now she'd have to make good on that. If Shunnar thought he couldn't trust her, she'd never find out who was behind Rensberg's death. His superiors had backed her play against the local police investigator—she owed them. She owed them a hell of a lot more than she owed the five strangers. Except maybe Matthews. Yes, he had saved her life and she owed him a debt of another kind, that, given the chance, she would try to repay.

But the rest of them she would have to keep away from Shunnar until she'd obtained what information she needed. Then they could have him, do whatever they pleased with him. In the meantime, the security of her nation came first, even over the needs of the Americans. She bore them no ill will; she just believed her mission had become more important than theirs, and she would do what she had to do. Jeanne Marais would protect her own.

CHAPTER SEVEN

Boston, Massachusetts

Fortunately for Nootau Hightree, Rosario Blancanales was a skilled medic.

After a thorough assessment and treatment with ice, bandages, a forearm splint and some antibiotics purchased from a medical office in the projects—the kind where the more money, the less questions asked—Hightree was as good as new.

"You'll need to rest up at home for a couple of days, but I think you'll be fine," Blancanales told the big Fed.

"I owe you guys a lot for pulling me out of the fire," Hightree replied.

"You should have followed orders and stayed out of sight," Lyons grumbled.

"Consider us even," Blancanales told him. "If you hadn't provided that distraction we might not have made it out of there with our skins intact." He gave Lyons a you-know-I'm-right look, and the blond warrior decided to shut it down. He couldn't be too hard on Hightree. The guy had saved their asses just buying them the few extra minutes Schwarz had needed to download the information from the onsite computer systems. Now they would just see if this was actually a peaceful Qibla cell or a terrorist faction trying to gain a foothold for whatever operation was coming down the pike.

Lyons looked at their prisoner on the other bed. "What about sleeping beauty there? You think he's going to wake up soon?"

Blancanales rose from the chair he'd placed at Hightree's bedside and conducted a quick assessment. Finally he stepped back with a satisfied grunt. "He's got some superficial burns, but nothing that can't wait for treatment a few more hours. And I don't see anything that makes me suspect he suffered any internal injuries."

"Good," Lyons replied. "I don't want to turn him over to the locals before we've had a chance to question him. Is there something you've got in your bag of tricks to revive him?"

"Assuming the absence of a closed head injury, I think some anti-emetics and smelling salts ought to do the trick."

"And if that doesn't work?"

Blancanales flashed a wicked grin. "Then I'll try a pitcher of cold water."

"Well, don't go that route without me. I want the honors."

The Able Team leader nodded, then Lyons left the main bedroom of the Stony Man safehouse and made his way to one of the three spare bedrooms. This one had been converted by Kurtzman's cybernetics team into an operations center. It had two computer workstations tied into a central server connected with fiber-optic, high-speed data/voice-over-Internet-protocol lines to Stony Man's secured network housed in the Annex.

Gadgets Schwarz sat in front of one of the workstations, his face reflecting the intensity of a skilled professional. His technical skills had saved the lives of his companions on occasions too numerous to count, and Lyons was glad to have him as a colleague and a friend. Frankly, he didn't know what they would do without Gadgets. Lyons wasn't afraid of technology—he didn't have much use for a lot of it. Some of the high-tech toys were great, and Lyons was always up for testing the latest in weapons systems, but he just couldn't get into all the other jazz.

"What's the story, Wizard?" he asked. He spun a nearby chair so its back faced the terminal, and plopped down.

"I'm waiting to get something back on the information I uploaded to the Bear."

Lyons furrowed his eyebrows. "What's taking him so long?"

Schwarz turned and studied his friend. "Give him a little time, Ironman. D-Day wasn't won overnight, you know."

"Would've been if we'd been there," Lyons quipped. "I—"

"Wait up," Schwarz cut in. "There's something coming through now."

At first, Lyons couldn't tell if anything was happening. The screen was completely black. Abruptly, information appeared on the screen, the text dancing by almost too fast for him to make anything out. Schwarz didn't seem to be having the same trouble. Lyons watched as his teammate's eyes moved quickly, seemingly scanning the data and then hitting the Return key to take in more of the same. After about four or five pages, Schwarz sat back, folded his arms and grinned like a Cheshire cat.

"Well?" Lyons finally prompted.

"According to what we pulled off those systems, the Qibla group has definitely been involved with activities of those companies in South Africa. It seems our friends on this end were sort of the business side of the operation. Their books show not only a ton of donations from investors, but also some significant outflow to as yet unnamed sources."

"So they've got entrepreneurs, businessmen and sympathizers financing their cause," Lyons said. "Big deal. Terrorists have been doing that for aeons. There's nothing new about that."

"Maybe so, but there's an interesting twist here. All of these companies specialize in one thing—salvage. They bought up a bunch of old freighters, solely for the purpose of refitting them for active shipping duty. At least, that's what was written on the bills of lading when they were delivered into Qibla hands."

"Yeah, but transport what?"

"Well, we might have a clue to that, too." Schwarz wheeled in his chair and blasted away at the keys. No more than ten seconds elapsed before he had a new screen, this one with a scanned image of some type of document. He emitted an "aha" of triumph and gestured at the screen.

Lyons squinted, tilting his chair forward so he could see what was displayed. "A shipping manifest?"

"Not just any shipping manifest," Schwarz said.

"South Africa," Lyons replied.

"Yeah, Cape Town, to be more exact, which is where they sent David and the boys to take a look-see.

"Lovely," Lyons replied. "Well, the Bear will get that information on that company to them, and they can check it out."

"That's not what bothers me," Schwarz continued. "I know they can take care of themselves. What worries me is some of the equipment listed on that manifest. Oh, sure, there's a lot of the normal stuff you'd expect to see there, but also a ton of stuff that by itself probably wouldn't draw a lot of attention. But I know those materials well."

"What are you talking about?"

"Oh, come on, Ironman," Schwarz said. "Ultrathin aluminum sheeting? Steel slide rails? Electronic and

GPS equipment? Titanium-alloy pallets? Oversize hydraulic lifts with portable loading capabilities? Use that hard head of yours and think about it."

"This hard head of mine has an ache," Lyons grumbled. "I don't want to think about it. Just tell me already."

"That's the kind of stuff you collect when you're plan to build launch pads. Remember all that fuel we saw in those pics Rensberg took? I couldn't really make out the symbol because of the quality, but—" he turned and brought them up on the computer "—looking at them now, I can make an educated guess. Those, my good man, are the markings of rocket fuel."

"Oh, shit," Lyons muttered. "Missiles."

"And you can just bet that they're probably loaded with that cholinesterase Calvin managed to scare the living shit out of us about. Now we—"

Both men looked down simultaneously as their pagers went off.

Damn! That was all they needed right now. Lyons had wanted to question their prisoner, but now that would apparently have to wait. They had done their duty, and delivered the information Brognola and the rest had asked for. What the hell more could they possibly want?

Lyons picked up the phone and punched in the security number that would connect them via a series of cutouts to Stony Man. When Price finally answered, he said, "What's up?"

"We need you to get over to the main Coast Guard headquarters at Boston Harbor." She gave him the address.

"Do we have to? We just ordered out for pizza."

"Leave it for your contact," Price said, giving back as good as she got. "Your country needs you."

"What's going on?"

"Our shores may be under terrorist attack."

USCG GROUP BOSTON'S motto was "Birthplace of the U.S. Coast Guard." It was the unadulterated truth. The Group's operational area extended from the New Hampshire state line border with Massachusetts all the way to New York. Three agencies, all formed during various periods in America's history, had merged to form the USCG. Massachusetts had been at the heart of those mergers. Five lighthouse stations and one command area made up the unit, along with the Coast Guard Cutters *Grant* and *Lockett,* and a small boats interdiction team. LantArea Command was the Group Boston command authority out of Portsmouth, Virginia.

They were a proud and able bunch.

Captain Samuel Bryant, commander of the *Lockett* was at the top of that proud and able list. When the call came in, he scrambled his crew and stood stiffly on the foredeck as they were the first to put out to sea. According to his orders, a heavy commercial freighter originally headed north in international waters had turned and was now inbound. Despite repeated requests for the ship to identify her crew and cargo, the freighter had failed to reply. She had also apparently refused all requests to turnabout—or to halt and prepare for inspection—and was now approaching the twelve-nautical-mile border of U.S.-international waters. Bryant was nearly halfway to intercept when he was called to the communications deck and handed a confirmed message to return to Boston Station to pick up three specialists with the Department of Homeland Security. The orders dumbfounded him.

"Captain on the bridge!" Commander Jude Sherman called as Bryant stepped through the hatchway.

"Orders from LantArea. Come about and put back to station." He turned to the helmsman and added, "Best possible speed, mister."

"Aye, sir," the seaman replied.

"What's the story, skipper?" Sherman asked, ordering a chief petty officer to take control of the bridge before following Bryant out the door.

Bryant got out of earshot of the bridge before stopping and swearing under his breath. "I don't know, Sherm, but I'd guess it's some fat-assed bureaucrat who doesn't trust us to not cause an international incident. Command insists we return to let these landlocked simpletons tag along. They don't seem to care that I have a goddamned job to do here, and I don't have time for this."

"But we're more than halfway there," Sherman said, the tone of his voice indicating he thought it was as preposterous as his superior.

"Tell it to LantArea, Number One. You've got the bridge. I'll be belowdecks. As soon as they're aboard, come get me."

"Aye, sir."

THE SHIP'S COMMANDING OFFICER stiffly studied the men of Able Team as they crossed the gangplank from the dock onto the cutter. Carl Lyons could always tell when someone was scrutinizing him, and this beanpole captain acted as if he should be commanding a Navy cruiser instead of a sixty-four-foot cutter. Well, the Able Team leader didn't have time for a turf war.

"So you're the three with Homeland Security I was ordered to come back for," the captain announced as Lyons extended his hand and introduced himself as Carl Irons. "Great."

Lyons felt his blood begin to boil as he glanced briefly at the man's name tag. "Yeah, nice to meet you, too. Listen, Bryant, as far I'm concerned, you're the boss on this ship—"

"You're sure as shootin' I am, mister," Bryant replied, whirling to call up to the bridge. "Get us under way ASAP and lay in a course for that freighter! Best possible speed!"

"Aye, sir," the big man called. He tossed a salute, then disappeared inside the bridge.

Lyons got close to the officer and showed him a wan smile. "I see you like to get right to the point. That's good, I like that. In fact, my friends here will tell you exactly how much I like that."

"Ironman?" Blancanales said very slowly and deliberately. "Be cool."

"I'm cool," Lyons said, not taking his eyes from Bryant's. "Before I was interrupted, I believe I was saying that you're in charge of this ship. But I'm in charge of making sure whoever or whatever is aboard that freighter never reaches American shores. So, you decide what happens on this ship, but that freighter is our department. Now I could go into exactly who it is we work for, but... I think you can probably guess. So I'll spare needless dick-flexing and summarize by saying that when it's time for us to take that thing down, if I say jump, you ask how high. You got me?"

Bryant's face went beet-red and he became visibly rigid, his lips pressed tightly together. He looked as though he wanted to haul off and hit Lyons, but the uncertainty in his expression said he knew he didn't stand a chance. He simply replied with a stiff nod, then spun on his heel and headed for the bridge.

Lyons turned and joined his friends in preparing their equipment. On the trip to Boston Station, Gadgets had loaded several more spare clips of the SS109 ball ammo for his over-and-under, and checked the workability of the two MP-5/40s Lyons and Blancanales would carry into action. The smoker grenades, along with some high-explosive rounds, would provide an extra-heavy dose of firepower if they should require it. The three

Able Team warriors then slid into their LBE—load bearing equipment—harnesses. Lyons figured their best bet would be a direct approach. The terrorists, if there were any, were expecting standard USCG troops and were hardly prepared to go against experienced antiterrorist veterans like Able Team. Lyons figured that gave them the advantage.

They had just finished donning their equipment when Blancanales noticed Bryant approaching with the perfunctory stride of someone who considered himself more important than he really was. "Look out, Ironman, thy girlfriend draweth nigh."

Lyons started to mutter a rejoinder but thought better. He didn't want Bryant mistaking their banter for infighting.

"What?" Lyons asked.

"We're a half mile to target," he replied. "There's a Jayhawk that came out of Cape Cod already on scene and they're attempting to raise the ship by radio."

"If the freighter continues to fail responding to radio hails or manual signals, what would be your next step?" Blancanales asked, ignoring Lyons's surprised look.

"By the numbers, we'd fire one warning shot across the bow."

"You're equipped with heavy weapons?" Lyons asked.

Bryant shook his head with an expression like a kindergarten teacher who had grown impatient with a child. "Hardly. We're a sixty-five-foot tug and boarding operations unit. Our support comes from the small boat teams, and the *Grant,* which are both under way, as well. But we'll probably be first to arrive."

"What's your armament?" Schwarz asked.

"Small arms only. And, of course, the Jayhawk's loaded with a pair of Mk 46 torpedoes, but that's fairly minimal armament against a freighter."

"And if she doesn't stop with the warning shot, what then?" Blancanales pressed.

"Then we'd take out her rudder and screw."

"Which would put her dead in the water," Schwarz said with a snicker.

Blancanales punched Schwarz in the arm for the pun. The Able Team leader then stood and said, "Well, I'm not against a warning shot, but if she won't heave to, then you'll have to get in close enough so we can board her while she's moving."

"While she's moving?" Bryant parroted. "Are you crazy, man? Why do that when we can stop her dead to rights and board safely?"

"'How high,' Captain. Remember?" Lyons warned.

Bryant remained silent, nodded then performed another perfunctory one-eighty and headed for the bridge.

With that business concluded, the men of Able Team checked each other's harnesses and then readied for their assault. They already had the general information on the freighter, her dimensions and such, which Stony Man had provided. However, that's all that the Farm had on the ship.

"So we haven't confirmed she's hostile," Lyons concluded.

"Not yet. According to Aaron's intel, she originally put out three days ago from Cape Town, with a manifest for lumber and other building supplies being delivered to a local construction firm in Yarmouth, Nova Scotia."

"Canada," Blancanales interjected. "So up to this point, she was basically on course."

"Yeah," Schwarz said with a nod. "But suddenly she turned and headed in our direction."

"Could be mechanical trouble, after all," Lyons said. "But I guess we can't chance it, and rightfully so."

"Especially since we now know that Qibla is connected with these remanufactured freighters," Pol added.

"Well, whatever happens, we'll be ready for it," Lyons said.

The sound of chopper blades commanded the trio's attention. They gathered up their equipment and headed to the foredeck, struggling to keep their balance as the cutter slowed rapidly and nearly tossed them to deck plates. Lyons cursed softly, trying to keep his balance.

They had the freighter in plain view now. She was pretty big—Lyons estimated about five hundred feet, stem to stern. He was no expert on freighters, but he knew enough from reading and training that the vessel was older. The majority of modern merchant ships had been increased to seven hundred feet to make up for industrial automation and to answer the economic need to transport the most cargo at the lowest cost. This automation had also allowed most merchant fleets to reduce manpower on larger ships from fifty men to around twenty.

The *Lockett* continued to decrease speed, and her loudspeakers squawked as Bryant's voice came on the line. It was difficult to hear him over the helicopter that continuously circled overhead, but he was able to make out something about surrendering and preparing for boarders. Lyons guessed that the crew aboard was most likely belowdecks and preparing to repel boarders.

"They're not answering, sirs!" the cutter's executive officer called to them from just outside the bridge.

"Take us in!" Lyons shouted back.

It was time to collect their pay.

CHAPTER EIGHT

Cape Town, South Africa

It was nearly four hours before the men of Phoenix Force returned to their rooms at The Table Bay Hotel.

Jack Grimaldi and Rafael Encizo were waiting in the three-bedroom suite they shared with David McCarter, which adjoined an identical accommodation occupied by the remaining members of Phoenix Force. The entire team now waited in the suite for McCarter, who had gone to meet Jeanne Marais.

No doubt about it, the South Africans were certainly pulling out all the diplomatic stops. Through some reading material and brochures, T. J. Hawkins had noted to the rest that they were staying in a hotel with some of the most modern conveniences and amenities available in all of Cape Town.

"Wow," he muttered as he looked over the room-service menu. He'd wanted to sit out the evening for a delicious T-bone with all the trimmings, but McCarter put the kibosh on that, ordering them to clean and check weapons, and to change into more "suitable attire," which was to say they were going to be out in public and needed to act and dress like the rest of the South African natives.

Hawkins looked at James and continued, "They have twenty-two kinds of pie in this place. Can you believe it?"

"Yes. What I can't believe is that you haven't ordered something to eat yet, T.J.," James replied. He made a show of looking at his watch. "And we're scheduled to leave here in less than an hour."

McCarter had just entered the room with Jeanne Marais and had obviously caught the last snippet of the conversation. "And I'm not going to wait for you to stuff your bloody face." McCarter looked at Encizo. "How are you?"

Encizo flashed him the okay sign. "Clean bill of health. Bumps and bruises, but nothing broken. I'm cleared for action."

McCarter grunted in way of reply, then turned to Grimaldi. "What about our ride? You got my message?"

Grimaldi nodded. "It's at a nearby helipad the SASS rented for us. Ten minutes by foot."

"Bloody marvelous."

"You know," Encizo said to Hawkins, "if you're going to order something, I could use a bite myself."

"He can order for all of us," McCarter said, conceding to his men.

The Briton obviously figured they deserved something to eat. They'd been giving practically nonstop since returning from their mission in Buenos Aires.

"So what's sticking in your craw?" Manning asked McCarter.

"Yeah, no shit," James added. "You're bouncing around here like you got fire ants up your ass. What gives?"

"Marais here has some news, so listen up," McCarter said, obviously intent on ignoring the gibes being tossed his way.

Marais cleared her throat. "The prisoner you took at the waterfront has been put into the protective custody of my government. You won't be able to question him."

"Say what?" Hawkins said. He dropped the receiver on the house phone before room service had a chance to answer. "What the hell does that mean?"

"Just what it means," Marais replied, firing him a harsh look. "And I don't want you to blame me, because I had no choice in the matter. This was a decision left to my superiors and they told me it was nonnegotiable."

"That's just great!" Hawkins slammed the menu onto a nearby credenza.

"I'm afraid I have to go with my friend here on this one, Marais," Manning said, rising from a chair next to the love seat where Encizo had planted himself. "What's the story, exactly?"

"As she already said, it's not her choice," McCarter cut in.

"The important thing is that I did manage to get some information in the short time before the prisoner was snatched away from me," Marais said. "I speak fluent Arabic. Apparently there is a warehouse near the wharf that contains the equipment you saw."

"Well, our trip through that airshaft sure didn't reveal much," James said, "so maybe this is the break we've been looking for. Only thing we found was a big open area where we think some trucks were parked, and it looked like perhaps some equipment had been unloaded."

"We've pretty much agreed that it's the same place we saw in the photographs Rensberg took," Manning added.

Marais nodded. "Well, then, I think you'll be very happy to know that we believe we may be able to tie those activities in Table Mountain with something the prisoner told me before some other SASS agents whisked him away to Pretoria."

The woman took a briefcase she'd brought over to a nearby table and opened it, unfolded a large sheet of what looked like cream-colored butcher paper, spread it on the table then motioned for Phoenix Force to gather around her. The men complied, and James noted on further inspection it was drafting paper, the kind used by architects. The paper had blue pencil drawings of some kind of architectural layout.

"These are the plans to a large, commercial shipyard about seven miles south of our location." She pointed to the small plot map in the lower corner to emphasize. "Here. This yard closed down a few years ago and was abandoned until it was recently purchased by an international shipbuilding company headquartered out of Portsmouth."

"Virginia?" Hawkins asked.

McCarter snickered. "Just like a Yank. Automatically assumes that she means America. She's talking about my neck of the woods, mate."

Hawkins nodded.

"Moving forward," Marais continued. "This contact told me that all of the equipment you saw in those pictures was moved from the location you discovered in Table Mountain to this shipyard. However, he couldn't say for sure where inside the shipyard it's being held."

McCarter added, "And it's a bloody well big place, so we've got our work cut out for us. I'll spare you boys the pep talk, and just say this may be our last chance to find a connection to Qibla and exactly what the hell they're up to. That's why I'm increasing our odds."

He turned to Encizo. "Gomez, you'll take Smith and Jackson and approach from the bay side. Matthews, you'll be with me and Marais in the chopper. We'll approach from the air and rappel down to the rooftop at the center of the shipyard."

The plan made sense, James knew. While all the men of Phoenix Force were skilled warriors by sea, air or land, every team member had their strongest and weakest points. He, Encizo and Manning had the most experience with underwater operations, and Hawkins would play it well, given his experience and training in Delta Force. But both Manning and McCarter were more naturally skilled with air assault operations. James wasn't sure where that left Marais, and as the party broke up to get their equipment together and prepare to leave at McCarter's urging, he decided to broach the subject as the Briton changed in his room.

"Yo, David," James said in a hushed tone.

"What's up, mate?" McCarter said as he began to shrug out of his fatigues in preparation for civilian clothes. "And close the bloody door. I don't need Marais seeing me in the all-together. She might not be able to control herself."

"Yeah," James said as he closed the door. "Well, it's her I want to talk to you about. Why are you letting her tag along? She's got no business—"

"She's got every business," McCarter cut in. "And I'm not letting her tag along, I'm including her as part of the op. She's got antiterrorist training and she knows the drill."

"You sure that's a good idea?"

McCarter stopped dressing, one leg in his pants, and scowled. "You questioning my judgment?"

"Yeah," James said with a stony expression. "I guess I am."

McCarter appeared to think about this a moment, then shrugged and continued dressing. James wasn't sure how to react to that—he had kind of expected McCarter to go off on him—so he stood there feeling stupid for a moment. It seemed obvious the conversation was over.

James wasn't ready to let it go that easily. "We going to talk about this or not?"

"You talk, I'll dress."

"I don't think it's a good idea to let Marais be involved in this."

"Why not?"

"I don't trust her," James said simply.

"You think she'd compromise our well-oiled machine."

"It's not that, exactly," James replied. "This has more to do with the fact I don't believe her about that prisoner."

McCarter shrugged as he buttoned his shirt. "So what? I don't believe her, either."

James did a double take. "Huh? What do you mean, you don't believe her?"

"Just like I said," McCarter said. "According to the intel Barbara gave us, Marais was in charge of this operation. Her people wouldn't have even known about the prisoner we took unless she told them. She doesn't strike me as the type of woman who would roll over so easily, even for her superiors. Right now I think she believes it's not in her best interest to let us interrogate the prisoner, so fine. But I figure eventually she'll be forced to tell us the bloody truth. And when she does, we'll have the leverage we need to get her cooperation."

"That's your plan?"

"That's my plan, mate. You see, it's all about the

truth. And as the Good Book says, the truth shall set you free."

"Amen, brother," James replied.

DAVID MCCARTER CHECKED the luminescent hands of his watch as he studied the area immediately ahead of them. Grimaldi had brought the chopper in three hundred meters offshore, and a mere three meters above the water, he dropped the scuba-clad trio that would approach from the water side. Encizo was still recovering from his minor injuries, but the Briton knew the little Cuban would have no problem leading his crew to the targets.

After dumping the frog team, Grimaldi swung the chopper south and moved away from the shipyard. McCarter wanted any sentries to figure that the chopper was simply ferrying about for some rich out-of-towners. By seeing the chopper move well away from the area, even the most alert observers would relax their vigilance. At that distance from the shoreline, only someone looking through a very powerful night-scope would have been able to detect the human cargo that had dropped from the chopper.

The Briton waited ten minutes before advising Grimaldi to make his move. The ace pilot flashed McCarter a wide grin, then swung the chopper in a wide arc. The Phoenix Force leader readied for his jump. He'd be the first out of the chopper and descending the thirty-odd meters to the ground. He'd then provide cover for Marais, who would come next, and finally Manning.

As they neared their destination, McCarter began to second-guess his decision to allow Marais to accompany them. Of course, she had provided this information to them, which he hoped paid off, but that was her job. She was either on their side and her superiors really were shafting her, or she was playing Phoenix Force like a five-piece band. Whichever way she swung, McCarter figured he had no choice but to use her in every capacity he could. There was too much at stake to ignore her, dismiss any suggestions out of hand. He just hoped for her sake that she was on their side, because the minute he knew otherwise she'd be done working with them. If there was anything David McCarter couldn't stand, it was a liar.

"Two minutes," he heard through the headset.

He nodded, gave the okay signal to Manning and removed the headset. There wouldn't be any further talk. McCarter had left strict instructions to maintain radio silence until they were on the ground and had cleared any immediate threat that might present itself. The middle of a firefight wasn't time for chitchat, even if it seemed like necessary traffic. He'd need all his wits about him when he touched ground, and what he didn't need was a bunch of yammering in his ears.

The chopper slowed very suddenly, then began to hover. McCarter took a quick look at the rigging, then bailed over the side. He felt the heat build under his thick, neoprene gloves as he descended the cable. The ground rushed to meet him, and a few feet short of impact he yanked on the brake, drawing the belay line behind his back. When he'd stopped, he snapped the quick release and free-fell the remaining distance.

McCarter had chosen an H&K MP-5 SD-6 for this mission. Several grenades adorned his LBE harness, including a pair of CS riot control grenades, two M-67 frags and an M-18 colored smoker. With the loss of their prisoner, the one lead they had to discovering the heart of Qibla's operations, the Phoenix Force leader figured to take some new prisoners on this trip if at all possible.

The Briton glanced upward to check on Marais's progress. It looked at first as if she were having trouble with the rigging, but a moment later her darkly clad form descended. McCarter moved away from her drop point and put the MP-5 SD-6 into battery, adjusting from safe to 3-shot firing mode. He swept the area with the muzzle of the machine pistol, hopeful no threat would present itself before all three of them were at ground zero, but ready if it did.

And it did.

Marais was still disengaging her belay line when motion alerted McCarter to trouble. Two men emerged from the shadows, both armed with assault rifles pointed in the Briton's direction. They rushed him, one branching away to try for a flanking position. McCarter took the flanker first, swinging the machine pistol into mid-level target acquisition and squeezing the trigger. The weapon coughed a report as the gases escaped through the two-chambered, integrated suppressor system. All three of the 9 mm rounds connected with the gunner's chest. Pink foam erupted into the air as the wounds punctured his lungs. The impact sent his body into a lazy spin and he died before he hit the ground.

Marais managed to clear her pistol from the hip holster she wore and tried to tag the other attacker, but he dodged to the left and her shot went wide. Before she could realign her sights, gunfire echoed above their heads. McCarter looked up to see Manning descending on the line, one hand controlling his speed while he fired his .357 Magnum Desert Eagle with the other. Two of the Canadian's four shots struck home. One punched a whole through the enemy's chest, and a second got him in the shoulder. The man's body flipped under the force of the heavy-duty Magnum loads and he sprawled to the cracked pavement, his chin leading the way.

Manning touched down as lightly as a goose feather. He freed himself from the belay line a moment later, then waved a signal for Grimaldi to winch it in. The line began to withdraw as the chopper turned and climbed steeply from their position.

McCarter slapped his friend's back. "Nice shooting, mate."

"New contacts," Manning quipped.

"Let's get to business."

The trio turned and moved toward the nearest building. When they reached the shadows, McCarter glanced at his watch. Only three minutes had elapsed since their insertion. Adding to that the ten-minute wait and two minute transit to the drop point brought the total to roughly fifteen minutes. That should have been enough time for Encizo, James and Hawkins to reach the shoreline.

Given the quick response of the now-dead pair of sentries, McCarter figured they weren't far from where the central group hid. The tip from Marais's prisoner had paid off. The Briton wasn't sure they would have been able to extract much more from the prisoner. Perhaps if her superiors had horned in on their operation, it hadn't been a bad thing. At least that took the spoiler off Phoenix Force's hands, and no one had to stay behind to babysit.

"Hey, Brown," Marais whispered over his shoulder, "are you waiting for an engraved invitation?"

McCarter jerked his thumb in the direction of the deceased. "Looks like it was already delivered."

"This year, team," Manning interjected.

The Phoenix Force leader nodded and then peered around the corner. There was no entrance on this side of the building, which meant they would have to find another way in. There was a lot of ground to cover and they didn't have time for a building-to-building search. McCarter was hoping they'd get lucky. He quickly spotted the door midway between the two corners, checked their flank one last time, gestured for his team to follow then sprinted for the door.

They reached it only to discover it was locked.

McCarter signaled Manning and immediately took up covering position in one direction, signaling Marais to take the other. She obeyed as the big Canadian stepped forward and reached into his bag of tricks. He withdrew a stick of C-4 plastique, which was already formed to take a blasting cap. He inserted a primer with a wire antenna attached to its end, then pressed it firmly against the bottom hinge. He repeated the procedure for the top hinge and then indicated the others should grab cover.

Manning traversed the wall back the way they had come, stopping maybe twenty-five yards from the door. McCarter and Marais quickly found cover behind some nearby crates. After the big Canadian verified they were clear, he withdrew a wireless detonator from his pocket, engaged the arming switch and pushed the button. The radio frequency spanned the distance and ignited the primers. The heat and pressure detonated the C-4, and in a cloud of smoke and red-orange flame it blew the heavy door clean off its hinges, taking some of the concrete and mortar of the building with it.

McCarter and Marais joined their teammate a moment later and the trio entered the darkened building cautiously, weapons held at the ready. The damp and musty smell of the interior signaled disuse. McCarter felt it highly unlikely they would find their quarry in this building.

The sudden muzzle-flashes and ear-splitting reports of autofire quickly changed his mind.

CHAPTER NINE

Rafael Encizo had just left the water and stripped off his gear when he heard the first sounds of gunfire.

He quickly gained his bearings and looked in the direction of the chopper, gauging its distance by the sound of its blades smacking the air. Encizo sensed McCarter and the rest were in trouble. For the briefest moment the Cuban warrior thought he saw flashes of light just below the chopper. Muzzle-flashes, perhaps? Or flaming equipment? Whatever the hell it was, it signaled something had gone awry.

Encizo turned to see his teammates exit the water, their heads appearing over the edge of the dock. Fortunately, a small boat pier with a ladder at its end led from the shipyard docking and storage area. Encizo reached over to help Hawkins out of the water, lent a hand to James.

"Damn, Rafe," Hawkins said, snapping the skintight

cap from his head. "You took that spill today, and you still swim like an Olympic gold medalist."

Encizo showed him a wry grin as he replied, "Yeah, well, save the scorecards for later, T.J. We've got trouble on the horizon."

"What's the deal?" James asked with obvious concern.

"Not sure," Encizo replied, "but I saw what may have been shooting or explosions near the chopper."

"You think they got made?" Hawkins asked.

"Possible," Encizo said. "But we won't know for sure until we find them, so I'd advise getting out of those wet suits ASAP, and getting geared up."

Encizo turned from his teammates and grabbed the waterproof equipment bag. The bag was adorned with air bladders that kept it afloat during their swim. Encizo released the air-tight seals and zipped the bag down to reveal their weapons. He'd opted for an MP-5 A-3 subgun and .45 caliber Colt M-1911 A-1 as his side arm. Unlike his teammates, he'd chosen a Cold Steel Tanto fighting knife over the standard Ka-Bar.

He checked the load and action on the MP-5 A-3, slung it then wrapped a Sam Browne belt around his waist. Encizo then turned to the other weapons. He handed four spare magazines loaded with 5.56 mm ammo and a satchel of 40 mm HE grenades to James, followed by an M-16 A-4 assault rifle with attached M-203. He passed Hawkins an H&K G-41—a modern variant of the HK 33 optimized for SS109 hardball ammo that could be fired in 3-shot mode—and a Beretta

93-R. The trio quickly checked their weapons and moved toward the main shipyard with Encizo on point, James at center and Hawkins on rear guard.

They moved with stealth in spite of the fact that it sounded as though the other trio's cover had been blown. There was no reason to alert the enemy to the fact they were being stormed on more than one front. The threesome kept to the shadows, and Encizo was optimistic that their advance had gone undetected so far. He wasn't the least bit sure what would have blown the operation so early in the game, but then he didn't have any evidence to suggest it wasn't simply the terrorists' response to the sudden arrival of the chopper. It still seemed like a hell of a quick response for an insertion that they weren't expecting. Who knew how long the terrorists had operated here without interference? They would have grown lax, perhaps even become a bit lazy in their security. Well, he needed to stop worrying about that and focus on the task at hand.

McCarter and Manning could take care of themselves and Marais with their eyes closed.

The Cuban stopped short when he heard a stifled yelp of pain. He crouched and turned, seeing Hawkins rubbing his ankle and James moving to his position to check the injury. Encizo took a moment to scan the ground and noted that there were some cracks and deformities in the pavement of the dock area. The concrete here was old, weathered from years of salt-laden sea air. Its integrity was compromised with rubble in places where cracks and potholes had developed.

"Is he all right?" Encizo whispered.

James nodded as Hawkins replied, "I'm fine, just turned my ankle a bit."

"Both of you watch your step," James counseled them. "The ground's uneven here."

They took up their original positions and continued toward the shadowy outlines of some wrecked-out forklifts. Encizo signaled them to regroup as he studied the area ahead. The first building they encountered stood some sixty yards from their position, surrounded by an open area of more broken pavement. The little Cuban knew they couldn't move that fast across the treacherous area, and the poor lighting served as both blessing and curse.

Before Encizo could formulate a plan for crossing the expanse as quickly and safely as possible, he saw movement. He squinted, not sure if he'd seen what he thought he'd seen, but his patient vigil paid off. The movements were too calculated, too precise, to be those of animals. What he saw was a group of black-clad forms shifting positions, leapfrogging from one position of cover to the other. Their backs were to the Phoenix Force warriors, so Encizo figured they were waiting to spring an ambush on McCarter's team.

Encizo motioned his two friends to draw close. "You guys see what I see?"

"I see London, I see France, I say it's just about time to dance," Hawkins cracked.

James nodded. "I count five, maybe six."

"Ditto," Encizo said. "And there could be more."

"What's the gig?" James asked.

"Well, we can't just walk into the open. The terrain's too unpredictable." Encizo looked in all directions and eventually spied a series of commercial shipping crates stored end to end. "I say you two go for those, try to find a way to flank. I'll stay here and cover you. Go now."

Hawkins and James moved away quickly and silently. Encizo was sorry he hadn't packed a night-vision scope for the MP-5, but then they hadn't been given a whole lot of time to prepare. McCarter had put the op together as efficiently but quickly as he knew how. Encizo always believed thorough planning was the key to any such insertion exercise like this. But then sometimes planning had to be thrown to the wind and warriors simply had to, as Carl Lyons was fond of saying, "just nut up and do it."

Encizo figured the closest target he could detect would pose the greatest threat if James and Hawkins were spotted, so he steadied the MP-5 against one of the forklift's skids and trained his sights on that area. Fortunately his friends made it to the crates unchallenged.

Less than a minute passed before Encizo caught just the hint of two outlines emerge from the far side of the crates and proceed slowly but deliberately in the direction of the enemy. The Cuban counted to five, then rose and moved toward the enemy's position, keeping his eye on the closest target.

There will be no ambush tonight, boys, the Cuban thought.

When he was within fifteen meters, Encizo went prone, raised his MP-5 and squeezed the trigger. His target turned at the sound of Encizo hitting the ground, but it was too late for an effective response. At the same moment the terrorist opened his mouth to shout a warning to his comrades, the Phoenix Force commando's rounds punched through the gap. The man's skull blew apart under the short-range velocity of the slugs, his body slamming against the large, upturned chunk of pavement he'd used for cover. He slid soundlessly to the ground as his deadened legs folded under him.

A flash of light on metal in Encizo's peripheral vision caused him to turn and ready for a flanking attack, but he quickly saw it was James and tempered his near reflex action to defend himself. A heartbeat when he noticed that James was triggering his weapon on the run. A second later Encizo understood the fervor. The Cuban warrior had been so focused on taking his first target by surprise, he hadn't noticed another terrorist lining up his sights to claim Encizo as a prize. James's timing saved his life, and it was one of the first times Encizo could remember the distinctive autofire of an M-16 A-4 being music to his ears. His would-be executioner danced under the hail of high-velocity rounds that spit from the assault rifle and ripped gaping wounds in tender flesh. The man fell to the ground in an untidy heap.

Encizo got to his feet, tossed off a salute of thanks then indicated they should proceed. James tossed a similar gesture of acknowledgment and started forward.

T. J. Hawkins was the next one to score on a terrorist. Several of the remaining gunners had fled, moving in the direction of the building ahead, but one stood his ground. He took turns firing on Encizo and James, apparently unaware that there was a third party in the game. Hawkins managed to flank the shooter on his blind side, just to his left and slightly rear. His adversary never saw it coming as Hawkins raised his G-41 and triggered a single round through the back of the man's head. The forehead erupted in a gory exhibition of blood, bone and gray matter. The nearly decapitated corpse slumped forward, rifle clattering from its desensitized fingers, then slumped backward.

The trio continued toward the building, moving in a fire-and-maneuver drill they had practiced a thousand times and probably executed in battle half as many. The terrorists continued sprinting toward the building, but one of the three stopped suddenly and turned, obviously intent on covering the escape of his comrades. His bravery was commendable, but at the cost of his life. All three Phoenix Force warriors brought their weapons to bear and let loose at the same time. Bullets smashed through the man's guts, chest and skull; the flesh-shredders decimated his upper torso mercilessly and the impact flung him off his feet and slammed him to the pavement.

The other pair had now reached the building. One gunner appeared to fumble with the lock in the door while the other whirled and opened up on the trio with a fusillade of rounds. The weapon barked with the familiar reports of an AK-74S.

Encizo and Hawkins went prone, scraping hands and knees to avoid being ventilated, but James was lucky enough to find cover behind a large chunk of broken pavement. He retrieved a 40 mm HE grenade from the satchel, slammed it home and closed the breach of the launcher. He then aimed the grenade and squeezed the trigger, not even bothering to engage the leaf sight, rather trusting his experience and intuition with the launcher. The grenade landed just as the one terrorist got the door open with a cry of triumph. The high-explosive round blew on impact, ripping the door from the hinges and separating appendages from its intended targets. Flaming wreckage and debris still fell as the three Phoenix Force veterans reunited.

"Well, looks like that's the end of that," Hawkins said with a drawl.

"Yup," James agreed.

"Nice work, boys," Encizo said. "Now come on, let's find David, Rafe and Gary."

WHETHER SKILL, FATE OR some other unexplained phenomenon saved David McCarter and Gary Manning might never be known. The fact remained that they were spared from the swift and violent assault of a group of terrorists lying in wait for them.

Unfortunately, Jeanne Marais wasn't.

She took three slugs, two in the stomach and a third

through the right upper chest, before Manning—for the second time in as little as twenty-four hours—pulled her to safety. The big Canadian had managed to find cover to shelter both of them, and moved clear with her before the area where they had stood was rife with bullets. Even in the poorly lit building he could see the dark stains of blood spreading rapidly across her blouse. She coughed several times, flecks of the blood appearing on her mouth and chin as she struggled to breathe.

Manning held her tightly, her head resting in his lap, and smiled at her. He shouted to be heard above the cacophony of gunfire. "Hang tight, lady! You're going to pull through!"

Manning realized McCarter was otherwise occupied, although he couldn't be certain whether the Briton had seen Marais get hit. Either way, it didn't matter because McCarter never showed his belly to the enemy. In fact, the Cockney warrior responded in just the opposite fashion, returning the terrorist fire with a furious volley of his own. A moment later, over the din of the sporadic firing, Manning heard the unmistakable ping of a spoon leaving a grenade body.

Covering his own ears, he wrapped his thighs around Marais's and shielded as much of her body with his own as he could manage. It occurred to him even as he did that he was risking his own life to shield that of a potentially dead woman. Still, he couldn't take the chance.

The room was rocked a moment later by a hot explosion. Superheated glass and metal fragments whooshed a few meters over his head, followed by the sound of autofire as McCarter put his MP-5 into action. The explosion and subsequent gunfire caused Manning's ears to ring, threatening to disorient him, but the big Canadian kept it in control. He gently moved Marais's head from beneath his lap, then joined McCarter in spraying the area with high-velocity slugs.

After nearly thirty seconds of continuous fire, sustained only by the fact they were intermittently changing out magazines at different points, the two men ceased the assault. The vast room they had entered fell into silence—so quiet, in fact, that Manning could hear the blood rushing through his ears as his heartbeat began to slow as the sudden surge of adrenaline abated. After more than a minute, when no further threat presented itself, McCarter emerged from his cover and stepped into the half-light emanating from the doorway Manning had blown open.

"You all right, mate?" McCarter asked, just the slightest shake evident in his voice. He had also suffered some effects of their near-death experience.

"I'm okay," Manning replied, turning his attention toward Marais. "But I think Jeanne's in trouble."

McCarter moved to Manning, who had knelt and was now holding Marais's head in his hands once more. Her breathing was ragged, wheezy, and her eyes were starting to glaze. She was going into shock—probably from all the blood loss or due to what was obviously a punctured lung—and Manning knew there wasn't a thing they could do. Suddenly he heard the sickening, wet crackling sound of a sucking chest wound.

"We need Calvin here. Now."

McCarter shook his head. "Can't risk the radio contact."

"Are you kidding me?" Manning asked. "They're already onto us. They already know we're here. The operation is compromised, and now, as I see it, Cal's her only chance. We have to help her. We owe her that much, David, and you know it."

The Briton finally nodded, the look in his eyes surrendering to Manning's logic. The big Canadian realized McCarter's hesitation wasn't caused by heartlessness, but rather by devotion to duty. They had no idea where Encizo's team was at, or what they might have encountered. To break radio silence after McCarter had strictly ordered them to forgo radio communications could have a very negative impact on the mission. But then, they had to have enough faith that their transmissions wouldn't be intercepted. It was a risk, but it was one Manning felt was worth it.

McCarter started to reach for the switch but Marais raised her hand and shook her head slowly. It was a gesture for him to stop what he was doing.

Manning looked at McCarter, a bit puzzled, then turned his attention to Marais. "We're going to get you help."

"Don't," she said. There was a high-pitched rasp in her voice. "He wouldn't get here in time."

"That's bullshit, Marais," McCarter said, kneeling next to her, opposite Manning. "You're going to pull through this. You're a tough woman."

Marais smiled, but the look in her eyes said she didn't believe him. "You...always were...full of it, Brown."

She coughed twice more and fresh blood oozed from the corners of her mouth. There was little question in Manning's mind that Marais was right. She probably wouldn't last long enough for James to arrive. The sucking noises in her chest had stopped. That meant there was no longer any air moving through the right side of her chest wall. It wouldn't be long before she lost consciousness, assuming she didn't succumb to the shock of acute blood loss first.

Either way, she was about to check out.

"Well, we can't just—" Manning began.

"Listen," Marais cut in with a hoarse whisper. She managed to reach up and palm his cheek. Her hand was cold and damp. "It's not... your fault. But you need...to know something before I go."

"You're going to pull through," McCarter said between clenched teeth.

"I wasn't forthright with you," she continued. It was obviously becoming more difficult for her to talk. Her words became slurred as she continued, her speech pattern broken with bouts of coughing and more blood. "The prisoner's name is Fadil Shunnar, he's with the Qibla. They are responsible for Rensberg's death. You...you must stop them. Please...swear you will stop them!"

"We swear it."

"They have…four freighters," Marais said. "They are loaded with missiles they plan to launch from portable systems. You must find them. You must…find…"

And then Jeanne Marais coughed her last breath.

For just a moment, as her hand started to fall, Manning grabbed it and held it against his cheek. This hadn't been the plan at all. They were going to have to explain her death, which was bad enough, but they had also involved her in something she wasn't trained for. They had allowed an innocent to fall. Manning looked at McCarter and expressed the accusatory nature of the look. The Briton picked up on it immediately. He knew what Manning was thinking.

"She was a big girl," McCarter said. "She could take care of herself, make her own decisions."

"Except dying," Manning replied coolly. "We made that one for her."

"She went the way any of us would prefer to go. She went out hard and she went out large. She died defending her country. She died defending what she believed in. So if you want to bloody blame someone, blame the terrorists. Blame the Qibla. And then let's take that with us, and go find them and blow their bloody arses back to hell."

And Gary Manning agreed.

It was time to take the fight to the enemy. Up to this point, he felt they were the ones who'd been taking the ass-kicking, and it was time to start dishing it out. There was nothing Manning wanted more. He couldn't dismiss the lump that formed in his throat as he took Marais's hand from his cheek and laid it at her side. He couldn't understand his sense of loss, but that didn't mean he didn't feel it. He hadn't known her that long, but for some reason in that short period of time he'd come to respect and appreciate her. She was another example of the costs tallied in battling the terrorist threat.

Jeanne Marais had paid the highest price.

Yeah, McCarter was right. It was time to go on the offensive and stick the knife right into their hearts, whether that meant the Qibla or whoever was responsible for this travesty. It was time to exact retribution, time to make the terrorists behind understand that there always came a day of recompense for each and every one of them.

CHAPTER TEN

Washington, D.C.

Harold Brognola sat, chomped on a cigar and waited for the Man.

The situation wasn't good, and Stony Man had been slow to crack this one wide open. Then again, what the hell did they really have when they started?

Well, at least they'd made some headway. Able Team was in Boston with a prisoner taken from the Qibla seaside house, and McCarter had called to tell him about their planned operation against the shipyard. Both groups had to cooperate with outside agencies and simultaneously keep local jurisdictions at arm's length. That wasn't always an easy task, especially in foreign countries. McCarter had told him and Price of his distrust where Marais and the prisoner were concerned, but they'd agreed that to ask presidential interference so soon wouldn't help their cause.

Brognola pondered his decision when his cellular phone rang. It was Aaron Kurtzman.

"Have you seen the Man arrive yet?" Kurtzman asked.

"No," Brognola replied. "Please tell me you'll have better news for me to give him."

"As a matter of fact, I do. We just heard from David."

"And?"

"They found Qibla operatives at the shipyard and seized some information they think will help us disseminate their plans."

"So we're pretty sure it's Qibla behind this?" Brognola asked.

"There's no doubt about it," Kurtzman replied.

"So that confirms Jabir al-Warraq's complicity."

"Check. We've also identified the other guy he's playing footsies with, one Mahmed Temez."

"What do we know about him?"

"Former Iraqi army officer and escapee from the war," Kurtzman replied. "He's been on our most wanted list for a while, apparently."

"How come we didn't flag it sooner? We had a picture."

"Yeah, but there were no previous photographs of him we could compare with those we had, boss. His military records were destroyed during the early bombing campaigns. We got lucky because one of Barb's contacts at the CIA managed to scrounge up a description in an archived database. Something I guess we'd obtained

from prisoner interrogations of Iraqi soldiers during
Desert Storm. A cross-check confirmed the rest, so now
we're positive of our identification. And check this out.
You know what Temez did in the Iraqi military? He
was a medium- to long-range field artillery officer, an
expert with missile ballistics and equipment."

Brognola grunted. "Well, if we add that fact to what
we already know from the information Gadgets sent us,
it stands to reason they're planning to launch missiles
from portable platforms aboard those freighters they
are refitting at the shipyard."

"Bingo."

"Okay, where do we head from here? What does
Barb think?"

"Well, I have descriptions of four freighters that
Phoenix Force seized in Cape Town. I'm cross-
checking them now against all known commercial shipping registrations past and present. It shouldn't take
long to narrow down."

"Okay, then what?"

"Well, once we know what type of ship we're looking for, we have to determine how many ships are presently at sea that match the criteria, then start discounting
those least likely to be a Qibla freighter."

"Process of elimination," Brognola said with a sigh.

"I know it's not the preferred method, but with the
information I have that's all I can go on. Our GPS satellite system should be able to make the job easy. Most
of the newer freighters are around seven hundred feet

in length, which means we're looking for older and smaller ships."

"They'll also be faster," Brognola suggested.

"Right," Kurtzman agreed. "Not to mention that we have a certain number we can eliminate immediately, since we know all four of these freighters came out of Cape Town. That should narrow our search considerably."

"Assuming that they didn't file bogus shipping manifests," Brognola said.

"Well, even if they did, it won't matter because every ship that leaves port must undergo a safety inspection just prior to departure. This also includes a GPS signal record, and each one is unique. Any ship to leave port must transmit a signal at all times. Any loss of signal would be cause for immediate investigation by the nearest military naval unit."

"That's all well and good, Aaron, but we're assuming that they even left Cape Town by normal channels. These are terrorists we're dealing with. They don't do anything by conventional means."

"They do if they don't want to attract attention," Kurtzman reminded him. "And the fastest way to do that would be four freighters suddenly leaving a busy port in the dark of night without any warning or clearance, particularly in today's environment of heightened global security."

"All right, I'll concede that point," Brognola replied. "And I'll leave it up to you and Barb on how to proceed here. But keep me informed every step of the way. And call me as soon as you hear anything further from Able Team. Was there anything else?"

"Yeah, um…just one more thing, so you're not surprised if the Man mentions it."

"What's that?"

"I'm sorry to report that Jeanne Marais bought it during Phoenix Force's assault on the shipyard. She was shot and killed."

"Shot and killed?" Brognola echoed. "Christ, what the hell was she doing there? She shouldn't have even been involved."

"I don't know, Chief," Kurtzman replied. "That, I would think, would be a question for McCarter. Barb's nearby. You want to talk to her about it?"

Brognola sighed again, a longer one that had "tired" written on it. "Not right now. I think I hear the Man. I'll be back there within two hours."

The door of the small White House anteroom swung inward. Four men in suits entered, eyes scanning the interior. A fifth man followed them, this one well-dressed, also, but he seemed disinterested in the activities of the Secret Service. The President finally appeared.

"Hal, good to see you," the Man said, crossing the room and extending his hand as Brognola got to his feet. They shook hands and the President introduced the man next to him. "You know Frank Lusk, my national security adviser."

"A pleasure," Lusk said, shaking Brognola's hand.

"Likewise," Brognola replied uncertain,   mpletely taken aback by Lusk's presence ... turned to the President. "Uh, Mr. President, no disrespect intended, but I don't understand why Mr. Lusk is here. We don't—"

"I know this is highly irregular, Hal," the President said. He gestured at the table. "Why don't we all have a seat and I'll explain."

When they were comfortable, the President said, "Frank here is aware of who you are, Hal…at least indirectly. He is not aware of the exact nature of your additional duties, because he doesn't need to be aware of them, and he understands that. I invited him because in addition to being my adviser on policies of national security, he also has some 'special duties' of his own. He works very closely with Homeland Security, and I think under the present circumstances his input will prove valuable. In a nutshell, that's why he's here, it's at my request and I will take the brunt of any security risks in that regard.

"In return, I would ask that you be candid about anything you know regarding our situation, but be discreet on the particulars of your people and their operations. Fair enough?"

Brognola nodded.

The President smiled, then turned to Lusk. "Frank, as we discussed on the way over, Hal here officially holds a high-ranking position within the Justice Department, but he has some additional duties assigned by my predecessors. The exact nature of this work is classified from everyone, both for the sake of the country as well as the Office. I would ask that you respect that."

"Of course, sir," Lusk said with a nod.

"Good," the President replied. He looked at Brognola. "I'm all ears, Hal. Tell me where we're at."

Brognola took a deep breath, appraised Lusk once more and then, "I just received word that we have confirmed Qibla is behind our assessment of a possible terrorist attack, and that we have now identified the major players. As it stands, we expect one or more attacks by missiles possibly containing chemical or biological agents. We think that the Qibla have built mobile launch pads on four different freighters now currently afloat in international waters, and each bound for their own respective targets."

"Any idea where they plan to strike?" the President asked.

"Unfortunately not, sir," Brognola replied. "What we do know is the specific types of freighters, so my home team is presently looking at ways of assessing all vessels in the present commercial traffic and narrowing it to the best possible candidates. We also have it on good authority the freighters got under way in only the past twelve hours, so that should make it a bit easier."

"You mentioned we've identified the major players," the President said. "Who are they?"

"Well, one we had already known and suspected of collusion, Jabir al-Warraq, is now confirmed. The second man has been identified as Mahmed Temez."

The President looked askance at Lusk, who nodded. "I'm familiar with both of them. Al-Warraq has been the figurehead of Qibla since I started as a pup with the Company. He's wealthy and influential, and has the will to use both if he thinks he stands to gain anything for his cause. The South African government's biggest trouble has been connecting him to any domestic crimes. For the most part, the general sociopolitical views toward Qibla center on the idea that they are a predictable and peace-loving lot. There are never any violent outbreaks at their demonstrations, at least none they have been known to incite, and they are apparently quite generous to many of the underprivileged."

"Doesn't sound like we could easily convince the South Africans that Qibla's involved in acts of international terrorism," the President said.

"Very doubtful," Lusk replied.

"What about Temez?" Brognola said. "What do you know about him?"

"Well, now, his background is murky," Lusk admitted. "You could almost say he's the exact opposite of al-Warraq. He'd avoid publicity of any kind at any cost, and he's a radical supporter of al Qaeda."

"Our intelligence says he's an Iraqi army officer," Brognola interjected.

"Used to be," Lusk replied. "He went rogue after Baghdad fell and fled the country along with a whole bunch of his fellow officers. We do know that during the evacuation he was involved in either the destruction or sequestering of WMDs and that he participated in the terrorizing of smaller villages during the early phases of the war. He's also well connected in Syria and Iran. He has lots of friends in high places, and more terrorist leaders who would be willing to hire him than you could shake a stick at."

"Could one of those be al-Warraq?"

"Are you kidding?" Lusk said. "Like I said, al-Warraq loves to rub elbows with Temez's kind. I could see them getting together and cooking up something like you're describing."

"So we're all in agreement that Qibla and Temez have conspired to commit terrorist acts," the President interjected.

"Yes, Mr. President," Brognola replied. "We've established the who, what and how, now we just need to figure out the where and when."

"That will be the real challenge," Lusk said. "Given that Mr. Brognola here is assigned the task of looking for needles in the proverbial haystack, I would advise we put the Navy and Air Force on full alert."

"That could prompt a lot of very uncomfortable questions from the press corps and Congressional leaders, Frank," the President said. He looked at Brognola. "What do you think?"

"I don't have enough information yet to advise you best, Mr. President," Brognola replied. "But if you want my opinion, I think that putting the military on full alert is a bit premature, and could cause some unnecessary grief for you. You wouldn't be able to write that move off as a training exercise."

Brognola noticed the furious look Lusk gave him, but he didn't let it affect him. In most cases, guys like Lusk had some other agenda, and usually the first item on it was protecting their own asses. The difference between him and Lusk was that Lusk's duties didn't usually involve sending men he'd known for many years into the heat of battle. Brognola had become very used to his position in Stony Man, but that was something he'd never been able to become accustomed to. If it were his choice, he would have lived in a world where good men like those of Able Team and Phoenix Force didn't have to risk their lives every day to keep the country secure. Unfortunately, that was his job and he'd do it the best he knew how.

And he sure as hell wasn't going to try to make someone else the scapegoat.

"I hear a 'but' in there, Hal," the President remarked.

Brognola shrugged. "Well, I do agree that perhaps you might consider upping the readiness status of a few small and select units. Perhaps you might even consider sending them out in an alert, combat-ready state. But any major deployment this early would be tantamount to political suicide, not to mention the panic it might cause."

"You're suggesting your people can handle this, then?"

"I have no reason at this point to think otherwise, Mr. President," Brognola replied firmly.

Lusk snickered.

The President looked at him. "You disagree, Frank?"

"I'm afraid I have to, sir," Lusk replied. "I mean no disrespect to Mr. Brognola here…or his people. And I certainly don't want to talk out of turn. But as your National Security Adviser, I would think we should consider a military response as the first and best approach."

"And why is that?"

"Well, for one thing, I've not seen Mr. Brognola present any evidence whatsoever to suggest there's anything substantial in his theory regarding these freighters. I realize that perhaps I don't have all of the information but—"

"That's right, Mr. Lusk," Brognola cut in. "You don't have all the information."

"Hal," the President said, raising a hand. "Please. I don't want this to turn into something bad. Let's hear Frank out."

"Thank you, sir," Lusk said. "And even if we are to assume his theory's correct, I'm not sure he has the resources necessary to cover the area we're talking about. These ships could be anywhere, and if we don't start dispersing our fleets now, we might not be able to respond in time if an attack should come. We could have another disaster on our hands. And it could be a lot worse if they fire warheads loaded with chemical or biological agents."

Damn, but Lusk was good. Of course, he did have a couple of accurate points, such as the disaster a chemical attack would cause, and the time to respond. But what Lusk didn't know was the steely resolve of the Stony Man group. He didn't know the cybernetics team that worked tirelessly, disseminating row upon endless row of data records. Every scrap of information that came through Stony Man computers was analyzed, cataloged and warehoused in an appropriate archive. When the men in the field needed intelligence or the White House assigned a new mission, Lusk wasn't there to watch Barbara Price sit long hours with Aaron Kurtzman, drinking gallon after gallon of bad coffee as they dotted every "i" and crossed every "t" to insure the safety of the men.

But mostly, Lusk didn't know Able Team and Phoenix Force. He didn't know these men personally. He didn't know their dedication to their country and devotion to duty; didn't know all the losses and sacrifice they had endured for so many years to protect the American way of life; didn't spend the many hours pacing the floor with Brognola as he worried about his friends and their selfless acts of daring, all in the name of freedom and justice. That's what Lusk didn't know. And how could he? Nobody could, because they didn't come home to ticker-tape parades and awards ceremonies. Instead, they usually returned to a bleak farm in some nameless location, perhaps lucky if they could grab a hot bath, decent meal and good night's sleep before having to go and do it all again.

But Hal Brognola understood it—all too well. He understood because he'd lived it far longer than he cared to remember. The celebration of his birthday the day before made him realize just how lucky he was. He commanded the most elite counterterrorism unit in the world, and he had the privilege of friendship with people like Barbara Price, Aaron Kurtzman and Mack Bolan. Almost daily he was forced to decide the fate of eight men, among whom he counted as comrades-in-arms, and he had immediate access to the most powerful man in the free world.

So, yeah, he took it a bit personally when guys like Frank Lusk interfered. Hell, he probably knew more about Lusk than Lusk knew about himself. He could have told Lusk what his temperature was at his last physical if he really wanted to know, and yet now he had to sit here and put up with this bullshit. Well, he'd take it only out of respect for the Man, and not for any other reason. Brognola studied the President. He could see the wheels turning behind those sharp blue eyes. Finally, the President looked at Brognola, and obviously saw something behind the Stony Man chief's expression that told him what Brognola was thinking. He turned to Lusk and smiled gently. "Frank, would you excuse us a moment?"

Lusk started to open his mouth, looking as if he were going to object, then he rose, nodded to Brognola and left the room. The President nodded, indicating that the agents should leave, as well.

"I'm sorry about that, Hal," the President said. "Frank's a good man, but at times he can be a bit too…

anal retentive. He does mean well, though, and I can tell you with certainty that he always has the best interests of this country at heart."

"You don't owe me any apologies, sir," Brognola replied. He grinned, adding, "Unless, of course, you tell me I have to start working with him on a regular basis."

The President chuckled and raised a hand in mock defense. "I promise not to do that, but I do believe he has a point. It would be difficult to mobilize any kind of effective response if we wait until this Qibla threat, real or not, was on top of us."

"I promise that won't happen," Brognola said in a quiet, firm tone. "I won't let it happen, and I speak for all of my people when I say that."

"I believe you." The President cleared his throat. "But I had other reasons for bringing Lusk in, as well. Reasons that are on a need-to-know basis and none of your concern. The important thing is that you know I'm ultimately inclined to trust your judgment. You believe the men can neutralize this before it's a problem?"

"They're already on it," Brognola said. "In fact, Able Team is investigating the freighter that suddenly changed course and headed for Boston Harbor. And it won't be long before we've located the other three Qibla targets, assuming that freighter is one of them. Once that's accomplished, the field teams will do exactly what they've always done."

The President nodded with a knowing wink. "Shoot first, ask questions later. I got it."

"We won't let you down, sir," Brognola said. "I promise."

The Man nodded, then rose. The meeting was over, and he extended his hand. "Well, unless you have something else, then, I have another engagement. I assume at our next contact you'll be advising that this threat has been neutralized."

"Understood, sir."

"And just so we're on the level, Hal, I do plan to advise the Joint Chiefs I would like to increase air patrols in all key coastal areas. If these terrorists somehow do manage to get a missile off, I intend to make sure it never reaches American shores. And as you don't have the resources to stop such an attack, it seems only defensible I employ military means to run interference."

Brognola grinned at the reference. The commander-in-chief was a huge football fan. "Any help is always appreciated, Mr. President."

The Man nodded and left.

CHAPTER ELEVEN

Boston coast

Rosario Blancanales was first aboard the freighter.

A stiff ocean breeze tugged at the small tufts of hair that protruded from the black stocking cap. Black cosmetics covered his face, lessening the chance that slivers of moonlight would betray him to the enemy. He could sense they awaited him and his fellow warriors. Yeah, he could actually feel it.

Death waited somewhere on that freighter.

The sound of the USCG chopper overhead, its searchlight piercing the night, caused Blancanales to throw himself against the nearest wall and crouch, his MP-5/40 tracking the area around him. He glanced backward and saw Schwarz, who had been next up the ladder, freeze. His gritted teeth were visible in the reflections carried by the massive searchlight built onto the Jayhawk.

Blancanales keyed the transceiver. "Hey, Ironman, tell those hombres to cool it with that chopper. I want it at two hundred yards back, and no lights. I don't feel like getting my dick shot off because they're itching for some action."

A single click acknowledged that Lyons had received his message, and thirty seconds later the light winked out and the chopper moved away, the sound of its blades fading on the wind.

The freighter had continued moving despite repeated warnings to stop. Finally, Lyons had given permission for the chopper to take up a position where they could take out the rudder and screws, if necessary, but they still insisted on boarding the vessel while it was moving. Naturally, Captain Bryant had argued against the maneuver again, cited a half dozen Coast Guard regulations, but Able Team ignored him. They were the experienced antiterrorists, and it would still be another ten minutes before the small-boat teams arrived.

Lyons got his way.

"You're clear, Pol," Lyons said. "Proceed on mission."

"Roger."

Blancanales eased forward, staying at a crouch as he came up on the port side of the bridge tower. They had approached in the *Lockett* from the rear, and once the cutter had matched speed, Able Team attached a grappling ladder and easily ascended to the deck. Such an assault was more treacherous at night, but this had been one of those situations where they hadn't been afforded a time of their choosing. Besides, dawn would be here soon.

Blancanales willed himself to relax. His ears were attuned to every sound. He sensed the deep rumble of the freighter's engines beneath his feet; listened to the lap of the waves against the slow-moving ship; took note of each and every element and then filtered it so he could hear anything out of the ordinary. Occasionally he would crouch and raise a fist to signal Schwarz and Lyons that they should hold position.

Finally he reached the base of the bridge tower and studied the darkened windows. There wasn't a single light on inside the bridge and he considered the oddity of that. It seemed like a ghost ship, yet he couldn't shake the feeling something was amiss. He suspected a huge threat loomed close. If the terrorists were hiding somewhere aboard this freighter, they were waiting for just the right opportunity. According to Bryant's report, the crew aboard the Jayhawk had nearly missed the ship because of its blackout condition. Blancanales considered his enemies for a moment, tried to think as they might, assessing every possible move. It was like a game of chess. The pieces had to be in the right place, but a player had also to consider the real objective of the game. It wasn't to put the player's king in checkmate, as most laypersons might suspect; that was simply a reward for the victor. To control as much as possible the four center squares of the board was the true objective. To do that was to control the game, and ultimately the key to winning.

That thought came to Blancanales at the same moment as an explosion on the port side of the freighter. The Able Team commando threw himself to the deck instinctively and he heard and felt the heat as the massive explosion rocketed debris and flames over his head. The ball of superheated gases lit the night as effectively as a flare, and flaming debris rained onto the deck a moment later.

Blancanales turned and felt relief to see that both of his comrades had survived the blast.

He keyed the transceiver. "What the hell was that?"

"The *Lockett* just biffed it!" Lyons roared. "They blew it to hell!"

Blancanales didn't need any more information than that. The enemy had played the game correctly, and they had control of the center of the board, that being the freighter. With the *Lockett* out of commission, the Able Team warriors were trapped on the freighter, with only the Jayhawk as a saving grace. Blancanales got to his feet and raced to the nearest railing. In the wash of light from the flames that licked up from the cutter wreckage and reflected off the freighter's hull, Blancanales could see several small boats, painted black as the night, zip past his position and circle the freighter like birds of prey did carrion.

Lights winked from the boat and Blancanales staggered back in time to avoid the flurry of hot lead that buzzed past his ears. He landed hard on the deck, his right shoulder taking the brunt of his weight on impact, and bit his tongue. He cursed and spat blood, then scrambled to move farther from the railing. He looked toward his comrades, seeing Schwarz make a beeline for his position.

The relief was evident in his friend's eyes. "You okay?"

Blancanales nodded. "Where's Ironman?"

"Right here," the Able Team leader replied, joining them. He'd obviously taken a circuitous route to reach the pair.

"This iron rust bucket's nothing but a decoy," Blancanales said.

Lyons nodded. "Oldest trick in the book."

"And we fell for it," Schwarz added.

"Well, it's not over yet," Lyons stated. "Let's start giving back. I've radioed for support from the chopper."

As if on cue, the Jayhawk roared overhead, spotlight sweeping the area around the freighter. It wasn't armed with any cannons, but there were two crew members aboard carrying M-16 A-3s. They began to fire on the smaller boats, which Able Team could hear buzzing past them. Gunfire erupted from the boats in response and some of it sounded louder and heavier than standard AR fire.

"Machine guns?" Blancanales asked.

"Afraid so," Schwarz replied. He slapped the launcher on his M-16/M-203 over-and-under, and added, "We need to put some heavy fire on those boats if we can. Our boys aboard the chopper won't have unlimited ammo."

"Well, then," Lyons said with a wicked grin, "let's see if we can show them how it's done."

The pair assisted their teammate to his feet, then split up, each heading in a different direction. Blancanales moved toward the front of the vessel, keeping as close to the center of the freighter as he could to avoid exposing himself before he was ready. He couldn't help but feel a pang of regret for the loss of brave souls aboard the Coast Guard cutter. Bryant and his men hadn't stood a chance, the poor bastards. Blancanales would make sure the terrorists knew that the spilling of American blood came at a very high cost. Theirs.

He reached the foredeck and sprinted to the portside railing. He grinned at his good fortune. One of the speedboats approached from his right, visible in the half-light of dawn now breaking the horizon. It was a twenty-foot, high-speed powerboat, its sleek lines accentuated by a forward mounted machine gun. A figure dressed head to toe in combat fatigues manned the weapon. Blancanales extended the MP-5/40 in his right arm and squeezed the trigger, using his well-conditioned muscles to steady the SMG. Sparks flew from the boat where the rounds struck the fiberglass and metal bow. The Able Team commando adjusted his aim on the fly, continuing with a steady barrage of .40 S&W slugs. As the boat went past, he managed to take the machine-gunner, the impact knocking the man from his berth and dumping him off the side. The terrorist's body hit the water hard, the wave dissipating in the wake of the boat as it rocketed past his position.

Blancanales dropped the magazine when the MP-5/40 went dry, watching as the speedboat zipped ahead of the freighter. Another terrorist climbed up to the machine gun, balancing himself precariously as the boat turned a wide circle and made a return run for the freighter. The Able Team commando steadied the weapon with two hands on the rail, pressed his cheek to the stock and aligned his sights on the helmsman. Weapon snug against his shoulder, he moved the selector to 3-round bursts and squeezed the trigger steadily. The first burst went high, but the second caught the helmsman straight-on. All three rounds in the second volley punched through the guy's face and his head exploded under the impact. His body dropped from sight and Blancanales raised his head long enough to determine the boat was headed straight for his position.

The collision occurred moments later, the speedboat smashing just portside of the bow and exploding as sparks ignited the aft fuel tanks. Once more, just as with the cutter, Blancanales felt the heat as wreckage sailed overhead.

IT TOOK HERMANN SCHWARZ less than a minute to acquire his target.

The Able Team commando flipped the leaf sight of the M-203 into action as he ducked in front of a large vent protruding from the deck. The vent served more as a blind than cover, and an effective one at that. The numbers ticked away, but Schwarz held steady. His patience paid off. The armed speedboat zipped past, apparently rushing to assist another boat in some kind of action going down forward. He couldn't see his teammate from his vantage point, but he could imagine the kind of hell Blancanales was probably giving the new arrivals.

Schwarz stood, steadied the leaf sight on the freighter railing, quickly assessed wind speed and triggered the M-203. The weapon kicked against his shoulder with the recoil of a 12-gauge, but the results were much more dramatic. The HE M-383 round was superior in design to its predecessors. The RDX/TNT filling was propelled by a standard high-low pressure system, but with increased velocity given the expanded length of the propellant casing. The grenade hit the rear of the speedboat and exploded. The force of the blast decimated the aft section and the superheated gases caused a secondary ignition of the fuel tanks. The aft section suddenly dipped, flipping the lighter front end of the boat skyward. The ignited fuel washed over the helmsman and his gunner, and they screamed as their skin and clothing spontaneously combusted.

Schwarz didn't bother with mercy rounds this time—that one was for the crew of the *Lockett*.

The sound of movement to his rear caused him to turn and kneel. In the dawn light he made out four figures as they emerged from a hatch set into the aft deck plates. Schwarz went prone as he swung the muzzle of the M-16 A-4 into action. He selected single-shot mode, took a half breath and squeezed the trigger. His first slug connected with the group's leader. The SS109 hardball round ripped open the man's neck and blood visibly sprayed from his torn arteries, subsequently dousing his comrades. The swiftness of the assault obviously confused the terrorists, as they reacted by looking in all directions instead of going for cover.

Schwarz pressed the attack, triggering three more rounds with the precision of a veteran marksman. The second man fell with a double-tap to the chest, the bullets punching neat holes and exiting just as cleanly. They knocked the man off his feet, flipped him into a comrade and both terrorists collapsed to the deck. The third round contacted the last man standing in the chin and blew out the back of his head in a wash of blood and brain matter.

The Able Team commando checked his flank, then scrambled to his feet when confident he was clear. He raced forward, not wanting to give the one terrorist a chance to extricate himself from beneath the corpse of his fellow. The man was still struggling to disentangle himself when Schwarz reached him. A quick butt stroke to the side of his head knocked the terrorist out cold. Schwarz reached into the hip pocket of his fatigues and withdrew a set of plastic riot cuffs. He quickly slapped them in place, then went about the task of disarming the terrorists and tossing their weapons over the side.

Once that was accomplished, he set off in search of his teammates.

CARL LYONS HAD SPLIT from his friends, heading for the freighter's starboard side, intent on making sure they repelled any flanking attempts. The first enemy he encountered approached by speedboat, one of the several he could hear circling the freighter and looking for a clear approach point. Lyons figured he'd give them the advantage—or at least make them think they had it.

The Able Team leader crouched as he heard a speedboat engine die down, and then the voices of its crew members talking to one another. He couldn't make out much, but he recognized the language as Arabic. So the bastards had somehow managed to fool them into boarding the freighter, then made their move on the cutter. What he couldn't figure was how they had managed to wait it out and still avoid detection, but that mystery would have to wait.

Lyons dropped to his stomach—the sling of the MP-5/40 wrapped against his forearm to keep the weapon from sliding on the deck—and risked a glance over the side. He spotted the terrorists ten yards aft of his position just as they fired a grappling gun at the railing. The small charge propelled a hook-and-rope system up to the deck. The weight of the hook led the rope over and around the railing, and it wrapped several times before the steel tines of the hook bit into the thick wood.

Lyons slid out of sight, slung his SMG across his back and reached to his LBE strap to retrieve an AN-M14 incendiary grenade. Filled with a thermate mixture known as TH3, the AN-M14 could burn up to forty seconds even under water and burn through a half-inch homogenous steel plate. That certainly made it adequate for Lyons's purposes. He yanked the pin, clutched the spoon tightly against the grenade body and crawled to a point below the grappling hook. He peered over the side and found himself nose-to-nose with a terrorist. The man opened his mouth to shout, but he never completed it because his lips were mashed over his teeth by a rock-hard punch. The climber lost his hold and dropped from the rope, descending to the boat with the AN-M14 chasing him.

Lyons ducked to safety as shouts of surprise were followed a moment later by shouts of terror. The grenade went off. Piercing screams died under the force of the blast as TH3 doused the speedboat occupants. Lyons didn't have to see the scene to know the kind of carnage he'd dealt. Sounds of splashing followed as they dived into the cold water for relief. It would do them no good; water wouldn't end their agony. Only the sweet arrival of death could do that.

The Able Team warrior rose and leaned over the side as he loosed the MP-5/40. Two of the terrorists were still aboard, out of how many he didn't know, both rolling on the boat deck in agony as they tried to beat out the flames in their clothes and hot molten iron burning into their skin. Lyons ended their agony with a few short bursts.

His victory was short-lived as the roar of another speedboat approached, this one coming from the front of the freighter. Lyons started to swing his weapon into play but held off when he was suddenly lit with spotlights. Just before the lights blinded him, he caught the Stars and Stripes rippling in the ocean breeze. It was the USCG Small Boat Team arriving from the Merrimac River Station. Lyons slung his weapon and raised one hand so as not to get his head shot off, reaching to the radio on his belt with the other. Bryant had loaned him one before they'd boarded the freighter and Lyons had interfaced it with a compatible jack built into his radio. He keyed the transceiver and called the Coast Guard chopper.

"Hey, boys, tell your small-boat teams I'm a friendly!" he shouted.

He could hear an acknowledgment before he switched to the internal band. "Ironman to Gadgets, where away?"

"Coming up on your six, Ironman."

Lyons turned to confirm Gadgets's approach, then keyed the transceiver again. "Pol, what's your status?"

"I'm still at the foredeck, and I'd guess we're clear."

"Meet us at the central lift area. The small-boat team has arrived and we—"

"Um, Ironman, I hate to interrupt," Schwarz cut in, "but I think you better check out the view at twelve o'clock."

It took him milliseconds to realize the reason for his friend's concern. Directly ahead, lights still gleaming against the orange-purple haze cast by a dawning sun, Lyons saw the Boston skyline.

Hell, they were still moving!

Lyons sprinted for the bridge, keying the radio on the fly. "Pol, you ever piloted a freighter?"

"Well, I—"

"Never mind that now!" Lyons snapped on afterthought. "Get below and see if you can find a way to manually shut down the engines. I'm sending Gadgets to the bridge and I'll meet you somewhere near the halfway mark."

"Roger," Blancanales replied.

"Ironman, what the hell do we do if we can't shut this thing down?" Schwarz hollered.

Without looking back, Lyons replied, "Punt!"

He continued for the center section of the ship that would get them below. He couldn't be sure when Schwarz broke off his tail, but he didn't realize the electronics wizard was no longer with him until he met up with Blancanales. The two men went belowdecks, descending into the bowels of the ship and hoping they were headed in roughly the correct direction of the engine room. Lyons whispered a prayer to whatever deity might be listening that Schwarz was able to shut the thing down.

"Worst-case scenario," Blancanales said between pants, "is that we run aground."

"I'm more worried about running into something," Lyons shot back.

They reached the engine room five minutes later and there was no indication the powerful machine was slow-ing. Life hummed through the antiquated freighter, the basso sounds reverberating torturously in Lyons's ears. His eyes took in the massive boiler-style diesel engine at a glance.

Lyons keyed the radio. "Ironman to Gadgets."

"Go."

"What's the story?" he called, overemphasizing each syllable.

"Controls are sabotaged, boss. You're going to have to shut it down there."

"Any ideas?"

"Nothing comes to mind. And the coast is getting pretty big in the window here."

Lyons took another look at the engine and tried to calm his sense of helplessness. Neither of them was exactly a freighter engines expert, and it was a pretty big engine, which meant they could spend a half hour throwing levers without results. Lyons wondered a moment if the terrorists wouldn't have the last laugh after all. Of course, they didn't have it in mind it would go this far. Perhaps Bryant had been right and it would have been easier to stop the ship first.

No use crying over spilt milk, Ironman, Lyons thought.

"Well?" Blancanales demanded, breaking his train of thought. "What now, genius?"

Lyons scowled. "I hadn't thought this far ahead."

"You mean, you don't know how to disable this thing?"

"Not really," Lyons replied. "Do you?"

Blancanales responded with a blank look.

"To hell with it," Lyons finally muttered. He switched to the Coast Guard frequency and said, "Irons to the Jayhawk, do you copy?"

"We read you, sir."

"You still have those Mk 46s ready and waiting?"

"That's affirmative."

"Good. We can't stop this thing from in here. Shoot out the screws and engine."

"Are you crazy?" Blancanales shouted.

"Not according to my last psych eval," Lyons replied with a maniacal grin. He keyed the radio for the Coast Guard chopper as the pair turned and headed topside. "And Jayhawk, just for safety's sake, you guys might want to give us a minute to get the hell out of here."

And a minute was all they got.

CHAPTER TWELVE

Off the Venezuelan coast

Mahmed Temez stood on the deck of the freighter and stared at the rising sun. He thought of his mission and how soon his view wouldn't be so peaceful. In less than twelve hours, the Americans and their allies would be suffering horrible losses. They would be ill-prepared for the disaster to befall the city called Dallas.

Temez was pleased with their progress and with the fact that Jabir had kept his promise. He knew a large part of that success was attributed to the sacrifice of his brothers. According to the latest reports he'd received, the Americans were involved in a vain effort to engage their decoys, totally ignorant of his people's true plans. At that moment, Jabir was on another freighter, far away and bound for the English Channel. The snide, cynical dogs would pay for their interference in his homeland.

Outside of culture and location, there existed absolutely no difference between the Americans and British in Temez's mind. They proclaimed to love freedom, but were first to take it from others. They stood on their pedestals and preached peace and tolerance, but they were the most single-mindedly intolerant and warring nations on the face of the Earth.

Nonetheless, it had all come to this moment. They would emerge victorious. Days and weeks of planning had turned to months; months had realized more than a year of execution. Temez had smuggled the missiles and equipment out of Iraq and into Syria. Under the protection of friends and sympathizers, they disassembled the materials, then shipped them by various means into South Africa. Temez had personally overseen their delivery to Cape Town, where his cousin awaited them. The most important element, of course, was musrah. Its effects were devastating on the human body, as witnessed in the response of the South African military agent's exposure. Now they would implement the poison on a large scale. The death toll would be catastrophic. It wouldn't have the effect on thousands, but on tens of thousands. The operation of September 2001 would seem minor by contrast. This was the first time a plan of this scale would encompass the targeting of civilian populations by military means.

Their chances of success were increased tenfold by Jabir's noble efforts. He had gleaned the support of many allies and stemmed the tide of risk. Financial and technical contributors to the Qibla cause hadn't been aware their efforts would only work to further the success of this operation. They would launch a coordinated attack from four separate locations. By the time the Americans and British realized they were under attack, it would be too late. Yes, they would pay for their interference in Iraq. Allah had willed it long ago. It was destiny.

The sound of throat-clearing brought Temez back from his daydreaming. He turned to see Karif Bhati, his trusted friend and aide. Temez smiled.

"You are lost in meditation," Bhati observed. "I shall leave you."

"No, my friend," Temez replied. "Please stay. I was just thinking of how our moment of victory approaches."

"It will be to the glory of our people," Bhati said.

"It will be for Allah's glory," Temez reminded him.

Bhati bowed. "Of course."

"However, it is also, as you say, that tomorrow will be a day for all our people who have suffered at the hands of the Westerners. They do not realize what they have done. They sleep now in their large homes and warm beds. Most of them have never known what it means to be cold, to be hungry, to be parched under the hot desert sun while awaiting your enemies when you would kill for a few drops of water from their canteens. No, Karif, they have chosen the path to eternal damnation. They have enriched themselves on the suffering of the Islamic nation. I intend to make sure they understand the cost of their actions."

"I know you will succeed," Bhati replied.

Temez smiled at him again. "You are a good friend. But I assume you did not come to listen to my idle banter. What have you to report?"

Bhati stepped aside and gestured for Temez to lead them from the bow to where they worked on completing the platform. "We have been working in shifts to complete the launcher. All of the material is in place and the missile is ready for mounting. I thought you might like to witness the fruit of your men's labor."

"Our men, Karif, our men," Temez replied. "You sometimes forget that one day I expect you will succeed me. When that day comes, I trust you will carry on with our mission. Do not let this be an event of closure. I want you to treat this as a mere preview of what is to come. Should I not survive this operation, you will need to carry on with greater acts. You shall be a bolder man than I, for I've seen it in my dreams."

"Please do not talk of your death, Mahmed," Bhati interjected. "It disturbs me greatly."

"It is a fact of existence," Temez insisted. "We will all die, my friend. But it is how we die that is most important. One can only hope that it is in the cause of Allah, and that we do it not for our reward, but because we are striving to make this a peaceful world for our children. They are the future of our people. If the Americans and British were to have it their way, we would all suffer and die without honor or reward. They would eradicate us if they could."

"Perhaps you are right," Bhati said. As they came to the edge overlooking the pit in the center of the freighter, he added, "But we will not permit extinction. It is not the will of Allah, and it is not our destiny. We are a great people. Witness the triumph of that greatness."

Temez took a sharp breath. The construction was finer than he could have imagined it. The massive lift was supported under hydraulics, and atop the main plate they had slaved for hours to complete assembly of the launcher. At the moment they were working to move the missile into place. Temez was hard-pressed not to show his pride. It was a glorious weapon of war, this device. Long and sleek, it could travel more than six hundred nautical miles with a reserve fuel capacity for another hundred or so. It could carry a nuclear warhead with a thousand-kiloton payload, but in this case it was loaded with an explosive charge capable of leveling several city blocks. The dispersal of musrah would encompass approximately three square miles. Given its target, a heavily populated area of downtown Dallas, Temez's engineers had predicted an exposure of five to eight thousand people.

Temez had been trained to fire many such warheads, but never afforded the opportunity to do so. The chemicals used against the coalition forces during his country's invasion of Kuwait hadn't proved as effective as would musrah. First, they had been dealing with short-range field missiles at the time, and the Patriot missiles had proved quite effective against their Scuds. Temez had once recalled meeting Saddam Hussein during a field inspection, appealing to his great military mind by suggesting more effective ways—ways just like this—to disperse chemical and biological agents. Saddam had considered the idea but never chosen to invest funds in further research.

Temez's colleagues in the Iraqi military liked his ideas. With their connections, they had managed to find some rich oil tycoons to fund exploring the concepts in greater detail. Unfortunately the search by NATO inspectors had effectively halted measurable progress. It was in the months just preceding the American invasion of his country that two scientists he had secreted at an abandoned bunker complex deep in the heart of the Syrian Desert discovered musrah. Subsequent tests of the agent proved promising, but it was Temez's knowledge of missile ballistics and funding by Jabir's associates that made the difference. Ultimately, this was the product of their efforts.

"When will we be at complete operational capability?" Temez asked.

"Our experts tell me they expect to have the missile ready for launch within a few hours," Bhati declared.

Temez nodded. "That is about all of the time we can afford them. We have the greater task of full preparedness in a much shorter span than my cousin. All three of the ships must be ready. Everything depends upon this, Karif. I do not want to be the one who is lacking when it comes time to strike."

"Understood. I give you my personal assurances we will be ready."

"Excellent."

Temez couldn't have asked for more, and knew his friend well enough to know that they would make their deadline with time to spare. He was only sorry they wouldn't be able to witness the destruction firsthand, although he was quite aware of the effects of musrah. It was a viable agent, to be sure, and he had made certain that all of their crew leaders were well informed of its dangers.

The chief antidote was a drug called atropine. It was carried by most medical facilities, but required large quantities to counteract the effects of musrah. While a good number of these medical facilities carried substantial amounts for the very purpose of treating exposures to cholinesterase poisons, it wasn't maintained on a per capita basis. Exposures were uncommon except in farming communities, but even the medical facilities around these areas didn't stockpile atropine with the idea of treating mass casualty incidents. In fact, a good number of countries around the world had severely limited its manufacture, further reducing the chances of treating the masses. Finally, America and its allies would understand what it meant to be starved for medicines and other essential elements for sustaining life.

Yes, the results would be devastating. The aftereffects of such an incident as they had planned made the idea doubly pleasurable. Emergency systems would be unable to handle the flood of patients seeking treatment. In all probability, the national disaster systems would break under the initial burden, and it would take many months, perhaps years, to recover. Bodies would clog the streets and businesses and residences of Dallas. Panic would ensue. There would be riots and the economy would suffer. The results would be like nothing ever witnessed in the history of the Islamic jihad.

Soon, the very face of the world would change. Forever!

Off the Moroccan coast

JABIR AL-WARRAQ WATCHED as the freighter *Thurayya* departed for the Strait of Gibraltar. Its final destination: Israel. Thus far, they were proceeding on schedule. Al-Warraq had to admit that his confidence in their plan was stronger than it had been when his cousin had first approached him. Still, he couldn't help but pledge his loyalty and support for the operation. Mahmed Temez was one of Jabir's few living relatives, most of the remainder having died in defense of his Iraqi homeland in one fashion or another.

Still, al-Warraq wasn't motivated by quite the same religious fervor as Mahmed. In some ways he'd fallen from the pure Islamic faith long ago. Al-Warraq was a realist, a product of the times, and not given to the passion and emotions of religious fanaticism. No, this operation was about revenge against a mutual enemy.

Since moving to South Africa and befriending members of the Qibla, al-Warraq had been profiled by every major police authority in the world. His notoriety and constant scrutiny in the public eye was by design. He'd considered his choices carefully, ultimately realizing that if he were to become actively involved with a small, conceivably nonthreatening group like the Qibla, his visibility would provide the very front he needed to cover his real motives and activities. The spy they had discovered in their cavern hideaway—a man who a short time later he learned was an SANDF agent named Kern Rensberg—had caused him considerable worry.

Al-Warraq had convinced his cousin to accelerate the operation and launch the freighters immediately, not out of any desire to complete the operation but simply to protect his own assets. Now that there was a chance his most secretive activities would be uncovered, he ran a severe risk of failure. Until now, al-Warraq had managed to use the public profiles as a tool to manipulate others into believing he was a victim of ethnic stereotyping. That would have changed drastically if the South African government had published tangible proof of his affiliations with wanted war criminals, thereby causing supporters to back out and withdraw the funds he so desperately needed to succeed in the operation.

Good fortune had smiled on al-Warraq to this point, but the terrorist realized that wisdom was founded in practicality, not prayer to an uncaring god. Despite his upbringing, al-Warraq didn't believe in Allah or the rewards of fighting an Islamic jihad. He was a terrorist, yes, and he knew it. All of his plans and schemes had finally come to fruition, and it was from this point forward that he had to prove his efforts and methods were just as effective as those, like Mahmed, who insisted on supporting what they thought to be a nobler cause.

When the *Thurayya* had become just a speck against the Moroccan coastline, al-Warraq turned and headed to the bridge. He found his second in command, Aban Sahar, sitting in the command chair and watching the activities of the helmsman and navigator. As soon as al-Warraq made his presence known, Sahar jumped from the chair and stood stiffly.

"We can dispense with formalities, Aban," al-Warraq replied with a wave. "We are freedom fighters, not soldiers."

Sahar relaxed, but not entirely. He was unusually tall for an Arab. Syrian-born and raised by a foster family, Sahar was one of the few destined for life as a desert fighter. His foster father had served in the Syrian army, a career officer, and his mother worked as a civil servant as an analyst, a very unusual position of prestige for a woman. Like most Arabs, Sahar had followed in the footsteps of his father and participated in the fighting in Lebanon at the tender age of sixteen. Eventually he'd become discontented with his life, deserted the military and defected from Syria to live in Cape Town. It was then that al-Warraq met the big and impressionable man and eventually convinced him to support his efforts with the Qibla.

Part of that deal included an understanding that Sahar could act anonymously and with complete autonomy.

Eventually, al-Warraq had discovered his friend's unique abilities and talents for dispensing pain. When anyone threatened their cause to lend aid to terrorist groups, he would dispatch Sahar to apply his distinct methods of persuasion. When that didn't work, Sahar would simply satisfy his "autonomy"—the word he chose to describe his bloodlust—and murder them in cold blood.

Like al-Warraq, Sahar also chose not to concern himself with the path to eternal paradise. It was a farce in his mind, which made him particularly useful in al-Warraq's chosen profession. Sahar had been waiting for this operation many months, and his eagerness to hand down death on such a massive scale was present even now in his coal-black eyes.

"Our associates are under way for Israel," al-Warraq announced.

"Yes."

"And yet we're still sitting here, not moving," al-Warraq continued. "I assume there is a good reason for that?"

"We were having some difficulties with the engines," Sahar replied.

"But we aren't now?"

"No."

"Then I would suggest you give the order to get us under way. I have no desire to sit here and wait for them to become wise to our activities."

"I was about to give the order to continue, as you request," Sahar said, "but we have another issue that has recently come to our attention."

"And that is?"

"There are reports that the British have dispatched a battle convoy from one of their southeastern ports. It is a large convoy. We're told several ships, including an aircraft carrier and destroyers. Our intelligence experts believe its composition signals an armada suitable for blockades."

"You think they are on to us," al-Warraq concluded.

"It is a possibility we must consider."

"To what end?"

Sahar expressed confusion. "What do you mean?"

"Do not answer a question with a question, Aban. It is most annoying. I am trying to make a point. You have said we must consider the possibility that the British know of our plans to attack Portsmouth, and that they may attempt to intercept us or the missile. I asked you to what end will this consideration benefit us? Pondering the invariable number of possibilities will not accomplish anything. There is no action in considering possibilities. Do you understand me? The only thing that our enemies understand is action, swift and precise, because it is only until after the action is taken that they discern the message. They have repeatedly demonstrated their inability to accurately predict when or where or how we will strike, and yet we continue to promote the notion that somehow, by some miracle, perhaps, they will spontaneously become enlightened of our methods. The very notion is ridiculous and beneath me. Now, if there are no other issues, let us move this ship and cease any further discussion of insipid and ambiguous details."

Al-Warraq noted with twisted satisfaction that the muscles in Sahar's jaw clenched. There were times when his trusted lieutenant took things a little too far and al-Warraq was forced to put him back in line. There were close friends who had accused him now and again of pontification, but the truth was al-Warraq was simply an educated man. In addition to formal education equivalent to a doctorate in philosophy, al-Warraq was also well-read and extensively traveled. He had walked on every continent, and served as a spokesman for whatever cause would pay him the highest. Men of al-Warraq's ethnicity didn't attain such a status easily, and it was less than rare for anyone to win an argument with him.

Sahar whirled, and in an abusive tone ordered the helmsman to get under way.

Al-Warraq nodded with satisfaction, then left the bridge to clear his head and take in more fresh air. He didn't like enclosed spaces. It had taken a considerable amount of discipline to spend the time he had inside the caves back in the foothills of Table Mountain. The open air suited him, and he'd found any reason at all to escape those confines to take in the views of Table Bay on a regular basis.

He thought of Cape Town now. It had been his home for the past fifteen years, although he doubted he would ever be able to return. That was all right, as he was prone to neither sentiment nor habit. The most important thing about Cape Town was that the false clues he'd arranged to leave behind for the American group that had arrived there would be sufficient to keep them occupied until Qibla had accomplished its mission.

Al-Warraq felt the attack on their group at the waterfront, solely devised so they would take a prisoner, had been an especially nice touch. He had subsequently heard it was Fadil Shunnar who survived the fight on the docks. That was good news. Fadil had always been a reliable party, even since the earliest days of al-Warraq's Qibla influence. He would do exactly as instructed and send the Americans down a dead-end path. By the time they figured out what had happened, it would be too late.

The one thing that seemed troublesome—nothing he saw fit to fret about, but it still nagged at him—was the involvement of the Americans so early. His spies in the SASS said that they were a multicultural team of troubleshooters, but little was known beyond that. Given the proximity of their arrival to the death of Rensberg, al-Warraq could only assume they had missed something vital. Rensberg either had somehow managed to send a message to his people before they caught up with him, or they had found something on him postmortem that had led them to investigate. Other spies said that the mysterious group of men had discovered the abandoned caverns in Table Mountain on the same day they'd arrived in Cape Town.

But al-Warraq refused to let it worry him. As he'd told Sahar, conjecture and rhetoric would serve no purpose. It was time to act, and act was exactly what he planned to do.

"Soon," he whispered as he watched the ocean. "Soon."

CHAPTER THIRTEEN

Stony Man Farm, Virginia

Barbara Price leaned over Aaron Kurtzman's shoulder and watched as he worked.

The Bear's keen mind never ceased to fascinate her. His fingers danced over a keyboard, entering specific codes into the software program created by his team. In front of him was a twenty-five-inch LCD monitor that displayed a three-dimensional image of the Earth's surface. The system was interfaced to the Stony Man group's satellite for their exclusive use. With a combination of the latest technology available from the NSA—National Weather Service, U.S. Navy and NASA—the system could pinpoint the location of any seafaring vessel utilizing a GPS transmitter. The system could also locate vehicles, planes, military equipment and civilian transportation systems that were GPS-equipped.

At present Price could tell Kurtzman was frustrated by the volume of clacking keystrokes. They had so far had little luck in determining, outside of the point of origin, which freighters had the greatest potential. That didn't worry Price to any great degree; she knew Kurtzman would eventually nail it. But it was going to take time, and that, unfortunately, wasn't a luxury they had. The clock was ticking and they still weren't any closer to finding the correct targets.

The other pressing matter was how to prepare a response if they couldn't locate the freighters in time. There was no question the threat was chemical in nature and everything she had learned from medical experts at the Surgeon General's office and FEMA painted an ugly picture.

The effects of the chemical compound, a cholinesterase poison of some complexity, acted on the muscarinic receptors in red blood cells. Victims of cholinesterase poisoning would exhibit signs and symptoms that included profuse sweating, nausea and vomiting, uncontrolled urination and defecation, as well as severe reactions from the central nervous system. The onset was minutes, and mortality was based on the dose and method of exposure. In short, Price was no doctor, but it didn't sound very good.

The other problem was the ability of medical facilities to effectively treat anyone exposed to the cholinesterase poisoning. All the experts Price had consulted concurred on the preferred treatment, which was the administration of high-dose atropine.

That was all well and good, but there were no stockpiles large enough to handle a major number of exposures. The key, then, was to insure that the Qibla terrorists never succeeded in their plans. The only way to do that was to find the freighters and, if necessary, to dispatch military units to blow them out of the water. The greatest difficulty would be keeping such activities quiet and stemming public scrutiny. Even if the President were forced to give the order for such an operation, it wouldn't go over well in the view of public opinion to have naval and air force units blatantly sinking commercial freighters. A lot of tough questions would be asked, much tougher than had been posed at the 9/11 hearings.

They had to make sure it never came to that.

Harold Brognola's weary voice intruded on Price's thoughts. "Greetings, team."

She turned to see that Brognola had entered the Computer Room. His face was as haggard as his suit. He had finished his meeting with the President and opted to go home to catch a couple hours of sleep before returning to the Farm. Price had argued with him over that, pointing out that if he returned immediately, as planned, he would be too tired to continue working effectively. Eventually, Brognola had taken her advice.

"When I told you to get some rest, Hal, I didn't mean for you to sleep in your clothes," she said with a grin.

Brognola chuckled. "Well, I did take off my shoes and jacket."

"Uh-huh," she said, expressing her doubts about even that. "Coffee?"

He nodded, and she went to the pot and poured him a cup.

Brognola crossed to where Kurtzman continued to work. The computer expert hadn't acknowledged him, but that was okay. They all knew the pressures he underwent in an operation of this kind. It was a matter of pride for him. Kurtzman's mind was like a steel trap and he tackled every assignment with the ferocity of a hungry grizzly.

As Price handed him his cup, Brognola asked, "Any more word from Able Team?"

Price nodded. "They stopped the freighter."

Brognola sighed with relief.

"They also managed to ward off an ambush," Price continued. "They discovered the terrorists had been hiding inside an internal hatch in the aft section designed to support small-boat transport. They were attacked once they got on board. Unfortunately, the USCGC *Lockett* was lost in the battle."

"They didn't find any missiles?"

"No, unfortunately," Price replied. "Ironman thinks it was a decoy."

"Which means the threat still looms," Brognola said. He inclined his head toward Kurtzman. "Are we getting anywhere with finding the other freighters?"

"No, and the Bear's been working it three hours straight now," Price said. "I've been trying to get him to take a break."

"No time for breaks," Kurtzman stated, never breaking stride in his typing. "Our teams don't get a break, so I don't get a break. Simple."

Kurtzman returned to his work.

Brognola went to a nearby conference table and dropped into a chair. He took a careful sip from the steaming cup of coffee, then said, "What do we know from Phoenix Force?"

"They left Cape Town about two hours ago, and Jack's filed a flight plan due north near the Western shores of the African continent, but far enough out to be in international airspace. And I'm afraid I have some unfortunate news."

"About Marais?"

Price responded with a curt nod.

"I heard. Aaron told me." He shook his head as he set the coffee cup on the table. "I'm sorry that it happened. I'm sure the Man will want to issue some sort of formal condolences to the South African government. I'll advise him as soon as possible."

"Speaking of which, how did your meeting go?" Price asked, taking a chair next to him.

"Not as well as I'd hoped. At minimum, I think the President feels like it's in the best interests of national security to alert military units specially trained in this kind of thing. He's also alerted the British prime minister and allied governments in Europe and the Middle East, particularly Israel."

Price shook her head. "Why Israel?"

"I think he's concerned Qibla has plans to hit multiple targets," the head Fed replied with a shrug. "An idea he probably got from Lusk."

"Lusk? You mean, as in Frank Lusk, his National Security Adviser?"

"Yes. He brought him to the meeting."

"That seems a bit out of character for the Man," Price said.

"Possibly, but I'd guess he's just covering all of his bases. Actually, he made it clear that Lusk didn't need to know the details of my position or our operation, which I appreciated. My largest concern is what he's told Lusk. It's at the President's discretion, I suppose, but I'd be concerned about Lusk talking to others in less well-informed circles."

"You'd think by now the politics in Wonderland would have ceased to amaze me, Hal," Price said. She sighed. "I get the sneaking suspicion there's more to this than the Man's letting on."

"Well, it doesn't affect us in either case. Lusk advised him to put the military on full alert. Fortunately the President balked at the idea. He'd prefer we handled this and do it damn quick, so no more pressure than we're used to. My chief concern now is coordinating our efforts in the information-gathering process and dispatching the field teams to do what they do best. That makes locating the freighters our number-one priority."

As if on cue, Kurtzman let out a victorious shout. "Got it!"

Price and Brognola exchanged puzzled glances before rising and rushing to Kurtzman's workstation.

"We're not completely there," Kurtzman told them, "but we're a damn sight closer than we were six hours ago."

Kurtzman tapped a few keys and projected the image at his terminal onto a large view-screen mounted against a nearby wall. He then gestured with the mouse to multicolored dots and squares scattered throughout ports and oceanic bodies worldwide as he briefed them.

"This shows the current layout and positions of all known commercial freighter traffic in the world. The total count of full-container freighters based on the top twenty merchant marine fleets is just over three thousand. The yellow lines show the most common trade routes. All the green squares represent freighters that do not match the freighter type or configuration parameters we received based on the intelligence Phoenix Force seized in Cape Town. If I eliminate those, which includes all roll-on/roll-off, passenger, break bulk and refrigerated, that takes the number down to just over twenty-one hundred."

He tapped a key and the green squares disappeared. "I then factored in on the remaining ships that are currently in port and are not expected to leave within the next twenty-four hours. That knocked another large chunk off it, and gets us below the one thousand mark. Those I assigned are the red dots you see." He clicked the mouse and the red dots were removed from the screen.

"As you can see, the blue dots represent the remaining ships currently at sea. Based on the manifests and navigational plans, I cross-referenced all ships that were headed to ports of call we might consider nonessential targets."

"You realize, of course, that doesn't necessarily provide good criteria by which to quantify a prediction of this sort," Brognola interjected.

"In most situations I'd agree with you, boss," Kurtzman replied, with the grin of man who was bursting to tell a secret. "But not in this case. Since all commercial maritime craft are required to file a complete manifest and shipping-lane permit for any commercial maritime operation, I figured the terrorists would most likely falsify these documents. Based on that, I used an algorithm Hunt developed on the fly to map navigation routes against GPS signals and let our mainframe run the calculations against sensible routes."

"I get it," Price replied. "Home ports barely have the time to validate that the contents being shipped and all of the other necessary paperwork is in order."

"Exactly," Kurtzman said. "Which means they certainly don't have time to make sure the navigational plotting submitted by the freighters seems sensible in contrast to the departure and destination ports. The best they can do is to validate that the estimated time to arrive at the destination is within reasonable limits. After that, they rely on companies to tell the truth about where they're going, how they're going to get there and what they're transporting. Certifying agencies can't be everywhere all of the time."

"So if I get where you're going with this, this computer algorithm you and Hunt devised looked at departure port and arrival port, then mapped that against the navigation plan on file to see if it made some sense."

"You've got it!" Kurtzman cried. He clicked the mouse once more and the blue dots were removed from the screen. "That algorithm just completed its run, which left us a whopping fourteen freighters!"

"Fine work, Bear," Price said.

"Damn fine work," Brognola agreed. "So that leaves us only fourteen freighters to contend with. Those are pretty good odds. Now tell me how this breaks down."

"Well, two freighters are currently in the Indian Ocean, and according to the information we have, they're owned by the same company and traveling together. Two more are freight-forwarding vendors in the Coral Sea. In all cases, none of these left a port in South Africa."

"Not to mention I can't see what good it would do Qibla terrorists to hit targets in these areas," Brognola said. "So I'd say it's safe to eliminate them as suspect. But I will ask the Man to contact the Australian government. Perhaps they have ships in the area that could investigate, just to be sure."

Brognola squinted at the screen. "Looks like the remaining are scattered between the Atlantic and Pacific."

"Correct, and all of those left out of Cape Town in

the past seventy-two hours. Three are scheduled to arrive at various ports in the Mediterranean by midnight Zulu. The remainders have filed their destination ports as being in the British Isles, Panama, Newfoundland and, of course, the United States."

"I hate to ask," Brognola said, "but I have to. Are there any other criteria we could apply to pare the number down any further?"

"Nothing tangible, Hal, and I wouldn't attempt it even if I could. We're in a much better position than we were, and I'd take this for what it's worth and find a way to physically investigate the remaining freighters. The other factor we have to consider is that these freighters aren't even transmitting GPS signals. They could just turn them off."

"Not likely. It wouldn't make sense for them to do that. They would want to remain as legit as possible. Anything less and they know it might risk drawing attention. Too many governments monitor these very same things. At the very least, if one of those freighters was bound for a U.S. port, the Maritime Administration would have been alerted to a sudden loss of signal or cessation in communications." He paused and shook his head, then on afterthought, added, "No, I'm sure they're out there transmitting their signal. The trouble is that we just don't know which signal belongs to our Qibla friends."

For a long moment nobody said a word. They just stared at the screen, each lost in his or her thoughts and probably trying to come up with something else they could sink their teeth into. Price was still impressed by Kurtzman's work. It made sense. Of course, some of the information they had gone on was shaky, at best, but there were no other ways she could think of to improve the computer wizard's projections. No, this was about as close as they could get.

"So where do we go from here?" Price finally asked.

"Well, I think the first order of business is to get Phoenix Force in a position where they can start their own investigation," Brognola replied. "They're sure a hell of a lot closer to some of these freighters than we are. What do you think?"

"Well," Price said, looking at the screen again, "you said the President had some reason to be concerned about Israel. That seems like a defensible position. Lord knows the Arabs and Israelis certainly aren't bosom buddies. With those three freighters in the Mediterranean, they could probably make contact in the shortest period of time."

"Good idea, Barb," Kurtzman interjected. "Get the most bang for your buck. I like it."

"Yes, I like it, too," Brognola said. "All right, the Mediterranean it is. Let's get on the horn with David and get him up there immediately. But I want to talk to him personally."

"I'll set it up right now," Price said, rising and heading for the communications system where she'd make the video-audio satellite link.

"Bear, the ships bound for U.S. ports number how many, and where are they scheduled to arrive?"

Kurtzman turned and referenced a printout hanging from a clip attached to his monitor. "One's bound for Boston and scheduled to arrive tomorrow morning, and the other's got a zero-two-thirty ETA to St. Petersburg."

"Okay, then I would think we'd want to get Able Team on that last one, since we're assuming the terrorists are planning to execute their attack using missiles. Assuming a standard medium-range missile can travel six eight-hundred nautical miles, and it's now almost 10:00 a.m., we don't have a lot of time left. I think we better put Able Team on a plane."

"We could have them fly into Miami, get Charlie Mott to meet them there."

Brognola nodded. Charlie Mott was another pilot Stony Man used on an irregular basis when Jack Grimaldi wasn't available. He wasn't an overly skilled combatant, but he was reliable and talented behind the stick.

"Let's do it. I'll let you coordinate the details with Barbara."

The screen image they had been watching suddenly flickered and was replaced by the tired, bleary-eyed face of David McCarter. The fox-faced Briton yawned and scratched his head. Obviously they had woken him from his slumber. Price returned as McCarter mumbled something about it having to be important. She felt sorry for the Phoenix Force leader. They'd been through a lot.

"Wake up, David," Brognola quipped. "Nappy time's over."

"And I was just dreaming 'bout a nice tropical beach somewhere, sipping on a Coke, guv." As if to demonstrate, he popped the top on a can of Coca-Cola Classic, drank half of it down then belched.

"Oh, that's lovely, David," Price said with a droll expression. "Sometimes you have the social graces of a gorilla."

"I think you're confusing me with Ironman," McCarter replied.

"Cut the clowning and listen up," Brognola said. "We've narrowed our possible targets to fourteen. Three are in the Mediterranean, and I understand you're not too far from there. I'm going to be contacting the Man shortly to tell him where we're at, and I need you guys to shag your butts up there and find out what's what."

McCarter was now wide awake. "What about the others?"

"For now, there are no others," Price answered. "There isn't anything you can do about it, anyway, given your location. Four of the fourteen freighters the Bear narrowed us down to are most likely not a threat. The remainders are headed for ports in the Mediterranean, Great Britain and Central and North America."

"Fair enough," McCarter said. "What's the order of business?"

"Get to each freighter, get aboard and see what you can find out," Brognola said. "It doesn't matter how you do it. I'll take responsibility for any backlash. Right now, the President's counting on us to pull this off, and I've promised him we'll deliver. Do what you have to, but try to exercise some measure of control. In other words, do it as quietly as possible."

"Oh, of course we will," McCarter said. "I'm sure a bunch of commandos boarding a commercial freighter in the middle of the Mediterranean in broad daylight will be discreet enough."

"I understand that I'm asking the impossible," Brognola replied. "I just don't want you scaring a bunch of maritime sailors to death. So assess the threat, and if you find it, deal with it in any way you deem fit."

"That we can do," McCarter replied. "We owe these Qibla blokes more than a couple. The boys are champing at the bit to deal out some real arse-kicking. Gary's especially broiling about Marais."

"I don't mean to sound insensitive, but she knew the risks," Brognola said.

"That's what I told him, but I don't think he's much in the mood for logic."

"Just leave him be for now," Price told him. "He'll snap out of it soon enough if I know Gary."

"I can't say as I disagree with you," McCarter replied.

"Able Team will be on a similar mission south of Florida," Price said. "Coordinate with them directly if you discover anything you think might be of value."

"Acknowledged."

"And, David?" Brognola called. "You and the boys watch your asses. I want every one of you back here in one piece when this is over."

"Oh, we'll all come back in one piece," McCarter replied with a lopsided grin. "You can bloody well bank on it."

CHAPTER FOURTEEN

Atlantic Ocean

"Okay, let's get down to business," David McCarter said, dropping copies of maps on the table.

The Phoenix Force leader had printed them off an upload transmission from Stony Man's satellite. It depicted the Mediterranean Sea and pinpointed the three freighters they were to inspect. McCarter wasn't yet exactly sure how best to conduct the operation. He had originally considered splitting up the team; two of them taking one freighter, two more on a second and he and Grimaldi intercepting the third. He dismissed the idea, concerned about thinning their numbers. It had nothing to do with the capabilities of his men. What bothered McCarter most was what he didn't know, and that was the potential enemy count they might be fighting against. He didn't consider it a good idea to execute the operation short-handed.

Encizo picked up the maps, selected one and passed the rest to James. Phoenix Force was ranged around the small table aboard the Gulfstream C-20. They all looked tired, but the flight had afforded them a couple hours' sleep and most were feeling rejuvenated in spite of how they looked. McCarter intended to make sure they got a decent break when this mission was over.

"We have our work cut out for us on this one, chums," McCarter continued. "Hal and Barb are concerned that one of those three freighters could be toting the terrorists and a missile. Our job is to get in, inspect and move on to the next one. The positions you see they're in is current as of fifteen minutes past."

"This is strange," Manning interjected, studying the map carefully.

"What?" Encizo asked.

"Well, we're pretty certain from the intelligence we have so far that these freighters are carrying medium-range missiles."

"Yeah?"

"Well, all of these ships are within range of any number of viable targets already, so why haven't they launched?"

Silence ensued. McCarter had to admit that he hadn't thought of that. Manning had a point. The terrorists could have launched the missiles long ago, but they hadn't. It meant something, but McCarter couldn't quite put his finger on it.

Hawkins could. "I have a theory."

"Let's hear it," McCarter said.

"Well, there isn't really any evidence to support it, but it might explain a few things anyway."

"I'm open to anything right now in the absence of any better ideas," James said.

"Okay." Hawkins looked at the map again, as if it were helping him to collect his thoughts. Finally he said, "If one of these freighters really does have terrorists aboard, it stands to reason that they haven't attacked because they're not ready to attack. They're moving into position, sure, but that doesn't mean a damn thing. We know there are at least two freighters that left Cape Town with missiles aboard. At least, that's a pretty safe assumption, and the number could be even higher than that. And either this al-Warraq or Temez have gone considerably out of their way to try to throw us off the track, even to the point they made sure we found those documents at the shipyard."

"That's true," Encizo agreed. "If we consider just the amount of smarts and patience it would take to plan an op like this, I can't understand why they'd be so sloppy toward the end."

"So you think we were supposed to find that information," James said to Hawkins.

"Well, doesn't it make sense?" Manning cut in. "I've spent hours combing the library and databases at the Farm. As you know, those archives contain a hell of a lot of data, and the work of many a CIA analyst. I happen to think a lot of that stuff is pretty valid in the sense that it describes the general MO of most terrorist groups.

"Understand that one of the main theories behind terrorist planning is coordination. The days of hit-and-git are over for most of them. They've grown smarter, faster and more organized. It wouldn't surprise me in the least if this was one of those times where it's all about coordination."

"Well said, Gary," Hawkins replied. He looked at McCarter. "That's exactly where I'm trying to go with this. If the terrorists are in the Mediterranean and they haven't attacked yet, it's most likely because they can't attack yet."

McCarter nodded, completely understanding now. "In other words, they're waiting."

"You nailed it," Hawkins replied.

"Well, evidence or no evidence, your theory doesn't sound like bunkum to me, mate. I'd say we go with that and see what falls out, no pun intended."

"You know, of course," James said, "this likely means they have more than one target. If they're waiting, it's because they plan to launch the missiles at the same time. It would make it much more difficult to retaliate against a coordinated strike. If even one of those things lands where they want it to, we're going to have one big global shitstorm to deal with. The fallout will be felt worldwide."

"And God forbid they hit more than one target," Encizo added.

"So maybe what all this means is we have some extra time," Manning said. "Trouble is, we don't know how much, so we're going to have to move like wild horses on this deal. Where do you want to start, boss?"

McCarter frowned. "I think we have to assume the ship closest to a port is our first priority."

"From what I see here, that would be the ship headed to Israel," James observed.

"That works for me," Encizo said.

"And it seems like the most viable target, as well," Manning said. "The other two are bound for Tripoli and Naples. Unless Qibla has a beef with some fellow Arabs or a gripe against the Vatican, it seems our best bet would be Israel."

"Israel it is," McCarter replied. "Now, let's talk about the lovely swim we're all going to have."

Miami, Florida

"HEY!" CHARLIE MOTT CALLED as he stood near the hangar and waved at Able Team.

Gadgets Schwarz returned the friendly greeting as the three warriors, all in mirrored sunglasses, crossed the tarmac to join the pilot. Unlike Grimaldi, who spent a good part of his time flying members of Stony Man from one end of the world to the other, Mott took contracts outside official channels. Jobs like this didn't come often, but when they did, it seemed Mott was more than happy to oblige.

Mott had brought his personal plane, a Raytheon

Beechcraft King Air 350, its nose barely jutting from the front of the small hangar. Although built on the same style as the original King Air 90, this craft was considerably larger and faster, and most of the electronic modifications it had undergone had been financed courtesy of Stony Man funds. It was forty-six feet long, with two Pratt & Whitney Canada PT6A 60A free-turbine engines, each rated at over one thousand shaft hp. It wasn't as fast as a jet, its top speed being about 315 knots, but fully loaded it could travel almost two thousand nautical miles before refueling. Stony Man had added some advanced electronic surveillance equipment, including a Honeywell H-423 ring laser gyro Inertial Navigation System, a GPS receiver and two digital computers with dual-redundant multiplex buses. The craft's white hull gleamed in the noonday sun, and sunlight reflecting off the tarmac made its red-and-gold striping iridescent.

Mott pumped the hand of each man in turn with an enthusiastic expression. "Good to see you fellows again. It's been a while."

"Likewise," Schwarz said. "How's it hanging?"

"I'm getting by," Mott replied gregariously. "You know how it goes, same old, same old."

"You get briefed by our friends?" Lyons asked, having dispensed with the pleasantries and getting to business.

Mott nodded. "You bet. I understand we're looking for a freighter."

"Not just any freighter, Charlie," Blancanales said.

"This one's carrying a warhead loaded with some very nasty chemicals."

"Yeah," Lyons added. "And we've been assigned the lovely task of trying to find this needle in a haystack, so I hope all your equipment checks out."

"No sweat," Mott said, patting his aircraft's nose as gently as he would a baby's bottom. "The crew in Wonderland fixed up King Fish just fine. She's running like the champion she is, and I've already done all the preflight checks. So if you gents will just climb aboard, we'll be up, up and away before you know it."

Lyons nodded and then joined his teammates in stowing their equipment in the luggage compartment, located in the rear of the plane. While capable of seating eight in the main area, four of the seats had been removed, leaving an open space for the special equipment belonging to Stony Man. Brognola had insisted it be portable, so it was only loaded when Mott had a job to do with the team. Otherwise, Mott kept it locked safely away at an undisclosed location. Even Able Team didn't know where it was kept, which was fine because they didn't really have a need to know.

As they were taking their seats, Mott squeezed past them in the aisle and climbed into the cockpit. It was a two-seater, but Mott didn't need a copilot. He'd flown the little twin-prop probably as many times as Lyons had shot bad guys.

Mott taxied onto the terminal and got airborne as soon as the tower had cleared his departure. Meanwhile,

Gadgets had turned his attention to setting up the reconnaissance equipment. According to their intelligence, there were two ships bound for the U.S., one going to St. Petersburg and the other to Boston. Seeing as the terrorists had sent the decoy to Boston, Able Team agreed it was unlikely they would send a second freighter there. Security would be tight. The UCGC *Grant* had arrived shortly after their friends in the Jayhawk had stopped the freighter, and the Harbor was shut down for hours while they towed the freighter to a secure location. They still hadn't opened the harbor to general traffic when Able Team left.

The prisoner they had taken at the Qibla house refused to talk, so Able Team turned him over to Nootau Hightree's custody. Actually, the FBI agent would recover from his injuries with no permanent damage, and the capture of a terrorist insurgent would do wonders for his career. Able Team decided to give Hightree full credit for the capture, which also kept them far removed from any public scrutiny.

Lyons watched with fascination as Schwarz easily moved from one piece of equipment to the next. The guy's expertise with electronics was second only to that of Aaron Kurtzman, and that knowledge had been crucial since their first days together. It had certainly served Mack Bolan well during his war against the Mafia, not to mention how valuable it had proved to Able Team since its birth and the origins of Stony Man.

"What are you doing?" Lyons finally asked, no

longer able to quell his curiosity.

Schwarz stopped what he was doing long enough to look at Lyons with surprise. He knew why his friend was taken aback; Lyons had hardly ever shown much interest in anything technical above a menial sense of duty. Lyons was only interested in those things that could help them in combat, so he knew Schwarz would probably be taken a bit off guard by his genuine interest.

Schwarz went back to his work, not hiding the smirk on his face. "Yeah, like you really want to know."

"I do want to know," Lyons said, trying to sound hurt, "or I wouldn't have bothered asking."

Schwarz stopped once more to look at his friend. "Really?"

Lyons sighed, exasperated now. "What, do you want me to swear on the Bible?"

"As a matter of fact—"

"Forget it," Lyons said, waving him off.

"No, I won't forget it. You really are interested in this stuff here. Aren't you?"

"I just said I was."

"Yeah, but…ah, never mind that. What do you want to know?"

Lyons made a generalized gesture at the equipment. "I want to know about that stuff. What exactly does it do? How does it work? You know, teach me something."

"Okay, well, let's see…let's start with this here." Schwarz pointed to a large gray box sitting on top of a swiveling column. He said, "Inside of this is what's called a Military Laser Inertial Navigation System. It was developed by Honeywell, and it's capable of working in conjunction with another system called a terrain painter. What this will do is give us a road map, if you will, of the area where the freighter is at. We'll be able to tell then what we might be up against should we have to bail out and make an assault."

Schwarz flipped some nondescript switches on the box and it started to recess into the floor. He then gestured to the two computer systems that took up the majority of the room. "These computers are MilSpec SNU-84-1 compliant, meaning that they answer to the F^3 spec of the Air Force."

"And that means?" Lyons interjected.

"Form, fit, function," Gadgets replied with a wicked grin. "F^3 may sound like a lot of mumbojumbo, but that very basic idea has propagated delivery of some of the best equipment the military has ever known, particularly in recent years.

"Anyway, none of that would be half as interesting if you didn't know what it actually does, and that's the cool part. These two innocent little boxes are state-of-the-art, my brother. I can transmit high-speed data to Stony Man at almost one gigabyte per second."

"Is that fast?"

Schwarz burst into laughter. "Does a bear shit in the woods? Hell yeah, it's fast, and certainly faster than anything the enemy's got. What we can do would make even military scientists green with envy. We get the latest in everything, Ironman. We get it before NASA, before MIT, even before the Company. Hell, we're a hotbed of testing. Remember when the ACR prototypes came out and we gave all of them the thumbs-down?"

Lyons nodded. Oh, yeah, did he remember. Who the hell could forget it? The Advanced Combat Rifle program had been the brainchild of the U.S. Army, designed to give the most promising manufacturers of assault rifles in the world the chance to compete for a contract to supply the latest in small arms arsenals to the American military. The four final designs came from AAI Corporation, Colt, Heckler & Koch and Steyr-Mannlicher. While most of the basic tests were performed by Regular Army and Army Reserve infantry units, the military also considered the possibility of using the weapons in special operations.

Following inspection by John "Cowboy" Kissinger—Stony Man's resident gunsmith and chief armorer—the weapon was put into rigorous field testing. Able Team, in particular, abused the hell out of the four candidates, even taking them on a secondary mission. When all was said and done, they considered every single one of the weapons as hardly an improvement on the M-16 A-2, and they told the Army to have their vendors go back to the drawing board. The M-16 A-4 turned out to be the net result of those efforts.

"But data transmit speed just scratches the surface," Schwarz continued. "Once we've located the freighter, we'll be able to pinpoint every single target on board. This terminal will show us the heat signatures, and the second will then take that information and map it so that we have a perfect picture of where the hotspots are."

"Very nice," Lyons admitted. "What about Phoenix Force? Do the guys have something similar on board their wings?"

"You bet," Schwarz said. "But none of them are as savvy on the technical side. You know how David is. He just likes to push buttons."

"Yeah, I know," Lyons cracked. "All thumbs."

"Aw, why don't you two knock it off?" Rosario Blancanales said. Lyons knew he was referencing the almost egomaniacal relationship between him and David McCarter. "You know you really like each other, so why don't you just kiss and be friends."

"Because he's a cocky Cockney, that's why," Lyons shot back. "I know his type."

"Yes, and he's just like you," Blancanales said. "All ego."

Lyons winked and returned his attention to Schwarz when Blancanales simply waved away the gesture. "So, what else can these hunks of junk do?"

"Well, first you might want to know that these 'hunks of junk'—is that what you called them?—set the old man back about thirty-five thousand dollars apiece."

"What!" Lyons exclaimed. "I don't know of any computer worth that much!"

"You don't know computers, then, because we probably got off cheap, government discounts and all."

"Well, if we did," Blancanales interjected, "it sure wasn't reflected in our paychecks."

"Come on, you know you only do this because the money's so good," Schwarz told his longtime friend.

"Yeah, right, whatever you say, Wizard."

Schwarz chuckled, then returned to instructing Lyons. "Okay, so you asked what else it does. Well, because The Bear can send us so much information so quickly, this thing can also tell us at almost any given point where the nearest military units are. We know about every aircraft, every seafaring vessel, every boat, plane, train and automobile. That also includes a visual linkup, so when we're in range we'll be able to fly at a ceiling of twenty-thousand feet and still look in the eyes of a sentry walking the ship."

Lyons whistled. He'd been trained on a lot of the stuff, but mostly it had been high-level overviews given by bespectacled students from MIT, the NSA or the Pentagon in some generic classroom setting. Most of it didn't make a lick of sense, but Brognola insisted on cross-training for all three members. That part of it Lyons understood, even if he didn't like it. If one of them was weak in a particular area, then that weakened the entire team, and yet Lyons just couldn't seem to get himself interested. He knew he should set the example as a leader, but then he figured Gadgets and Pol were interested enough in the stuff to keep up on it. If he happened to lose both of them in a mission then he had no team, and there was nothing weaker than a team that didn't even exist.

"So you're saying that when we encounter these freighters we'll actually be able to see them? Not just their infrared signatures or blips on a computer screen, but actual physical bodies?"

"Pretty much," Schwarz replied.

"That's damned impressive, indeed," Lyons replied. "I didn't think such a little box could do all that."

"Oh, yes, and it can do a hell of a lot more. But now I have to run some tests and I can't show them to you. But we can talk more about it later."

Lyons nodded, and left Schwarz to the job.

During Lyons's brief phone conversation to the airport, Brognola had told him of his talk with the President, the Man's choice to involve Lusk in the meet, and the findings of Phoenix Force and death of Jeanne Marais. And Lyons could only conclude that not a damn bit of it added up.

First, there was the decoy to consider. The Qibla had gone to considerable lengths to throw any would-be pursuers off their track, and yet they had been sloppy enough to leave allegedly critical intelligence behind. Second, they weren't a large outfit by any means, and yet they had decided to pool all of their resources for this mission. So they weren't a big group, but the threat they posed was monumental. Lyons had read up on the effects of the cholinesterase poison, and it wasn't nice.

They would definitely have their hands full if they got exposed to the stuff.

In response to their initial intelligence reports, Brognola had insured the issuance of chemical suits to all the field team members. Lyons had to admit that had been a wake-up call for him. He couldn't be exactly certain of all the possible variables where this attack was concerned, but he knew what it would mean for the country if the terrorists were even partially successful.

There was a low beeping sound in the cabin, and it startled Lyons from his thoughts. The Able Team leader realized he'd been dozing. He tongued away the pastiness in his mouth, shook his head to clear the cobwebs, then the voice of Charlie Mott filled the cabin.

"Ironman, it's David McCarter on the horn for you, Priority One channel."

Lyons grabbed a headset off the nearby rack, donned it and keyed up to the standard secure frequency. "It's me."

"Enjoying your nap time, mate?" the Briton's voice replied.

"At least I didn't get some cushy vacation in South Africa," Lyons replied.

"I'll trade you anytime you'd like."

"No, thanks. I like this side of the world better."

"I can't argue with a bloke like you on that one," McCarter said cheerily.

"So, I take it you didn't call to whisper sweet nothings in my ear."

"Actually, no. I called to tell you that T.J. came up with what we all agree is a solid theory, and since last word from the chief was that we coordinate directly with you, I think you better hear this."

"Uh-oh," Lyons said. "I can tell just by the sound of your voice that I'm not going to like this."

"Mate, you don't know the bloody half of it," McCarter replied.

CHAPTER FIFTEEN

Mediterranean Sea

Not quite six hundred kilometers off the coast of Tel Aviv-Yafo, Commander Jarred Blankenship—a commanding officer in the British Royal Navy—stood on the bridge of his destroyer and studied the oncoming freighter. Standing next to Blankenship was Lieutenant Commander Edsel Bedford, the ship's executive officer.

"Has she answered her hail to full stop for inspection?" Blankenship asked.

"No, sir," Bedford replied. "That was why I summoned you, sir."

Blankenship didn't reply, but instead lowered the binoculars and grunted. This was quite odd, although not any more peculiar than other situations he'd encountered since being assigned to the Mediterranean. Actually, he had to admit that he liked his assignment.

Blankenship would have never admitted it openly to anyone outside of his wife, Mary, but he found the climate and easygoing lifestyle preferable to the cold, stuffy environment back home in London. In fact, he'd spent the previous evening having dinner at the NATO fleet admiral's home, and considerable time charming the man in hopes of retaining another tour of duty here.

However, he now had more pressing matters demanding his attention. In most cases this type of situation was usually the result of either a malfunction in a communication system, or a ship that, in addition to its standard cargo—which should have undergone rigorous inspection at the Strait of Gibraltar check station— might be smuggling a spot of contraband to avoid customs fees. Such contraband might include anything from liquor to magazines to cigarettes or cigars. Blankenship took one more look at the freighter through the binoculars. The freighter still hadn't slowed, and it now appeared as if she were planning to glide right past his ship just like it was nobody's business. Well, they couldn't bloody well have commercial freighters just buzzing around the Mediterranean and refusing to answer to Her Majesty's Royal Navy.

"Number One, send the call for general quarters," Blankenship said. He then turned and went to a ship-to-shore phone. It would connect him directly with the harbor master in Tel Aviv-Yafo. When the harbor master's office answered, he said, "This is Commander Jarred Blankenship of Her Majesty's HMS *Newcastle*.

We are currently tracking a freighter that is refusing to answer hails or requests to stop."

He gave them the freighter's registration number, then requested to be connected with the fleet admiral as per standard operating procedure. It was a time-wasting process, but Blankenship also knew it was a precautionary one. Since the involvement of a number of countries in NATO had expended efforts to provide a security presence in the Mediterranean, protection of the political environment had seemed to become preferable to maintaining a show of military security and force to would-be privateers, saboteurs and terrorists. One didn't flex muscles here without regard for the rights of commercial shippers who delivered vital supplies to a number of the more disadvantaged and unfortunate cultures in the "fertile crescent" of the world.

"Admiral Stalworthe speaking."

"Sir," Blankenship began, "this is Commander Jarred Blankenship of HMS *Newcastle*."

"Yes, of course," the admiral said in an almost congenial tone. "How are you, Commander? We did enjoy dinner with you so much last night. I was just telling my wife again this morning how impressed I am with your knowledge of RN strategies."

"Yes, thank you, sir…very kind of you to say so, sir," Blankenship said, trying to keep the impatience out of his voice. "But I'm afraid I'm calling on a business of some urgency, sir. I wouldn't use an official line for any other purpose."

The admiral cleared his throat. "Of course not, Commander, and I would never assume such. What seems to be the problem?"

"Sir, I have an R-class commercial freighter approximately three hundred meters off my port bow that despite all attempts at communication refuses to reply for spot inspection. According to information in our computer systems, she left the day before last from Cape Town and listed her final destination as Israel."

"And you say she's refusing her call to heave to?"

"Aye, sir," Blankenship replied. "Now, she has made no hostile move, but she isn't stopping, either."

"It sounds like a simple communications malfunction."

"That was my initial assessment, as well, sir, but with the sun setting shortly, the nighttime wouldn't be a good point for a ship to be without communications. I also considered it strange that any such malfunction wasn't discovered in Gibraltar. She would have undergone significant inspection at Checkpoint Gibraltar before ever being allowed to enter our sector."

"Yes, but that doesn't mean there was a problem at that time. And it might be something as simple as her working off the wrong band. Why do you wish to detain her, anyway, Commander? Do you have some reason to suspect she poses a security threat?"

"Not actually, sir," Blankenship replied, a little

miffed at the question. "I would respectfully remind the admiral of his recent standing order to increase the number of ad hoc inspections conducted in this area."

"Ah, yes, of course, you're right," Stalworthe replied. "Well, I don't think it's anything to worry about, Commander, but Her Majesty's vessel is under your command. I leave it to your discretion to make the final decision as to whether to stop this freighter or simply to make a log that you contacted me. Off the record, I would caution you to tread carefully on this one, Jarred. We don't want it to appear as if the Royal Navy has turned into some sort of martial force bent on reigning once more on the high seas. Do you understand?"

"I do understand, sir, and I will be as conciliatory as possible within the limits of my duties," Blankenship replied with glee. "And I am equally confident the admiral is correct, and that this will turn out to be nothing."

"Good work, Commander," Stalworthe said. "Carry on."

As Blankenship hung up the phone, he turned to his executive officer. "Lieutenant Commander Bedford, sound the alert call and prepare to intercept that freighter."

"Aye, sir."

"I THINK WE MIGHT have trouble," Manning said, looking up from the high-resolution image created by the digital painter built into the onboard computer system.

David McCarter looked up from where he was inspecting his equipment at the table. "What's up, mate?"

"That freighter we're tracking now has a British destroyer moving into an intercept position, and I'm not sure we can beat them to the punch."

"Damn!" McCarter rose and moved to inspect the terminal. "That's all we bloody well need, an international incident involving British military right in the middle of the Mediterranean."

"That's not the worse of it," Rafael Encizo said, entering the cabin and catching the tail end of the conversation. "If that destroyer crew attempts to board the freighter, the terrorists might panic and decide to forego a coordinated attack in favor of an early attempt on the target."

"Oh, bloody hell," McCarter moaned. He looked at the screen. "And they're within target range, too. Shag it, boys, we're going in." McCarter slapped a switch on the wall that opened an inboard communications link directly to Grimaldi.

"We've got trouble below, Jack."

"I saw it," Grimaldi replied. "You're talking about that destroyer."

"Right-o, mate," McCarter said. "We're going to bail here. I need you to take us in as close and low as possible."

"Minimum ceiling in that area is ten thousand feet, David."

"We're going to need at least half that if we've got a snowball's chance of getting there before my countrymen do."

"How will they respond if they discover there are terrorists on the freighter?"

"It's not the RN's response I'm worried about, mate, it's the terrorists'," McCarter said. "Just get us down there, and quick-like."

"Roger that."

McCarter terminated the connection and rushed to pack his equipment. The weapons would have to remain inside waterproof bags until such point as they were aboard ship. If they played their cards right, they could perhaps parachute directly onto the freighter. A lot would depend on how low Grimaldi could go before NATO's Mediterranean Command Group simply decided to blow him out of the sky. He wasn't sure how the Stony Man top gun planned to handle that. Then again, it wasn't really his worry. Grimaldi would handle it, and that's all he had to concern himself with. His chief job was to insure that they neutralized the terrorist threat, if any.

McCarter wished he had more intelligence, but this was the game and the hand he'd been dealt to play with, and he wasn't going to get any more cards. He was taking an awful risk, hoping he was right about the ship. For all he knew, this could turn out to be a dud. Then where in the bloody hell would they be? Not only would it take time to explain their presence to the freighter's crew and the destroyer's commander, but it would require significant cooperation to get somewhere they could hook up with Grimaldi again. Well, they would just have to play it by ear and work out the details at a later point. Right now the most important thing was to get to the freighter before the British and, if necessary, put down any threat.

JACK GRIMALDI HEARD the voice in his ears as he brought the Gulfstream C-20 into position. He wondered if David McCarter had the first inkling of what he was asking for. To violate airspace in a volatile region like this was risky enough, but he certainly was asking for it when there was so much sea activity. It wouldn't take the NATO defense forces long to respond to anything they perceived as a threat, which Grimaldi was going to have to find a way to convince them he was anything but.

"ComFAirMed control to unidentified aircraft," the man said, "you are in violation of Mediterranean air space under the jurisdiction of NATO forces. Please respond."

Grimaldi ignored the Commander Fleet Air Mediterranean controller.

The controller repeated his message and Grimaldi answered him. "ComFAirMed, I read you. This is American aircraft N921SV. I'm having a serious horizon indicator malfunction, and my altimeter just went on the fritz. I am also losing height. Can you confirm my position and altitude?"

"Aircraft N921SV, stand by and follow your present course," the controller said. Dead air came through his headset, but it was less than thirty seconds before the controller's voice returned. "Aircraft N921SV, do you copy?"

"I copy, ComFAirMed," Grimaldi replied.

"You are way too low, sir," the controller replied. "You're presently at two thousand feet and continuing descent. Hard deck is ten thousand feet, N921SV. Do you read? You need to pull up now."

Grimaldi knew he meant it. Commander Fleet Air Mediterranean was the primary U.S. command authority presence in the area, and one of four stations responsible for all air traffic activities under NATO. Right at that moment they were probably scrambling the closest fighters and it wouldn't be more than five minutes maximum before they were in the air. He couldn't compete against F-16 Falcons and F-18A Hornets. They'd be on him like white on rice.

Grimaldi said, "N921SV to ComFAirMed, I will ascend as soon as I can, but right now I'm flying blind up here! Can you assist?"

"Aircraft N921SV, you need to pull up, sir. Do you read me? Pull up your aircraft! You are entirely too low. Pull up now, or we will be forced to intercept your craft. N921SV, do you read?"

Grimaldi killed the switch and moved the band to the inboard system channel. "David, you reading me?"

"I read you."

"We're a minute out from target. Are you ready for drop?"

"Affirmative, mate. What's our height?"

"I've got you to two thousand. I go any lower than that and I'm going to have NATO fighters all over my ass. You got forty-five minutes, no more. Then I'll be up and gone. Let me know when the last one's away."

"Roger that. Thanks, ace."

"Good luck!"

"CLOSING TO WITHIN standard intercept range now, sir," Lieutenant Commander Edsel Bedford announced.

Blankenship nodded with a satisfied expression. "Excellent work, Number One. Prepare boarding boats and load a blank charge to fire. But let's send up the all-stop flare first. That should give them an idea of the kind of business we mean. We shall not fire a warning shot across the bow unless they leave us absolutely no choice, and then only if I give the order to do so."

"Aye, sir."

Although Blankenship wasn't really required to explain himself to his junior officers, he did have enough respect and stock in the knowledge and experience of his executive officer to pull him aside for a private conversation.

"I don't mean any disrespect to you, Edsel," Blankenship told him. "But we're in a rather precarious situation here according to the information Admiral Stalworthe gave me. We are to avoid any sort of incident, if you take my meaning."

Bedford replied with a short nod. "I do very much take it, sir. I leave control of this in your hands."

"Good. I am going to have you accompany the patrol teams. I think it will be a sporting show if the second in command represents Her Majesty's interests, don't you?"

"Of course, sir."

"Good, then join the men and prepare to board. You're relieved of bridge duty for now. I will take it from here."

"Aye, sir." Bedford saluted smartly, turned and headed for the launch deck.

Blankenship returned to the main part of the bridge and ordered the helmsman to full stop. They were now less than a hundred meters from the freighter. He turned and nodded to the signalman, an indicator that they should send up the all-stop flare. The signalman called a shipwide alert, threw two small switches to the right of his console and palmed a large red button there. The sound of a topside flare gun firing was barely audible inside the enclosed bridge. The cluster shot high into the air, arced and exploded into a starburst pattern recognized by all maritime vessels as a stop request.

Seconds turned into minutes, but the freighter didn't even appear to slow. Blankenship advised the signalman to call on the helm and release the boarding parties, then ordered him to have gunnery standing by with the blank charge. It wouldn't do anything more than fire an inert cluster—one that acted very similar to the all-stop flare—but it was as clear a warning as to the consequences the ship would suffer if it didn't heave to. Such signals were the foundation of maritime and naval military operations. All crews and captains of every vessel on the sea knew what these signs meant. There would be no proclaiming ignorance.

Blankenship hoped it wouldn't come to that. The destroyer commander looked out the forward view port of the bridge and shook his head. The freighter still hadn't stopped, and now he knew that the boarding parties leaving the HMS *Newcastle* would be visible to the freighter crew. Blankenship hated to do it, but the bow warning shot was his last resort.

"Mr. Devine?" He addressed the fire control officer.

"Aye, sir."

"Load the charge and clear for battery," he said. "Give me your firing solution."

"Aye, sir," he said. He reached to the ship phone that would connect him directly to the firing team. Blankenship knew he had a fine crew. They were the pride of the RN and he knew they would perform admirably.

The fire control officer said, "Sir, one Seagnat 216 Mod 1 charge is loaded and targeted for across the vessel's bow, angle one-ten mark zero."

"Fire at will," Blankenship said with a nod. Certainly they would stop when they heard that boom of a heavier gun. The Seagnat was generally used for electronic countermeasure purposes, but could double for other such jobs as required. It was an excellent choice for this type of situation.

At the moment the weapon fired, an explosion occurred somewhere just in front of the bow. Through the bridge window Blankenship could see several bodies flying through the air, their charred uniforms obviously those of his crew.

"Mr. Devine, report! What the hell is going on? Did we hit our own people?"

"Checking now, sir!" Devine replied. "Gun battery team one, report! What did you do?"

A moment later the entire bridge crew watched in amazement as the Seagnat exploded just aft of the freighter's starboard bow. Blankenship's jaw dropped. They had fired exactly where they should have and at the target they should have. The source of the explosion had been near the small boats, which meant that either there had been an accident or a purposeful attack. Only seconds elapsed from the moment of that realization to when Blankenship got his answer.

"Sir, Forward Obs is reporting that several men on the freighter are at the railings and armed with missile launchers, some type of shoulder-fired torpedo or anti-tank weapons."

"That was no accident," Blankenship whispered, unable to stop the horrified expression on his face. "We're under attack! Sound battle stations and get me command on the horn!"

"Aye, sir!"

FAHD ABUFATIN HADN'T EXPECTED anything even close to what was transpiring at this very moment.

Right before his eyes, he was watching a British warship approaching fast and sending boats with armed men to board his ship. Damn Jabir al-Warraq! He had promised that this would be easy. Jabir had said that they would be able to reach the port in Tel Aviv-Yafo without incident, and that everything would be fine. He only had twelve hours remaining before they would launch their attack, but now this problem had arisen.

In response to the incident, Abufatin ordered three of his men to attack the smaller boats. Whatever happened, they couldn't afford to be captured. If at all possible, he knew that the captain of the destroyer would try to take them without sinking the ship. If he focused his efforts on the smaller boats, that would prevent them from boarding the ship.

"Whatever happens, Dabir," he told his second in command, "you must not let them board this ship. We will defend until the last man, and if we cannot get the missile launched in time, then we will blow it to bits. Have your men get below and start planting charges in key areas."

Dabir had gone to do his bidding, but Abufatin could tell he did it with some reluctance. Who could blame him? They weren't soldiers or fanatics; they were simply hired guns in the employ of Jabir al-Warraq. Abufatin had no desire to die this day, either in loyalty to Allah or al-Warraq. He was supposed to do a job and get paid for it. If he had known about the magnitude of the risks, he probably would have doubled the normal fee for him and his men.

It didn't matter, though, because he prided himself on his reputation. He was one of the finest mercenaries in the Arabic community, and he had never betrayed a customer. He and his men had been hiding in Cape Town when they were first approached by one of al-Warraq's closest friends and advisers, the mammoth Aban Sahar. Abufatin could remember how much Sahar intimidated him when they'd first met. He had the eyes of a killer, there was no doubt there, and Abufatin had wondered in that first meeting if it was wise to take the job at all. But then the offer had been too big and too generous, so he accepted for the sake of his men and their families, most of whom were back in Iraq and starving.

The first of his mercenary group to reach the port side of the railing didn't hesitate in the least. The man raised a rocket launcher to his shoulder, sighted the weapon on the approaching boats and fired. At nearly the exact same moment, one of the heavy guns on the British ship boomed, almost as if firing in response to the explosion that occurred on one of the boats. The sailors in that boat were decimated by the explosion. Even as the blast died, a second man set up his launcher and fired, but this charge missed, instead exploding about fifteen feet beneath the surface and showering the remaining boat's occupants with a harmless spray of seawater.

Abufatin could now hear Klaxons sounding on the destroyer. He knew they wouldn't be able to repel such an overwhelming force for long, and they were cer-

tainly outclassed by the mammoth warship, whose guns
were now swiveling in their direction. But none of that
could hold Abufatin's attention, because something even
more bizarre and puzzling demanded it.

It was the sound of something landing on the roof of
the bridge tower, then the subsequent burst of autofire
that raked his men below.

CHAPTER SIXTEEN

All five members of Phoenix Force had bailed from the Gulfstream C-20 as it made a low, sweeping turn and began a rapid ascent as soon as the last man had cleared the door. At that low altitude, the only way to jump was with a static line, which would pull the cord automatically. The average speed of drop from the peak of chute expansion was about thirty-three feet per second, so total jump-to-target time had only taken about seventy seconds.

Yeah...*only,* David McCarter thought.

Seventy seconds was a long time when he considered it took the enemy less than a second to pull the trigger. Then again, that was assuming the quarry knew where to look, and in this scenario they were able to take the terrorists by total surprise. McCarter had been first out the door and he steered his chute to bring him down on the fast-moving freighter as close to the bridge as possible. His luck held out and he made a picture-perfect landing, slapping the quick releases on his chutes just a few feet above the roof of the bridge.

McCarter brought his MP-5 A-3 off his shoulder, went to one knee and opened up with a steady barrage of 9 mm Parabellum slugs on the three terrorists holding rocket launchers at the railing. He had watched helplessly as they destroyed one of the small launches put forth for boarding, but he wasn't helpless now.

McCarter's first rounds caught the closest terrorist in the back, ripping his flesh with enough impact to drive him over the railing and into the choppy sea. The second terrorist met a similar fate, the rounds lifting him off his feet and slamming him to the deck. The third was smart enough to drop his now useless antitank weapon and attempt to go for the AK-47 assault rifle slung across his back, but he never had time to bring it to bear. McCarter ripped him open from crotch to throat with several corkscrew tribursts from the MP-5 A-3.

The Briton threw himself to his belly before being able to even think about his next move. The sky echoed with fire coming from one of Her Majesty's powerful destroyers. The ship's commander had obviously ordered a full retaliatory response, and McCarter couldn't say he blamed the guy. His years in the SAS also left no doubt as to what exactly that response included. The Vulcan 20 mm/76 Phalanx Close-in Weapons System was an invention of the Americans, and he knew it was a damn fine one at that. McCarter knew it was primarily used as an antimissile and antiaircraft defense system, but in this case the ship's commander had obviously found another clever use for it. While perhaps overkill, the weapon could clear any threat from surface ship decks faster than anything else, and in this case it did a bang-up job.

Still, McCarter didn't feel like getting shot. He kept his head down and keyed his radio.

"Papa One to Eagle One, do you copy?"

"This is Eagle One, loud and clear."

"We're taking friendly fire over here, mate," McCarter said. "I don't think my countrymen know yet that we're on their side, and I'm not even sure they care. Can you get with them and tell them to put a capper on the turkey shoot?"

"Roger, wilco," Grimaldi replied.

A moment later an earth-shattering boom erupted from the direction of the destroyer and was followed by an explosion that rocked the entire freighter. The blast was heavy enough to lift McCarter off his belly and slam him back onto the roof. Considering he was on the highest point, he was probably taking less of a battering than those below. Now it seemed the destroyer—which McCarter had finally identified as the HMS *Newcastle*—had finally put its gunnery departments in place. The blast had come from an Mk 8 just to the rear of the ship's bow, a 114 mm general-purpose gun that fired 25 kg shells at the rate of twenty-five per minute.

McCarter kept his head down as debris rained on

him. Yeah, he thought, it was bloody well time to get off this damn roof. The Briton slung his MP-5 A-3, grabbed the edge of the roof and flipped himself onto the catwalk that bordered the bridge. He kept low and moved to the entryway, stopping short as a smaller man with a dark complexion and a thick mustache emerged from the bridge. A pistol glinted in the red-orange light of the setting sun and McCarter could see immediately that he was facing a serious threat.

The man started to turn and McCarter realized in a heartbeat he wouldn't be able to bring his SMG or pistol to bear in time. So McCarter did the only thing he could, launching a snap kick that caught the man's wrist and knocked the pistol from his grip. The terrorist reacted quickly, withdrawing a long, curved knife and charging McCarter. The Briton dropped to his back and executed a judo circle throw, sending the man over the railing and plummeting to the deck thirty feet below. McCarter rose in time to see the terrorist land on some crates. He smacked his head on at least two or three—breaking his neck with an audible crack—before his body hit the deck with a sickly crunch.

McCarter nodded good riddance, and then continued on a quest to find his teammates.

T. J. HAWKINS DIDN'T GET much of a chance to recover when he hit the deck, because two terrorists with assault weapons charging his position suddenly became more important. The muzzles of their Kalashnikovs flashed and Hawkins rolled away from the hungry rounds looking to punch through his unshielded body.

Hawkins took cover behind a stack of flimsy pallets and brought his weapon to bear. He'd traded the G-41 for an M-4 Commando—the law-enforcement carbine version of the M-16 family—which Kissinger had modified just for him. The weapon fired the standard .223 Remington shell, but Kissinger had turned it into an even more compact weapon by detaching the stock and loading the buffer spring in a special casing beneath the forward handgrip. The result was a short, compact weapon with all the power and accuracy that had made Colt Defense, LLC and the M-16 rifle famous.

Hawkins moved the selector to full-auto, swung the weapon into action and sighted on the charging terrorists. He squeezed the trigger and took his first attacker with a short, tight burst to the chest. The rounds punched large holes in the man's back at that range, knocking him from his feet. He left a gory smear on the deck as his body slid away from Hawkins's position.

The second terrorist obviously realized his target wasn't helpless or unarmed, and quickly grabbed cover. The terrorist evaded death by laying down a merciless onslaught of autofire while going for cover. It was an old but still effective tactic, and Hawkins knew it well: keep heads down until you can get somewhere safe. The only problem in this case was that "safe" was undoubtedly a relative term, and one the terrorists obviously didn't understand.

Hawkins reached to his LBE for an M-67 fragmentation grenade. He thumbed away the pin, let the spoon fly, let it cook off for two seconds and tossed the bomb gently across the gap separating him from the enemy. There was a shout of surprise followed by a tremendous blast as the explosive ignited under the fuse. Hawkins felt something warm and wet smack his face before falling in front of him. A quick glance revealed it was a finger.

RAFAEL ENCIZO DROPPED TO the freighter's aft deck with the grace and speed of a combat veteran. He'd made more jumps like this than he could count, and this was just one more to add to his belt. He moved quickly to keep from being trapped under the parachute that fell in the wake of his landing, then crouched. He brought an MP-5 into play and checked his immediate surroundings. No one appeared to challenge him.

The Cuban warrior double-checked his flank, then waited for his backup to arrive. It came a moment later in the tall, lanky form of Calvin James. The ex-SEAL hit the ground and rolled in a perfect landing. He came out of the roll easily and retrieved his M-16 A-4/M-203. The over-and-under assault combo was a favorite of the warrior's, having served him well on many missions.

Encizo whistled a sharp, high tone and James moved over to his position as soon as he saw him. The two didn't speak at first, checking the immediate area one last time before risking to give each other their respective attention.

"Did you notice if the others got down okay?" Encizo asked.

"Don't know about David or Gary, but I saw T.J. run into some trouble as he set down."

"He pulled out of it okay?"

James flashed him a lopsided smile. "You kidding? He fragged one terrorist."

That figured about right, from what Encizo had come to know about the youngest, and in some ways toughest member of Phoenix Force. T. J. Hawkins might have played the game to the max, even applied a bit of overkill at times, but he was one tough guy and could take care of himself. There were few situations he wasn't able to handle, even in some of the toughest training scenarios they would run at the Farm.

"All right, so we stay on mission," Encizo said.

"Well, at least we picked the right freighter," James said, obviously unable to refrain from pulling some good humor from a very bad situation.

"You think?" Encizo cracked, not missing a beat.

The Vulcan Phalanx erupted once more and Encizo risked breaking cover long enough to check the position of the British warship. It was now approaching the freighter, and Encizo could see they had their Lynx MK 8 chopper rolled into position and the rotors beginning to wind up. Simultaneously there was another booming report from the MK 8 gun and this time the shell punched through the hull somewhere belowdecks. A moment later an explosion blasted through the deck plates about fifty yards from the Phoenix Force pair's position. Fire, smoke and heat belched from the hole left in the wake of the blast.

"What the hell is taking Jack so long to get that message from David through to the Royal Navy?" James asked, brushing dust from his closely cropped hair.

"I don't know," Encizo replied, "but it won't be long now. Come on."

The two emerged from cover and headed toward the forward berths. Their mission was simple: get inside the ship and see if they could find the missile. If they did, they would then have to sabotage the launcher with the heavy explosives Manning had rigged for them so that it never got off the pad. If they couldn't do that, then the missile would have to go into the murky depths of the Mediterranean Sea.

The trio reached a hatch on the starboard side of the ship, about middeck, and within seconds they were inside and descending the steps. Encizo knew they would have to go several decks before reaching the bowels of the freighter. According to their intelligence, the freighter's cargo lift—a massive hydraulic pad that sat just aft of the forecastle—would be the most likely place for them to build the pad unless they had performed major alterations to the freighter's configuration. Phoenix Force wasn't buying that, simply because the terrorists had obviously felt the pressure being exerted by the Stony Man teams and accelerated their plans.

Encizo could only hope their theory would hold long enough for the terrorists to make one too many sloppy mistakes. So far, they had proved to be clever and formidable enemies, and apparently intent on completing their mission no matter what. To this point, however, he hadn't witnessed them acting with the predictability of fanatics, but rather like a cold, calculating war machine of some considerable efficiency. The thought of going against such a well-trained terror group wasn't something to which Encizo looked forward.

He and James turned a corner and nearly ran into four terrorists coming from the opposite direction. The terrorists were still trying to figure out how to react while Encizo and James were in motion. Encizo slung the stock of his MP-5 with an underhand move and crushed the nearest man's testicles. The guy opened his mouth to shout in pain but quickly found it stuffed with the muzzle of Encizo's machine pistol. The Cuban squeezed the trigger, the single 9 mm Parabellum round hammering through the man's skull and blowing his brains completely out of his head. The flesh, blood and bone doused the two terrorists behind him.

Simultaneously, James took a second with a double punch to the face followed by a ridge-hand strike to the throat. The blow smashed the terrorist's windpipe, bits of sharp cartilage and bone continuing onward to lacerate his esophagus. The man tried to scream, but it came forth only as a bloody gurgle. James finished it with a snap kick to the breastbone that shattered the sternum and cracked the ribs with enough force to lodge bone fragments in both lungs.

The pair opened up on the remaining two terrorists with their respective weapons, shredding their flesh with a volley of 9 mm Parabellum and 5.56 NATO slugs. The sudden assault lifted the men off their feet and slammed them into the hatchway door to their rear. The deafening reports began to die down in the confined space.

Encizo shook his head to clear the ringing in his ears.

"That was goddamn close, brother," James said. "We come any closer to the enemy like that again, and I'll take my chances with those big-ass guns on that destroyer out there."

"Ditto."

"And nice moves there, by the way."

"Same to you," Encizo said. "Now, let's see if we can't find this big, bad missile we keep hearing about."

WHEN GARY MANNING SAW the carnage unfolding in front of him, he could barely contain his rage. That rage—the same he'd kept bottled up all this time over the death of Jeanne Marais—was now able to be unleashed. Manning was going to kill as many of them today as he could, and if he fell it would be most likely that he'd taken a bunch of them with him.

Unlike the rest of the team, Manning had a very special mission. His job was to get to the bridge and blow it to kingdom come, thereby leaving the ship dead in the water. But that was going to prove to become quite a challenge, because Manning didn't get lucky enough to land somewhere on the freighter, and neither had he touched down in the water. Oh, no. Manning had come down on the back end of the ship and got his chute hung up on its rearmost rail.

Manning let fly with a firestorm of obscenities before willing himself to get calm and think through the predicament. It stood to reason that to this point all of the terrorists were too occupied to have noticed his chute wrapped around the back of the freighter. What he didn't know was how long that luck would hold out, so it seemed reasonable that the first order of business would be to get out of his current situation as quickly as possible.

First, he gave thought to cutting himself free and dropping into the sea, then firing a grappling hook at the ship. Had he been hooked up at the bow or sides, such a tactic would have been impossible, most likely resulting in him being pulled under the freighter in its powerful wake and ultimately sucked into the screws. That would definitely have put an end to his career. Still, after some consideration, Manning realized that wasn't his best option. There was no guarantee if he hit the water that he'd be able to get back onto the freighter.

He watched the furious whitecaps directly below his feet, considering his other options. He couldn't dangle here all damn day. And then it occurred to him that he could cut himself loose from his harness, then climb the risers to the deck. The only problem would be the large satchel containing his explosives. One way or another, he'd have to dump it first. The churning water below wasn't an option, so Manning cut the satchel free and heaved it onto the deck, hopeful that a curious terrorist wouldn't come by.

Manning reached up to the right shoulder strap of his LBE and detached the Ka-Bar fighting knife. A minute later he had himself free of the straps and began to climb the bunched risers of the parachute. The ascent wasn't as easy at it might have looked to the outside observer. Hands grabbed at the thin risers and every part of the hand-over-hand climb was almost grueling, even for a commando as well-conditioned as Manning. By the time he reached the railing, his hands were bleeding, made raw by the unforgiving parachute cord.

Manning vaulted the railing and landed on the deck with the grace of a cat. He checked the area and quickly located the satchel. An inspection of the contents confirmed everything was still intact. A sudden shudder and lurch by the freighter, the result of an impact shell from a gun on the British destroyer, threw the Canadian to the deck.

It also saved his life.

A hail of slugs buzzed through the air where his head was only a second earlier. Manning rolled instinctively, not wanting to give the terrorist a chance to recover. He didn't, and Manning came to one knee with the satchel in his left hand and shielded by his body. A .357 Magnum Desert Eagle filled his right fist and he saw the terrorist's eyes grow wide just a millisecond before he pulled the trigger.

The steel-core slug drilled through the man's chest and slammed him against a venting stack. Manning followed with a second round, this one a head shot, although he knew the guy was dead even as he squeezed the trigger. The terrorist's corpse slid to the ground in a heap.

Manning rose and checked his flanks before proceeding toward the bridge.

FOR SOME REASON Jarred Blankenship couldn't explain, they had allies. At least, that's the way it was beginning to appear. At first, he hadn't noticed the men clad in black moving on these pirates or terrorists or whatever they bloody hell were with the tenacity of seasoned combatants. And they were doing a spot-on job of it, which was why it didn't surprise Blankenship when the ship-to-shore rang.

"This is Admiral Stalworthe."

"Yes, sir, Commander Blankenship here."

"What in the name of creation is going on out there?" Stalworthe demanded. "I just got off the phone with the prime minister's office, where I was ordered to order you to stand down. Apparently there is a gun battle in process?"

"They fired on us, sir," Blankenship replied. "We are simply defending ourselves."

"Well, stop defending yourself long enough to tell me if there are allied commandos on board that ship!"

Blankenship immediately felt a lump form in his throat. Had the admiral said "allied" commandos? That wasn't good. Here he was, blowing the hell out of them over there, and there were men now on board that were apparently on their side. No, he could kiss another assignment in the Mediterranean goodbye.

"You are hereby ordered to assist and observe in whatever capacity you deem fit," Stalworthe replied, "but for God's sake, man, stop firing on our allies. They might just put an end to this quicker than you think."

"I understand, sir. Of course, sir," Blankenship replied. He didn't enjoy having to kowtow to his superiors in such a fashion, particularly when he'd done nothing more than protect his ship and his men. Well, he would observe and assist, all right, but he wouldn't hesitate to sink that bloody piece of iron if provoked further.

Before Blankenship realized it, Stalworthe had disconnected the call.

CHAPTER SEVENTEEN

Rafael Encizo and Calvin James found their target.

The men took sharp breaths at the same time when they saw it there, a missile gleaming under the harsh worklights. The area surrounding the missile was poorly lit, lending an almost eerie quality to their surroundings. Well, it was no time for ghost stories. They needed to find and deactivate the missile controls, and hope that the terrorists hadn't thought far enough ahead to equip the missile with a remote switch of some kind.

A number of terrorists were scurrying around the missile, apparently trying to perform last-minute modifications that would allow them to launch it. The two Phoenix Force warriors exchanged glances and knew that the other was thinking the exact same thing. So, their arrival had caused the terrorists to have to accelerate their timetable, which could only mean that Hawkins's theory was correct—the terrorists had been waiting for something, most likely another attack that was to take place somewhere else.

Encizo surveyed the scene in front of him, taking the details in at a glance, then he and James hunched behind their cover.

"I saw what looks like a control panel connected to a power grid on the other side of the bay," Encizo began. "I think we ought to go for that."

"You think that's what controls the missile?"

Encizo shook his head. "I'm not sure it controls the missile, but I'd bet my next paycheck it controls that lift platform. I figure if they can't open the bay and raise the thing, they sure as hell can't launch it. I think I can take it out with one of Gary's little toys here, but I'm going to need a distraction."

"Great," James said. "How do I always get so lucky with the assignment of playing decoy?"

"RHIP," Encizo said. The old mnemonic of "rank has its privileges" was one that McCarter often used on Hawkins when the newest member of Phoenix Force would complain about having to do something he really didn't want to do. The reality was, of course, that they were all equal to one another—McCarter serving as team leader only because any military operation required someone to keep group cohesion in much the same way as a quarterback did for a football team—and none of them minded doing whatever they had to do to accomplish the mission. Bitching about it just helped to relieve some of the stress.

"Okay, so any ideas on creating a distraction, or would you like me to improvise?"

"It's your show," Encizo said. "Do what comes natural."

"If I did that, I wouldn't be here right now," James said. He extended his hand in a firm grip and added, "Good luck, bro."

"You too," Encizo replied.

And then James was gone.

While Encizo waited for his teammate to do his thing, he marked the location of each terrorist and tried to gauge how they would react. Not that it was an easy task, since he didn't have the first idea what James planned to offer up as a diversion. But whatever it was, it would be unique and original—more importantly, it would be effective.

Across the massive bay smoke suddenly began to roll from an area that wasn't too far from a set of drums marked as containing jet fuel. They had probably used them to provide fuel to the missile. Another moment elapsed and Encizo heard someone shout, "Fire," in English, someone who could only be James. A long moment of silence where it seemed to Encizo that time had stood still was followed by absolute pandemonium as the men working on the missile looked at one another with shock, then ran to extinguish the blaze.

Of course, Encizo realized something the terrorists didn't. James wouldn't have been stupid enough to actually start a blaze that couldn't be controlled easily so close to fifty-five-gallon drums filled with volatile chemicals.

Or would he?

Well, Encizo had no intention of finding out first-hand, because, as he had suspected, the diversion was perfect. The controls to the landing platform were left unattended, and after a quick check of his surroundings, Encizo slid from cover and ran, his body in a half crouch and MP-5 tracking ahead, to the target. When he arrived he stopped to check his flank; all the terrorists were obviously busy with the fire. Good, this wouldn't take long.

The Cuban warrior reached into the explosives satchel and withdrew a quarter-pound stick of C-4 plastique. The explosive was still a modern marvel of military science as far as Encizo was concerned. He'd been in love with the material ever since becoming an underwater demolitions expert, just because of its versatility and effectiveness. C-4 worked off a combination of heat and pressure, but was stable when subjected to one in the absence of another. Despite what they showed on television, shooting at it wasn't enough to blow the stuff. It was also quite flammable, but if ignited it would just burn. However, using it properly—that being attached to a fuse or some detonation cord—and then tripping the heat-pressure source, it suddenly became clear why C-4 was such an amazing tool.

Encizo withdrew an unsharpened pencil from the bag and shoved it into the end of the C-4 stick lengthwise. He then fitted it with a blasting cap, opened the plate covering the control panel and gently pressed it to the side of the panel. He quickly wired the fuse to a junction box next to the controls and in turn eased the wire through and twisted it against an inside screw of the panel, then sealed it up. The concept was quite simple. The wire running from the junction box was connected to an electrical source. However, the circuit was incomplete. When the time came for the terrorists to engage the lift and they opened the control panel door, the metal wire would touch the frame of the box, complete the circuit and...

A thick forearm suddenly snaked around Encizo's neck and yanked him backward, instantly and brutally cutting off his air supply. Stars danced immediately in front of his eyes with the sudden trauma, and the power behind the sleeper hold would have him unconscious shortly if he didn't react. But none of that went through his mind; instead his catlike reflexes took charge and a surge of adrenaline powered his body. Encizo bent forward and simultaneously dropped to one knee, taking his attacker off balance. He then measured that the attacker had his left arm around his neck, so he threw his left shoulder forward and rolled. For the assailant to maintain control, he would have to roll with Encizo. He did, and suddenly the attacker found himself on his back with Encizo on top. The Phoenix Force warrior hammered his opponent in the ribs with a double elbow strike, and the hold abated as the strikes forced air from the terrorist's lungs.

Encizo rolled away and got to his feet. He saw the terrorist now, rising with hatred in his eyes and an equally nasty-looking knife in his left fist. By his stance alone, Encizo knew he was dealing with an experienced knife fighter. Well, that was just fine, because the Cuban had learned a thing or two of his own over the years. He saw that he'd lost his MP-5 in the assault, which left him with his Colt M-1911 A1 pistol and the Cold Steel Tanto fighting knife.

The knife left its sheath with a rasp.

His enemy's blade was long and curved, and looked damn sharp. That didn't bother Encizo too much. It didn't intimidate him the same way it did most men. The most important thing to remember in a knife fight was that the likelihood of getting cut was high. In fact, Encizo had been cut badly on many occasions. But most cuts weren't fatal unless vital arteries were hit or the blade coated with poison, and so expecting to take a wound or two was just part of the deal. What ultimately determined the victor in a knife fight was who was most afraid. Fear was the real killer. Fear of being cut or stabbed was what did in the victim, and while having a healthy respect by not underestimating any opponent, Encizo had learned to conquer that fear long ago.

The fighters encircled each other for a long time, each looking for a weakness or opening in their opponent. Finally the terrorist lost his patience and moved in with a low slashing blow. Encizo easily sidestepped, having seen the maneuver many times, and countered with a slashing maneuver to the man's forearm. The Tanto blade went through the meaty portion of the terrorist's forearm like a warm knife through butter and opened a gaping wound. It also cut the tendons and forced the man to drop his knife.

The terrorist screamed and grabbed at his forearm, and Encizo launched a front kick that sent him sliding across the slick floor. The terrorist's body came to a stop and he looked at Encizo, fear now present in his eyes. Encizo rubbed his throat and then, in a single move of showmanship, kicked the man's knife to him. If the terrorist wanted to go out, Encizo figured he'd at least let him go out like a man.

The terrorist grabbed the knife, gripping it in his left fist, and rose. A pool of blood had formed quickly under his forearm and it dripped hot and fresh as he approached. The fear was gone once more, replaced by anger. Encizo figured that either way this went it wouldn't be good for the terrorist. The man couldn't control his fear or his anger, and both were sure killers in a contest of blades.

Encizo made a few feints of stabbing and slashing motions, goading his enemy. The terrorist got clever and used one of the feints to get inside and lay open a long cut on Encizo's right shoulder. The Cuban barely felt the smooth cut, instead dancing back so as not to expose himself more. The terrorist obviously took this for fear and decided to press the attack. It cost him more than he could have ever surmised. As he came in low, attempting to stab Encizo in the stomach, the Cuban latched on to his wrist. The Phoenix warrior twisted and delivered an upward slash to the left side of the man's throat, cutting away arteries, veins and some neck muscles. The terrorist's eyes nearly popped from his head as he realized he was finished. Blood spurted from the wound with every beat of his heart, its pace more frenetic than usual by the exertion.

The terrorist stood erect and dropped his knife, both hands now moving to the fatal wound to attempt to stem the flow of blood. It would do him little good, and he knew it. He just stood and stared at Encizo. Finally he went to his knees and his eyes began to glaze over. Seconds later he toppled to the deck, dead.

With his mission completed, Encizo collected his weapon and equipment, then set off to find James.

CREATING A DIVERSION FOR his friend came with its own set of problems for Calvin James. The Phoenix Force warrior quickly spied some wooden pallets cast aside, and immediately the idea came to him. He'd quickly tapped each of the barrels of fuel with the blade of his Ka-Bar until he found a full one, then punctured a hole in the top and then soaked the sleeves he'd cut from the T-shirt beneath his black fatigues. He tossed the two fuel-soaked pieces of cloth between two pallets and a quick touch of a match from his survival kit did the rest.

In the cover of the smoke, James figured he could make good on his escape. All was going as planned;

he hoped that the diversion was enough to give Encizo the time and room he needed to wire up the control system. It had been a pretty good idea, and James once more found it difficult not to have the utmost respect for Encizo. The guy was a sharp individual, sharper than many gave him credit for. James found a hatchway leading from the bay into an adjoining cargo hold.

James had expected trouble, but not of this magnitude. He spotted the quartet of gunmen just a moment before they spotted him, and managed to find cover behind a thick, metal filing cabinet. In the light streaming through a number of open hatches far above, James could tell he was in some kind of storage room.

The terrorists reacted with incredible enthusiasm and opened up with their AK-47 rifles, but there was no real attempt on their part to hit their target. For the moment, they seemed content to force James to keep his head down, which meant they were stalling, probably in the hope that if they put him off long enough they could arm the missile and launch it. If Encizo had accomplished the mission, and James had no reason to believe otherwise, then the terrorists were in for quite a surprise. So their strategy of stalling him worked as much for James as it did for the terrorists.

The Phoenix Force warrior brought his M-16 A4/ M-203 into play and slammed home a 40 mm white-phosphorous shell. He was about to teach his would-be Qibla murderers the one significant difference between gunning down a group of innocent bystanders versus going up against an enemy equal to the task.

Calvin James was just such an enemy.

James calculated the approximate area above his head, insured he had adequate cover, and fired the launcher. The weapon boomed in the confines of the storage hold and a moment later it was lit with a flash. The hot phosphorous fell on the area around the terrorists, but as luck would have it James managed to get only one man with the chemical that could turn iron into molten slag, or at least, he could only hear one terrorist screaming. That told him they had changed positions.

James checked the area around him, attempting to calculate the number of possible approaches they might take to surprise him. He didn't like what he saw—there were too many openings the terrorists could use to their advantage. In fact, one of them tried and James met him head-on with a controlled 3-round burst to the chest. An ugly blood pattern appeared on his shirtfront before the impact slammed him against a nearby crate and then dumped him face-first to the ground.

The terrorist's assault rifle clattered to the deck and slid in James's direction. The Phoenix Force warrior heard movement to his left, just around the corner from where his back was pressed to the filing cabinet, so he moved his foot enough to cause the weapon to ricochet off his foot. The sound of movement caused another terrorist to expose himself and open up with a flurry of

7.62 mm rounds. James took the advantage long enough to lean from cover, snap aim and squeeze the trigger twice. A volley of two 3-round bursts caught his opponent at hips and midsection, the M-16 rounds ripping mercilessly through yielding flesh. The terrorist danced backward in surprise, his weapon falling from limp fingers, and collapsed to the deck.

One to go.

James knew he couldn't hold position here forever. The remaining terrorist would likely get wise to the cluster of bodies in the area and find some way to flank him by weaving through the maze of stored junk. James decided to go one better, and use the junk to his advantage in a move the terrorist was certain not to expect. James leaped onto the filing cabinet and traversed to a tall dressing bureau. He crouched, tracking the area around him with the muzzle of the M-16 A-4, but saw no movement.

The terrorist would eventually show himself and he wouldn't likely expect James to launch an attack from above. Patience was the key to survival right now, and it eventually paid off. James waited for what seemed like forever, but in this case was only a few minutes, and soon spotted the terrorist who was keeping low and maneuvering his way through the storage-room maze. James froze in place, not breathing. Slowly and agonizingly he eventually let himself exhale as he watched the terrorist continue to search for him to no avail. His opportunity for a clear shot finally came. James slowly and steadily raised the M-16 A-4/M-203 to his shoulder, sighted down the detachable carrying handle, fixed his target and squeezed the trigger. The terrorist never saw it coming. A single SS109 hardball round punched through the man's upper lip and blew a large chunk of flesh and bone out the base of his neck. The man's eyes went wide with shock, then he fell. His body trembled and twitched to catch up as his brain had already told him he was dead.

James leaped off the dresser and quickly searched the three terrorists for identification. He found nothing that he believed would be useful. He then located the fourth terrorist, who had fallen victim to the WP grenade. He found the men with his eyes frozen open in mixed expression of horror and pain. A major part of the left side of the terrorist's skull had been burned away by the deadly chemicals in the grenade. James tried to ignore the ghastly look, to shut out the almost accusatory gaze. Again, he found no ID.

That accomplished, he turned to the task of finding his way out of there and back to the main deck. McCarter would be getting impatient and so would the others. He could still hear the shouting as the men in the adjoining compartment fought to put out the flames of his little diversion. He could even smell the remnants of smoke, although the hatchway leading to that compartment was shut tight. Those particular doors also served as fire doors and could be air sealed by the main systems of the ship if necessary for the very purpose of containing fires to a specific area. That fire wouldn't keep the terrorists occupied forever, but it would be long enough for him to find his way out.

James didn't really care where the exit was or how many terrorists he had to go through. It had just suddenly become very important for him to get as far away as he could from the WP victim, to escape that death's-head expression, to get far removed from those accusatory eyes peering sightlessly from a charred, mutilated skull. Yeah, it was a horrific look, one that James wouldn't soon forget.

CHAPTER EIGHTEEN

Gary Manning reached the bridge of the ship unmolested, which was probably nothing short of a miracle.

It probably shouldn't have surprised the big Canadian that much. The terrorists had been ill-equipped and unprepared to deal with a British war-class destroyer like the HMS *Newcastle,* and they certainly hadn't expected to have to deal with the arrival of Phoenix Force. Well, wherever they were hiding, Manning intended to make sure neither this ship nor any missile she might carry would reach their respective destinations.

Manning performed a quick inspection of the freighter controls that powered the big ship, then began to rig the panels with high explosives. He was about three-quarters complete with his task when he heard movement at the door. The Canadian whirled and brought his pistol into play, but he relaxed when he assessed he was looking down the slide at the face of T. J. Hawkins.

"Christ, T.J., you trying to get killed?" Manning asked. "Don't sneak up on me like that!"

"I wasn't sneaking up on anybody," Hawkins said. "I spotted your ugly mug through the bridge, and figured I'd give you a hand. And why the hell don't you have someone watching your six anyway?"

"Are you volunteering?" Manning asked, returning to his work as he did.

"In the absence of a better offer, I suppose so." Hawkins paused a moment, then added, "Sounds like Jack finally reached someone in charge on the Brits' side."

"Yeah, I noticed they stopped blowing holes in the sides of this kettle."

Manning then put the younger warrior out of his mind and focused on the job at hand. He couldn't be sure what the terrorists had planned, or what creative methods Encizo and James might conjure to attempt to put the missile out of commission, but he couldn't let that worry him now. McCarter had insisted they devise a failsafe plan in case one or the other sabotage mission proved ineffectual. Not that the Briton didn't have faith in his people. Since succeeding Yakov Katzenelenbogen, McCarter had proved himself worthy of position as top dog, yet he still valued the opinions of everyone on the team.

"Someone's coming," Hawkins whispered.

Manning turned and reached for his pistol again,

going to one knee as he did, but Hawkins pretty quickly recovered.

"False alarm," he called. "It's only David."

"Not 'only David,' mate," the Cockney said as he crossed the bridge toward Manning. "Try the one and only."

"Oh, brother," Hawkins quipped.

"You heard anything from Rafe or Cal?" McCarter asked Manning.

The Canadian shook his head as he began to stow his equipment. "Nada. But the job's done here. We can set this off any time you're ready."

McCarter looked at Hawkins. "How about you, mate?"

"I've seen neither hide nor hair of them," Hawkins said.

"Well, this is just not turning out to be my day, is it?" The Phoenix Force leader turned and stared hard at Manning. "We may have trouble."

"Sounds more like it's James and Rafe who might be having the trouble."

"It's a strong possibility, and one I'm going to have to act on if I don't hear something from them in the next five minutes," McCarter replied. "They were supposed to check in every fifteen minutes, and they're now ten overdue the first check."

"I know it got pretty hot and heavy when we were first coming down, boss," Hawkins interjected. "It's a good bet they ran into some trouble along the way."

"Well, there are one of two major possibilities," Manning said. "They're either dead or they're alive, and in the case of the former we know what to do. But I think we should wait at least—"

The headsets of all three men buzzed briefly for attention, then the voice of Encizo came through. "Green Three to Green Lantern."

"Green Lantern, here. Where away?"

"I'm out of the main cargo hold. Mission accomplished and charges are in place. I rigged them to destroy the lift if they try to prep the missile for launching."

Manning gave McCarter a thumbs-up.

"I'm on one of the lower decks," Encizo said, "but I'm not sure how to get out of here. I couldn't come in the same way I went out, and Green Four and I had to separate. Now I'm pretty sure I'm cut off. I think I hit the motherlode. There's a hallway directly ahead, and just beyond it I can hear activity. Lots. I'm guessing there are at least thirty targets in that area."

"Is that conservative, mate?" McCarter asked.

"Depends on your definition of the term, but I'd say yeah."

McCarter looked at Manning for help. The Canadian knew why. Manning could get a much more accurate picture of Encizo's position than anyone else, and would recall if there was an alternate way to the top of the deck. He'd studied the blueprints of the freighter very carefully, learning every inch in the event he had to rig the thing for demolitions capable of sinking it if all else failed.

"Green Two to Green Three," Manning cut in. "Do you see any landmarks, a corridor number, anything of that nature?"

"There are some markings on the wall, but they're in Arabic and I don't have a clue what they mean. I'm afraid my Arabic's a little rusty, Green Two."

"I swear, we're all taking a bloody crash course when we get back to the Farm," McCarter murmured.

"Do you know how many decks down you are?" Manning asked.

"That I did keep track of," Encizo replied. "I'd say I'm two decks below and maybe at midship."

Manning nodded. He could guess, based just on the description, that Encizo was almost directly beneath them. He told McCarter and Hawkins, adding, "The only trouble with where he's at is that there's no more an easy way out than there would be going in. There are two main hatches, one just below us, but he won't find them easy to gain access to."

"What do you recommend?" McCarter asked.

"That we tell him to stay put until we can get to him. He's right in that he's basically trapped. He certainly can't fight off a couple dozen terrorists by himself, and if he goes back the way he came, in the direction of the missile, it'll be out of the frying pan and into the fire."

"Green Lantern to Green Three," McCarter said. "Hold your position. We're on our way."

"Roger that, Green Lantern."

"Out, here."

McCarter switched off the radio and asked Manning, "How is this set to go off?"

"Just like we discussed," Manning said. "No timers, so I can only blow it remotely. But we don't want to be anywhere near it if I have to do that. In fact, I wouldn't even want to be on this thing when it goes."

"Good," McCarter said, then turned to Hawkins. "You stay behind and shut down the engines. Then I'd head to the main deck and wait for the cavalry. I'm sure the skipper of that destroyer over there will be sending a boarding party, and we don't want them to get any nasty receptions from our Qibla friends."

"Fair enough," Hawkins said, "but if it's all the same to you, I'd rather help you find Rafe."

McCarter shook his head and firmly replied, "No. I need you to look this thing over and see if you can pull any information on the other freighters. They have to be communicating with each other somehow, and as you've more electronics training than anyone else on the team, you're the most logical candidate. You know what to look for."

"All right, but what about Calvin?" Hawkins asked.

"He can take care of himself," Manning replied. "We'll either run into him going to find Rafe or he'll meet up with us here as originally planned."

"It's important you do this for us, T.J.," McCarter said. He added on afterthought, "Trust me. And don't worry about Rafe, we'll bring him back in one piece."

Manning could tell by Hawkins's expression that the

former Delta Force soldier didn't like the assignment, but he knew the young guy would give it his best shot. McCarter was right. There wasn't anyone more qualified to handle the radio systems than Hawkins. If there was something to be found, he'd find it, of this much Manning was certain.

McCarter turned to Manning and said, "Well, mate, you wanted your chance to dish out some of what we took in Cape Town. Maybe now you're going to get your bloody wish."

"Yeah," Manning replied as he followed McCarter out of the tower. "Goody."

ENCIZO WASN'T THE LEAST bit certain how he'd managed to get into his current situation, but he wasn't keen on having to ask McCarter and the others to come bail him out. Still, he supposed it was partially his own damn fault. When he and James had volunteered to go into the belly of this iron heap to rig that missile, they should have at least discussed a plan for getting out. Now, Encizo found these lower halls chilling and lonely, and he wished for nothing more than the arrival of familiar faces.

What he got instead was a series of angry faces, the anger evident by the wicked-looking weapons pointed in his direction. Six terrorists abruptly emerged from the hatchway leading to the area where Encizo knew his enemies were holed up. He had felt almost like a cat waiting at the proverbial hole for the proverbial rat. Most rats, however, weren't terrorist fanatics toting automatic rifles.

Encizo went prone as a maelstrom of hot lead passed over him. The Cuban warrior brought his MP-5 to bear and triggered a sustained burst that caught two of the six terrorists in the narrow hallway. Several rounds punched through the chest of one of the terrorists, the impact driving him back into his remaining comrades. Another's head exploded under the impact of the 9 mm rounds traveling at a muzzle velocity in excess of 400 mps. Encizo fired a second burst to keep heads down as he leaped to his feet and retreated down the corridor.

That did it. Before long, he'd have the entire group in pursuit and all the while not having a clue where he was going. As he rounded a corner, he finally got his wish to see a familiar face, this one black and sweaty, and a row of teeth that gleamed below a pencil-thin mustache.

"Glad you could make it," Encizo said.

"Thanks," Calvin James said. "I got your invitation and figured it would be a marvelous time."

"Well, I do know how to throw parties, darling. You got any idea how to get out of here?"

"Why, of course," James said, inclining his head in the direction he'd come. "This way."

He led Encizo down the corridor, keying his radio as they went. "Green Four to Green Lantern."

"Green Lantern, here," McCarter replied immediately.

"I've got our prodigal son and we're headed back toward the missile. I'd say cancel your approach and meet us somewhere near the entrance to the main cargo hold."

"Wilco, Green Four. But what's the plan?"

"No time to talk now," James replied. "We've got a whole terrorist posse on our tails. Just meet us there and I'll explain it then."

"Acknowledged. We'll be there, boys."

"Out, here," James replied.

As they continued toward the missile site, Encizo tried to imagine what his friend had planned now. It didn't make much sense why he'd want to go back to the missile. At any moment they might engage the box, and it was rigged with enough explosives that they wouldn't be able to go anywhere. Still, Encizo had learned to trust all of his teammates. If James was taking them that close to danger, then he obviously figured James had considered the risks and found them outweighed by the benefits.

And he couldn't wait to see what the Chicago badass had planned for the Qibla terrorists.

"YOU WANTED PAYBACK, right?" James asked Manning.

The Canadian nodded, a little puzzled as he exchanged glances with his teammates.

"Well, I'm about to show you payback like you've never seen before."

The foursome had finally met up and found a brief respite behind some stacked crates. Heavy wafts of smoke still clung to the air high above their heads, but the terrorists had managed to put out the fire and were now attending to their plans.

"Eventually, the other terrorists Rafe bumped into are going to find their way in here," James said. "Once they're ready to launch the missile, they're going to think this is the safest place to be. And when they do, we're going to have a little surprise for them."

"So what do you have in mind, mate?" McCarter asked. "Don't keep us in suspense."

James flashed him a wicked grin as he pointed to an area just barely visible through the gap between their cover and the freighter wall. "You see those two large plastic barrels over there? I've seen them before in pictures. When I worked with SWAT we used to have to train on hazardous materials emergencies, controlling scenes of chemical spills, things like that. Those containers are the same kind common to ships that regularly transport biohazardous waste and caustic chemicals. They're lined with plastic, and they have a small sheet of lead inside that is lined with more plastic. This provides an air cushion."

"I get it," Manning interjected. "You think that's what the terrorists are shipping this chemical in, this cholinesterase."

"Yeah, and I believe it's transmitted by airborne means. There doesn't seem any other plausible explanation."

"He could well be right about that," Encizo said.

"And I noticed something else," James replied. "They don't happen to have the first clue that all of the doors leading into this area are fireproof."

"That's standard on merchant marine vessels," McCarter said. "Hell, I thought everybody knew that. The bloody vendors won't let them ship materials on most freighters unless they're rated with such construction. It didn't used to be required, but in more recent years it's become a necessity on all maritime vessels, especially where oil tankers are concerned."

"Yeah, so we've been against odds like this before," James replied, "but why work hard? We need to work smart."

"Oh, hell," McCarter said. "I know what you're thinking, and I don't think I like it."

"I do," Manning said.

"What?" Encizo interjected. "Have you lost your mind, Gary? I mean, they're terrorists but they're still human beings, for God's sake. You can't actually be thinking of turning that shit loose on them."

"You're damn right I am," James said.

"Think about the moral implications of what you're suggesting," Encizo stated.

"It wasn't my idea," Manning shot back, "but I'm afraid I'm with James on this one. Do you think these Qibla bastards are in any kind of ethical dilemma about killing thousands of innocent bystanders with the stuff? And what the hell difference does it really make in the end, eh? Tactically speaking, and only speaking that way, we could turn this from their planning room into their tomb."

David McCarter was astounded at what he was hearing. It seemed like all at once the mission was falling apart on him. On the one hand, he saw a quick and easy way of eliminating the terrorist threat aboard this freighter in a very final manner, and he didn't really care how they did that if it meant the ends would justify the means. On the other hand, to expose the terrorists to something as deadly toxic as this poison made him feel as if he were no better than they were, in spite of how much poetic justice there seemed to be in the move.

Whatever the outcome, he knew that the men would look to him for the answers. The final decision rested on his shoulders and his shoulders alone. They certainly weren't equipped to take the terrorists one-on-one in a firefight. Both sides would run out of ammunition before that could happen. On the other hand, they could wait it out long enough, fighting where they had to, until he could contact the HMS *Newcastle* and ask them to dispatch their complement of Royal Marines. Then again, that was involving an outside force and they would have lots of questions to answer. They also had to consider the possibility that another freighter would need to be intercepted somewhere.

"Well, the way I see it," James finally said, "it's David's call. What do you say, David? Do you want Gary to wire those things for effect?"

And there it was. He knew it would ultimately come down on his shoulders.

"No," he said quietly, catching just a notion of the surprised look that crossed Manning's face. "I don't want it wired for effect. If we do that, we're no better than those we fight. We don't go to that level because we can't go to it. We have to draw a line somewhere, and as leader of Phoenix Force I'm the one who has to draw it."

He looked at Manning and added, "I know you want a piece of these bloody bastards, and so do I, mate. But I'm not willing to trade the objectives of this mission just for the satisfaction of getting my bloody kicks watching our terrorist friends die a slow and miserable death, despite how attractive the offer. We stay away from those chemical containers, period and end of story. Understood?"

It seemed everyone on the team let out a big sigh of relief, then McCarter continued, "But there is a viable alternative. We've got one of the queen's finest destroyers sitting right off the bow of this thing, and I believe that there is something about James's idea that has merit."

"What's that?" Encizo asked, simultaneously intrigued and relieved.

"We passed some lockers a little ways back that contained oxygen tanks and acetylene torches. We get them all inside here, or at least most of them, and then weld the doors shut. And I might point out that if the place would make a good tomb, then it will sure as hell make a bloody great prison."

McCarter looked at Manning. "You got anything left in your bag of tricks that you could use to guide our friends in the right direction?"

"Such as?"

"Well, I'm sure they've split up in what's probably some effort to engage us. If you can manage to blow out some major hatchways, you could eventually lead the majority of them in here. We can then seal this place from the outside."

Manning squeezed the satchel tighter and nodded, the determination evident in his eyes. "Consider it done."

"Good," McCarter said. "Get cracking."

The Briton turned to the two remaining faces eagerly awaiting his next instruction. "We chaps have the special honor of letting these Qibla terrorists chase us through this floating teapot. Are you feeling up to a brisk run?"

DAVID MCCARTER'S PLAN WORKED like a charm and they managed to get all but a few of the terrorists sealed inside the cargo area that housed the missile. The terrorists attempted to launch the missile once they realized they were trapped, but Encizo's handiwork on the lift controls squashed their effort. Several of the terrorists were wounded by the blast, and the one who had triggered it was killed instantly.

The remaining terrorists realized the futility of doing battle with the Phoenix Force commandos and quickly surrendered when they realized they were outclassed and outgunned.

As McCarter sent a message to the HMS *Newcastle* and Manning and James transferred their gear to a waiting chopper aboard an American aircraft carrier that had arrived a short time earlier, Encizo and Hawkins studied the data Hawkins had found in the communications system.

"According to this," Encizo observed, "there are a total of four freighters."

McCarter joined them at that point. "What's the story?"

"We were just talking about that," Hawkins said. "We need to get this information to Carl Lyons and the Farm as soon as possible. One of the freighters went out days before the rest. That was the decoy Able Team picked off outside of Boston. The other two appear to be headed for targets in the States and Great Britain."

"Do we know where, exactly?"

"No, but we definitely know which freighters they are now."

"Then time's wasting away," McCarter replied. "I'll have them give us a secure patch aboard the chopper. Navy's going to fly us to Hellenic AFB at Souda Bay, Crete. Jack will meet us there."

CHAPTER NINETEEN

Stony Man Farm, Virginia

Hal Brognola hung up the phone, yanked the unlit cigar from his mouth and sighed with relief.

After more than an hour on the phone with the Oval Office, he finally got the sense that some of the weight had come off his shoulders. While they were certainly far from a resolution in his mind, Brognola knew that Phoenix Force's job in the Mediterranean had gone a long way to put the President at ease and to demonstrate that his confidences in the Stony Man group weren't in vain. With the information of the location of the remaining freighters now in their possession—and assuming that this wasn't another elaborate attempt by Qibla to deceive them—Brognola figured they could safely proceed on the offensive.

Barbara Price entered the War Room, a cup of coffee in one hand and a sandwich in the other. "Time to eat."

It wasn't a suggestion, and Brognola knew it. While Price might have been a hardcore professional and mission controller for Stony Man, she also had a tendency to take on the roll of mother hen for everyone at the Farm. She even buzzed around the field teams when they returned from a mission, ensuring their wounds were treated and that they received baths, hot meals and as much rest as they could.

Brognola acknowledged Price with a grateful nod and waved her into a chair.

"I just got off the phone with the Man," Brognola said, taking a sip of the coffee followed by a bite from the sandwich. It was corned beef on rye, one of his favorites. "Mmm, this is great. Thanks."

Around a mouthful of food, he continued. "Anyway, the President wants us to continue the mission. He asked us to pass on his congratulations to Phoenix Force. He also said it wouldn't be too difficult to keep it quiet, given the remoteness of where it all happened."

"Thank God for small favors," Price replied.

"Really. What's our next move?"

"Well, I understand that David's already talked with Lyons, and Able Team's proceeding based on the information David sent to them. Aaron estimates they'll intercept the freighter somewhere near the Yucatán Peninsula."

"Now that's music to the ears," Brognola replied. "What about the other freighter?"

"Phoenix Force is on their way." She looked at the clock and added, "ETA about four hours. They think the target is a British port, but they can't be sure which one yet. But by the time they catch up with the freighter, nearly every southern port in Great Britain would be within striking range."

"Well, the prime minister of England has told the President that he's not going to recall the blockade in the interest of their national security. However he did indicate he wouldn't order the fleet to take action unless he felt the threat was imminent."

"What exactly does that mean?"

"I don't know, but the President seemed to think it was a reprieve," Brognola answered. "I get the feeling the political situation is shaky, but one thing they all seem to be able to agree on is that they would like to keep this as quiet as possible."

"For now, at least," Price said. "But if it doesn't go right, you know they'll all point the finger in our direction."

Brognola shook his head. "I'd prefer we don't concern ourselves with that right now. We've always done our best in the past to save the Oval Office any embarrassment, and the Man knows that. We'll do whatever needs to be done. It's business as usual, and I've told him as much. Now, where are you with my other little request?"

"Well, I did a thorough background check on Lusk."

"And?"

Price shook her head. "I wish I could say there was something more ominous there, but you'll probably understand when I say I'm glad I didn't find anything extraordinary. No great mystery, in fact. After getting his MBA from Columbia University, he turned immediately to politics. He was first elected for the state legislature in California, his home state, and eventually was accepted for entry training with the CIA. He went on to Langley with a few additional courses at Quantico and then he spent a year on special assignment in Kuwait during the first Gulf war. Following that, he worked a desk in North Korea and spent a three-year stint in Afghanistan immediately following 9/11. As you know, the President picked him to head up this cabinet position when his first adviser chose to resign. The only murky part of his background centers around a year he spent at an undisclosed assignment station for the Company under the title of field operative. That's information I couldn't pull without someone getting suspicious and alerting him or the Oval Office."

Brognola nodded. "To officially probe his service records while he was with the Company we would most likely need the Man's permission. I don't want him to know yet that I had us looking into Lusk's background. The year he was incognito is an item of interest, but it doesn't sound unusual for the CIA."

"Agreed. To be honest, Hal, I think we're barking up the wrong tree," Price said.

"You're probably right," Brognola conceded. "Let's drop that for now and focus on supporting Able Team and Phoenix Force. Where are we with their assignments?"

"Well, based on the details I managed to drag out of the Bear, I think Able Team will be first to reach their target."

"Well, we've all done what we can here," Brognola said. "Now it's in the hands of our friends in the field. I think for now there's little more we can do, so I'm going to suggest you get some rest. I don't want to see you anywhere near here or the Annex for at least six hours. Is that clear?"

"Hal, I feel fine."

"It's not a request," Brognola cut in sharply but quietly. Aaron finally caved in.

Price started to open her mouth again, almost as if she were going to argue some more, but then on afterthought she clammed up and smiled. She then rose, patted his arm and left the War Room.

Mouth of the Yucatán Channel

"I HAVE TARGET IN SIGHT," Hermann Schwarz announced. "We'll be on top of them in less than a minute. Did anybody realize that the water's pretty cold this time of year?" Gadgets remarked.

"It's the middle of the goddamn Caribbean Ocean, Wizard," Lyons replied as he secured the pockets of his wetsuit. "It's cold all year."

"Not actually," Schwarz replied.

"Spare me," Lyons said. He raised a hand to emphasize that he didn't want to hear all of the marine statistics quoted to him, especially since he was confident that Gadgets had every one of them tucked away in the sponge he called a brain.

Charlie Mott's voice came through the loudspeaker. "You guys are clear. Good luck!"

"Equipment goes first!" Schwarz shouted, attempting to be heard over the screaming winds of the now-open door.

Mott had brought them in low and slow, keeping the King Air 350 just above stall speed. They would have only a few seconds to get out and clear. The plane wasn't particularly designed for such airborne operations, especially given its speed. This would be much different from dropping out of a chopper, and Lyons knew even as he went out with their weapons and equipment that it was going to hurt like hell when he hit the water.

True to Schwarz's predictions, the water was quite cold if the sensation of his testicles drawing up instantaneously inside his body was any indication. Still, the main thing was to ensure that the weapons didn't get too far below the waterline, which hadn't looked quite as choppy when he'd bailed out of the plane. He yanked the cord on the equipment bag and the air bladders inflated immediately, driving the bag to the surface before it could sink to the bottom of the sea and drag Lyons with it.

The Able Team leader watched as Schwarz hit the water within about twenty yards of his position. Just like Lyons, his head disappeared beneath the dark waters, and Lyons held his breath and waited to see that familiar face break the surface. It seemed to take an eternity, but it was really only a few seconds before his teammate came up and gave him the okay signal. The pair went through the same exercise in watching Blancanales come down and then surface.

"Eagle Two to Able One." It was Charlie Mott over the radio. Lyons reached to his utility belt and keyed the waterproof receiver.

"Able One, here."

"Coming back on the second pass," Mott replied. "I'll try to get her as close as I can."

"Roger that. As soon as you've dumped the load, proceed to rendezvous point Bravo Two per instructions."

"Acknowledged, Able One. Eagle Two's out here."

And that was the last communication they were to have with Mott until they met up with him again in Cancun. Their plan was simple. If they could take the freighter without incident, they would arrange to have it towed or steered into Puerto Juarez at the edge of the Yucatán Peninsula. If not…well, Lyons chose not to think about the alternatives. The bottom line was that the freighter had to be stopped at any cost, and that meant that Able Team was to do whatever it had to, to avert another civil disaster.

Lyons watched as the King Air 350 buzzed overhead and something large and square dropped from the plane. It struck the water hard and at about a midway point between Blancanales and Schwarz. Bless Charlie Mott's big heart; the guy had damn near set the thing on top of them. While Lyons could have easily handled a swim of considerable distance, water this cold had a tendency to sap the strength much sooner than under more moderate conditions. Either way, it didn't matter because they would soon be visiting conditions that were a lot harder than some cold seawater.

Lyons began to glide toward the dropped equipment with long, smooth strokes, eventually catching Schwarz. All three of the Able Team warriors reached the massive, floating package at about the same time. Lyons quickly withdrew a Colt Combat Knife from his belt and cut through the straps.

"You want to step it up there, Ironman?" Blancanales called from the other side where he was performing similar measures. "I'm freezing my ass off."

Through gritted teeth, Lyons replied, "In the words of someone we all know and love, 'quit your bellyaching.'"

That shut Blancanales up.

The two men continued to work while Schwarz occupied himself with a compartment on the side of the package. Just prior to cutting the last packaging strap free, Lyons shouted a warning for all to clear away.

"Hold up one more second, partner," Schwarz said. "I'm almost finished."

"I've got a second, but I don't know if the sharks do."

Blancanales poked his head around the package. "Did you say sharks, Ironman?"

"Got it!" Schwarz declared, coming away with some little electronic trinket that Lyons was almost positive they probably could have lived without. "All right, Ironman, she's all yours."

Lyons ripped the knife through the last cord and the packaging fell away to expose the contents. Lyons immediately reached into the center and yanked a handle. Within a few seconds the contents fully inflated into a full-size assault raft, and buried within the center was a small, outboard motor easily powerful enough to propel the raft across the open water at a pretty good clip.

"All aboard who're going aboard," Blancanales announced, immediately reaching up and pulling his husky form into the craft.

Lyons followed and Schwarz was last in. The men quickly stripped off their wetsuits and dried their hair with a towel, then donned black stocking caps. It wouldn't do for them to remain wet and suffer from hypothermia before they had even completed their mission.

As soon as they were dressed, the trio went about their assigned tasks. Lyons began the process of getting the engine mounted, primed and started while Schwarz hooked up their electronic tracking equipment and GPS satellite link. Blancanales cleared the weapons from the waterproof bags and got them ready for action. Each man knew exactly what he had to do and just how to do it. Within eight minutes they were moving over the water and headed for their target.

As they buzzed along the open water, Blancanales moved up close to Lyons so he could be heard above the loud motor. "Have you considered exactly how we're going to approach this mission?"

Lyons shrugged, keeping his icy blue eyes focused on the water ahead. When they had landed they figured they were a good ten nautical miles from the freighter's current location. It would take them a bit of time to get there.

"Not really," he replied.

"So what are you planning to do then? Just make it up as you go?"

"I don't know yet," Lyons said. "But I'll have a plan before we get there."

"Well, I hope you don't think the Qibla are just going to let us power up to the freighter, grapple a railing and climb aboard!"

"No," Lyons replied with a wicked grin. "I've already taught them firsthand that approach doesn't work!"

"Actually, that's exactly what I was expecting us to do!" Schwarz offered, having now turned to face the other two men.

The pair looked at each other in amazement that Schwarz had actually been able to overhear their conversation with all the noise.

"And just how exactly do you suppose we do that?" Blancanales asked incredulously.

"Yes, please, do tell!" Lyons added.

"Well, one of the reasons I had to get that equipment out of that pack is because it's part of my plan! The way you get on board without being seen is to give the terrorists something else to look at! And that's exactly what I'm going to do!"

"And just how do you plan on doing that?"

"Well," Schwarz began, obviously savoring the moment, "I knew the odds were pretty good this freighter was our target. I read the other day that the Playboy cruise ship just so happens to be coming out of Cancun today, headed for the Bahamas! According to its navigational records, it would have gone right past our target! Only trouble was, it was an hour too early by my calculations. So I sent a message through the computer relay to the Caribbean Port Authority that it was believed the ship might have a faulty boiler system and should probably be inspected by the Authority before being allowed to shove off. That delayed it long enough that we should be seeing it right about…now."

He turned to look ahead of them and, sure enough, in the distance, the massive white outline of the cruise ship was becoming more distinct by the second. Lyons and Blancanales exchanged another series of bewildered looks, then stared at the back of their friend's head. Schwarz pretended not to sense they were watching him, but Lyons knew better. If there was anything he knew about his friend, it was that he liked to gloat.

Finally, Schwarz turned and looked at them. "It was a long shot, but I figured it was worth a try. Nobody, and I mean nobody, can resist being distracted by a beautiful body. Not even a terrorist."

CHAPTER TWENTY

Mahmed Temez watched with disgust as a number of his men cheered at the massive cruise passenger liner rolling past, the tops of its decks littered with the bronzed skin of at least a hundred beautiful women. Temez wasn't a eunuch, of course, as witnessed by the fact he'd fathered seven children. But he believed in the stories of the many virgins he would possess in Paradise, with the caveat that he keep himself pure from the women that would attempt to seduce him here on Earth.

Still, he couldn't fault his men for having an appreciation. He was pure but he wasn't blind, and he could tell even from here that these were women of extraordinary caliber, whom Allah had blessed and endowed with the loveliest of shapes. It wasn't as if they really deserved such an honor. Their skin wasn't naturally cured by the sun, as the women in his own country, and the fact they were emboldened enough to wave and show their faces—as well as other parts of their anatomy—to strange men only belied the falseness of their existence.

Well, he needed to relax and let his men enjoy what time remained, for in just a few short hours it would all be over.

Temez turned from the activities and strode to a hatchway that would take him into the bowels of the freighter. He hadn't heard anything more from either the *Thurayya* or the *Crescent,* and his ship—he had named it the *Fallujah* in remembrance of his home town—was ready to fire at a moment's notice and would be within position in a few hours.

The previous evening his men had used a special pressured system to load musrah into the warhead equipped with a dispersal charge. During the procedure, they had all been required to wear chemical suits to protect them in the event a hazardous spill or exposure accident occurred. Musrah was unforgiving, of this there was little doubt, and it would kill anyone. It didn't know enemies from allies. It was at that time that Karif Bhati had told him of his idea for increasing the yield, and after further debate he finally relented and allowed the men to perform the needed modifications.

They were now confident that they would be able to expose approximately ten thousand Americans to musrah. Temez wished he could have been the one to take credit for the idea, but he believed that credit was due appropriately for individual accomplishment. He wasn't the kind of leader to take credit for something done by one of his subordinates. There were moments he worried that Bhati was a little too ambitious, but he'd never had any reason to think the man would betray him, and he hadn't been ingenuous when saying he one day expected Bhati to succeed him. But he knew that day was still a long time coming.

Temez reached the hold and stared once more with fascination at their creation. Occasionally, crew members would approach and ask him if he needed assistance, but he would wave them on in reply. It amazed him that that innocent-looking cylinder, barely fifteen meters in length, contained within it the death of Americans and the victory of the jihad. He couldn't get enough of it, actually, and he was beginning to wonder if the warnings from his cousin about turning into a fanatic weren't true.

"Mahmed!"

Temez turned to see Bhati rushing toward him, an aide close on his heels. Sweat was covering his face and his eyes were bleary and tired. He'd volunteered to stay up during the night watch instead of letting Temez take over, citing that their leader would need to rest. He'd figured that Bhati had taken his rest with the changing of shifts, but apparently he was still up.

As his aide approached, Temez said, "Karif, try to get ahold of yourself." He looked around at the other men to see if they were watching. A hard look from Temez was enough to put them back about their business.

Temez returned his attention to Bhati. "You're not setting a good example for our men."

"I apologize, Mahmed," Bhati replied, "and beg your forgiveness, but there is a message from Jabir and he says it's urgent. It's about the *Thurayya*."

"He has broken communication silence?"

Bhati nodded slowly, trying to catch his breath. "He is waiting to speak to you now."

Temez turned and raced for the bridge.

He could now understand what had Bhati so concerned, although he still wished his aide had shown a bit more discretion. Bhati was his most trusted warrior, and he was charged with leading the rest of the men through an operation. He enforced discipline and executed any orders that Temez gave him. That alone was a tremendous responsibility, and being in such a position meant he was to maintain a certain level of control and demeanor at all times. But obviously Temez had had to make an exception here.

The only eventuality for breaking communications silence was at the point one or the other was in position and awaiting confirmation from the others for a coordinated strike. But in this case, Bhati had said Jabir's call had something to do with the *Thurayya*. Well, there was no point in attempting to guess. He would have to wait and see.

Temez reached the bridge in short order and took the satellite phone from where Bhati had left it. There was no sign of his aide, so Temez figured he had to have fallen behind during their jaunt to the bridge.

"Jabir, peace to you, my brother," Temez said, hoping that good nature would perhaps quell the blow of any potential bad news.

"Peace to you, cousin," al-Warraq replied. "I have some unfortunate news. I am afraid that the *Thurayya* has been captured by NATO forces. I do not know the details, but I am confident that Fahd Abufatin is now either dead or in the hands of our enemies."

Temez nodded in understanding, even though he knew al-Warraq couldn't see him. "I understand. It would seem reasonable to assume that they probably know of our plans. I believe we must consider accelerating the operation."

"That is my belief, as well. I also do not know how successful we will be. My spies tell me that there is a British naval blockade forming at the edge of the English Channel. We are going to try to go around it, but I do not know if we will be successful. When will you be within effective range of your own target?"

Temez let his eyes quickly scan the navigational panels in front of him, and a smile crept over his lips. He checked his watch and realized that they were within the window. "I could release at any time now. It would simply be a matter of reprogramming the coordinates into the navigational cone of the warhead. We have made excellent time."

"That's good," al-Warraq replied. "Your ship is a fine vessel. I think you took the pick of the lot. However, I would suggest that we keep to our plan unless we agree it has become infeasible, since it means the greatest chance of success. I expect my own ship to be in range within the hour. I will contact you as soon as we're in position."

"I understand," Temez said. "We will remain on course until I hear from you. Allah be with you, my brother."

"And with you."

Temez heard the click of a dying connection in his ear, then set the satellite phone in the charging cradle. That had not been good news at all. With the *Thurayya* out of commission, they had reduced their chances of striking a successful target by thirty-three percent! Before Temez could consider the next viable course of action, Bhati caught up with him and the look in his eyes told Temez that the impact of the news was written all over the terrorist leader's face.

"What is it, Mahmed?" Bhati asked.

"The *Thurayya* was captured by our enemies a few hours ago. She will not be participating in our victory. It is believed that Fahd Abufatin may have been killed, and Jabir and I agree that this could mean that those who would oppose us may know of our plans. We are accelerating the operation." For a moment Temez didn't say anything, still shocked by the fact that so many had been lost already and they hadn't fired a shot.

Temez shook himself and continued. "We must be ready to fire the missile within the hour. Get the men assembled and—"

The sound of gunfire interrupted him and he exchanged looks with Bhati before both of them nearly tripped over each other to get out the door and onto the observation catwalk of the bridge tower. Temez didn't see anything at first, but a moment later he watched as several of the sentries on the deck immediately below him took cover behind whatever they could find. His angle didn't afford him a view of what they were shooting at, but there was evidently an intruder aboard the ship.

"We are under attack! Take your men and lead them into battle, Karif. Kill your enemies. They must not survive this day!"

"What about the missile?"

"I will take care of the missile!" Temez waved him off. "Now go and defend our vessel!"

The man turned and rushed for the steps leading to the deck. Temez turned and entered the bridge once more. He ordered the helmsman to continue full speed ahead no matter what happened, then advised the bridge crew to seal themselves inside the bridge once he had gone. He went to a lockbox containing the passports and other information he had brought in the event he needed to make an escape. He had no intention of perishing this day.

No, Mahmed Temez would succeed in his mission for Allah and his people. And there wasn't anyone who could stop him. He would fire the missile now, and have to hope that Jabir could forgive him and try to understand his reasons at a later date. Temez wondered as he

stuffed his pockets with the fake credentials and identification who the invaders were, although it was of no
real consequence. Whoever had dared to oppose him
had made a critical error in judgment. He wasn't a weak-
minded fool like Abufatin had been, a man who could
not think for himself. To the contrary, Temez was a soldier first and foremost, and one who would go to any
lengths to complete his mission.

And most importantly, it was simply not his ap-
pointed time to die.

"'NOBODY CAN RESIST being distracted by a beautiful
body' you said," Carl Lyons mocked as a flurry of 7.62
mm slugs buzzed over their heads. "Yeah, this was some
plan, Wizard."

"What are you complaining about?" Schwarz replied.

Rosario Blancanales watched as Schwarz slammed
a fresh magazine into his SIG Model 551. A carbine variant of the Stgw 90 adopted by the Swiss armies, the SIG
551 was very lightweight and chambered 5.56 mm car-
tridges from magazines with sides that could be clipped
together. This permitted the carrier to effect a magazine
change out without taking time to reach for spares, one
of the chief reasons Schwarz chose the weapon.

Lyons scowled, obviously miffed at his teammate's
reply, then leaned to the side of the crates the trio was
crammed behind. He leveled the pair of MP-5s he'd
chosen for the mission and squeezed their triggers si-

multaneously. The air came alive with the reports from the machine pistols as Lyons kept heads down with a firestorm of 9 mm Parabellum rounds. He burned off both magazines in a matter of seconds, then dropped behind cover to reload.

"Well," Blancanales said, "we can't hold them off forever. I guess it's up to me."

He grinned as he popped a high-explosive grenade into the M-203 launcher mounted beneath the grips of his M-16. The high-explosive charge would take care of business quick enough, and if he left anyone out on the first go-around, the Able Team commando would definitely make sure he included them in trial number two. He came to his feet in a single motion, aimed the weapon from the hip for added stability and triggered the launcher. The 40 mm bomb sailed over the various objects in its path and came down just to the rear of the main assemblage of terrorists. The grenade exploded on impact, washing over the unsuspecting group with a destructive fury. Heat, smoke and intense flames engulfed the men furthest from the hit point, while the primary blast blew apart a number of others.

Blancanales took advantage of the carnage by following up with a second grenade just as planned. This one he delivered near the base of the bridge tower, putting a massive, scorched dent in the side that was mixed with the gory remains of two terrorists caught directly with the blast. Superheated shards of metal winged across the deck, a few of them contacting flesh while others sailed into the ocean and were extinguished. A shower of sparks followed this second blast, an indication that there had been some effect on the electrical system.

Just for good measure, the Able Team veteran put a third grenade into the launcher and this time aimed for an area just behind where he'd planted the first two. As he triggered the weapon he could make out a terrorist standing there, a leader perhaps, shouting orders to the men scrambling to find some kind of adequate cover. There wasn't a lot of that to be found on the deck of a commercial freighter. The terrorist apparently realized just a millisecond before the grenade hit that he was about to die, because Blancanales could actually see his eyes widen in shock and horror. A moment later, there was very little left to see as the grenade blew him and two other nearby terrorists to bits.

"Nice work, Politician," Schwarz said. His expression didn't do a thing to hide how impressed he was.

"How I love the M-203," Blancanales replied. "Let me count the ways."

"Count them later," Lyons said. "We have work now. Come on."

The Able Team warriors moved forward, obscured by the intense smoke and heat enveloping the port side of the deck near the bridge tower. Blancanales knew they would only have a minute or so to find a way to the missile before the terrorists regrouped. The sea breezes would make short work of the smoky devastation. Despite Lyons's sentiments, getting on board had been pretty easy. Schwarz's distraction had worked like a charm. They approached on the aft port side of the freighter and came aboard, leaving their ascension rope tied to the raft so the freighter could tow it. They had no idea if they'd need it later to get off the ship in a hurry, so they were planning for every eventuality.

What they hadn't counted on was the diligence of a pair of sentries. They had taken them down quickly but that ultimately led to attracting the attention of a few others, which provoked the firefight. So it really wasn't Schwarz's fault that they had been detected; it was simply part of the game.

They continued toward their target, Schwarz having identified the missile as being in the forward cargo hold. They were nearing the hatch when two terrorists sprinted around the corner of the bridge tower and spotted them. They started firing their AK-47s, muzzles flashing as the guns barked with their distinctive reports, but Able Team dived to the deck in time to avoid the onslaught of merciless slugs.

Lyons replied in kind by rolling, getting to one knee and triggering the MP-5s. The 9 mm Parabellum rounds drilled into both targets. One terrorist's head exploded under Lyons's expert marksmanship. The man's body staggered to and fro, struggling for balance, before finally dropping to the deck. The second terrorist took several rounds to the chest. They continued out the back and the impact spun the terrorist, slamming him face-first to the deck.

"Clear!" Lyons shouted.

Blancanales and Schwarz scrambled to their feet and went to the hatchway while Lyons covered them. They quickly got it opened and Schwarz was the first to descend. Lyons started to rise and rush the hatch when a terrorist came seemingly out of nowhere and triggered his AKSU-74, the weapon chattering as rounds danced at Lyons's feet. The blond warrior changed direction as he was running and tripped, the only thing that saved his life as rounds burned the air overhead. One caught him in the meaty part of the shoulder.

Blancanales was in such a position inside the hatchway that he couldn't bring his rifle up and acquire the target in time. His hand rocketed to shoulder leather and came away with the Glock 26. He triggered three rounds successively, a double tap for the body and a third for the head; all three connected. The terrorist's weapon went skyward, and he continued to fire even as the head shot punched him between the eyes and sent him falling backward. The remaining rounds in the AKSU were expended before the terrorist's body hit the deck.

"You okay?" Blancanales asked, looking at the wounded shoulder with concern as Lyons pulled away his hand, now slick with blood.

"I've been better, but I'll make it," Lyons said. "Let's keep moving."

Blancanales nodded and assisted his friend into the hatchway, then descended the rest of the way and closed the hatch behind him. He slammed the lock-bar in place, which would prevent anyone else from accessing the hatch from above deck. He didn't relish the idea of getting caught in a crossfire as they descended the ladderwell. Within a minute, they had all made it to the relative safety of the first sublevel deck.

"Okay, Einstein, which way?" Lyons asked, turning to Schwarz, who now had his equipment out.

The small device looked like something out of a science-fiction movie but it actually operated on a very simple principle. As Schwarz had explained, the systems aboard the King Air 350 had been able to draw a detailed map of the entire ship based on the previous intelligence they had gleaned. It wouldn't be a perfect map by any stretch of the imagination, but it would contain enough detailed information that the interface computers at Stony Man could then make a predictability assessment of the general layout. With that accomplished, Schwarz could then use a supplied PDA as a compass, thus providing an effectual way of navigating while in the labyrinthine-like bowels of the freighter.

"This way," Schwarz said, motioning for them to follow.

As they drew nearer to the cargo hold, Blancanales began to sense something he hadn't sensed earlier. It was subtle at first, nothing he could really put his finger on exactly, but as they got closer to the target it had become more obvious. It was a hum or vibration of some kind, a thrumming sound that seemed to reverberate through the freighter's structure. They went on another minute or so before he stopped the trio.

"Hold up," he said. "There's something wrong here."

Lyons stopped and turned to study his friend with a disbelieving look. "What, you mean beside the fact that a hundred or more bloodthirsty terrorists are somewhere aboard this heap with nothing more on their minds than hunting us down and killing us?" Lyons said.

"I'm not talking about that," Blancanales shot back. He was becoming a bit exasperated with Lyons's grouchiness. "I'm talking about that sound. Don't you hear it?"

"No," Schwarz interjected, looking up at the ceiling. "I don't hear anything. What do you hear, Pol?"

"I'm not sure. It almost sounds like…well, a humming noise."

Lyons rolled his eyes. "Oh, boy, he finally has lost it. Look—"

Blancanales shushed him. "Listen! Do you hear it?"

This time the two men stopped and listened carefully. They knew that Blancanales had the senses of a jungle cat. He wouldn't have risked stopping them if it was unimportant. This time, though, the humming was getting louder. It sounded like machinery, a cycling of some type, and then it hit Blancanales like a sharp knife through the belly. A cold lump formed instantly in his throat and the first thing he envisioned was a piled mass of dead bodies. The cargo lift!

"It's coming from the cargo bay!" he shouted.

"They're moving the missile into position. They're going to fire that thing now!"

And then the corridor ahead of them filled with terrorists.

CHAPTER TWENTY-ONE

North Atlantic

The mouth of the Bay of Biscay loomed directly ahead and Jabir al-Warraq considered his options.

They were within a hundred nautical miles of where they had to be in order to launch the missiles. The difficulty now was the naval blockade. There were just too many ships to expect they could get past the British fleet, and al-Warraq began to wonder if it would have been wiser to listen to Sahar. They could have altered course, but such a radical shift in the *Crescent*'s course would have most certainly alerted the maritime authorities.

Not that he and his men were left with a lot of options. They had a couple of choices. One was to launch the missile on a random target and take credit for the attack, but al-Warraq wasn't entirely sure what that would have accomplished. A launch against a European country would still have disastrous consequences, but al-Warraq doubted it would have the most desirable effect. The Qibla had very specific enemies, and such an attack didn't seem worth the effort.

The other option he'd considered was to dock at the nearest port and evacuate the ship, leaving its contents for the military to find along with a booby-trap. Al-Warraq ultimately dismissed the idea as pointless and cowardly. He wouldn't see their efforts come to naught in this operation. The *Thurayya* had already failed in her mission, and he couldn't be certain that his cousin would be any more successful. No, there had to be another way and it eventually came to him.

"The traffic in the bay is heavy at this time of season, with merchant ships bringing their wares and vacationers crowding the beaches," he told Sahar. "If we could lose the *Crescent* in that heavy traffic, we might stand a chance of getting close enough to the northern shores to come within range of our target."

Sahar appeared to consider the idea for nearly a minute, then nodded. "I believe it is possible as you say, Jabir."

"Excellent," al-Warraq replied. "Change course and get us to the north side of the bay. And do it quickly because the British blockade will be closing soon and sending their advance helicopters to pinpoint our exact position."

"As you wish, Jabir," Sahar replied. The massive Syrian headed for the bridge to carry out his orders.

Al-Warraq studied the water as it swirled against the freighter, bubbling into whitecaps before disappearing beneath the massive wake of the ship. It was so pure and clean, unlike the world he lived in. Al-Warraq had fallen from the Islamic faith many years earlier because of the impurity of life. It was an impossible task to live by the rules of Islam. In many ways, al-Warraq considered the Islamic faith barbaric and arcane. He knew that he risked eternal damnation at death but simultaneously he believed he had been forced to live a kind of damnation here in this plane of existence. There was nothing about his life that he cherished. He had enjoyed the spoiling pleasures of sin, the women and wine, and he had even walked among a very powerful and influential circle of friends.

But what did that really mean? What had he accomplished in his life outside the collection of wealth and social standing? There was nothing permanent in that any more than there was in his cousin's ridiculous faith in an ancient religion. Al-Warraq had made it his life's work to pursue something more and he had eventually determined that the key to happiness and longevity in life was power. But not in the sense of the word such as most might consider it. He wasn't talking about power as given to useless world leaders or even the kind of power bestowed on monarchs. That was authority, not power. Power in al-Warraq's mind was the kind that came from an ability to oppress others. He believed that only the most powerful men were those who knew how to use their wits and resources to bend the masses to their will. And that was his absolute goal.

"I THINK WE'RE GOING to have a real problem on our hands, mates," David McCarter said. "I was just talking to Hal, and he tells me that a British blockade is on the move. Jack confirmed it through some military channels he was monitoring."

The men sitting around the table aboard the Gulfstream C-20 let out a chorus of moans and groans. It had been one big nightmare trying to sort through all of the details of the first freighter with the British and American forces, and now it looked as if they were about to jump right into an identical situation. One thing they couldn't do in an assault was predict how any military force would respond to a perceived threat on the security of its nation. It not only endangered their operations, but it increased the risk of something going very wrong. They had nearly had their heads blown off in the Mediterranean. As if that wasn't bad enough, they now faced the potential of an entire naval blockade armed to the teeth and ready for a fight.

"If the British are given the green light to fight it out," Manning said, "they will most likely respond with a force equal to the task of blowing that freighter clean out of the water."

"Which also brings the inherent risk of potentially releasing toxic chemicals into the environment," Encizo reminded them all.

"Not to mention the publicity," James added. "Can you imagine seeing that one on television? The press would have a field day with it." He sat up straight, mocking a television announcer, and said, "Today the British navy blew a commercial freighter in the Atlantic to bits. We don't know why yet, but we'll have the full story and film at eleven."

"So the PM plans to sink this freighter?" Hawkins asked.

"He's the only chap holding them back, mate," McCarter replied. "I believe the words that Hal used were 'if they suspect an imminent threat, they will respond.'"

"I can't believe it," James said. "We've come this far and now they're talking about doing the very the thing we're trying to prevent. Why don't they just back off and let us do our job?"

"Does anybody here suppose that this is possibly what the terrorists wanted to happen?" Manning said.

McCarter furrowed his brow.

"What do you mean?"

"Well, let's assume that they never figured to get these missiles off. Nobody has fired a shot and yet they already have major governments quibbling with one another, and everyone's ramping up to deliver hellfire and brimstone if anybody so much as performs a course correction. I understand that the request from the White House to investigate those other freighters near Australia turned into a first-rate fiasco. Apparently the shipping company started asking all kinds of uncomfortable questions of the Aussie government, and so far nobody wants to take the blame for detaining a commercial shipment."

"Well, whatever the political situation is right now, we can't make that our problem," Encizo said. "We need to stick to the plan and finish this mission, British blockade or no British blockade."

He looked to McCarter, who nodded a grateful acknowledgment.

"Well?" Encizo asked.

"Well what?" McCarter replied.

"What's the plan?"

"Well, we were thinking we'd have to try for another topside landing, but it seems we might get lucky. The ship has shifted from a north to northeasterly heading."

"She's changed course?" Hawkins asked.

McCarter nodded.

"Most likely they figured out they weren't going to get past the British blockade and decided on an alternate course of action," Manning said.

The demolitions expert turned to the nearby computer terminal and punched up the tracking system on the keyboard. McCarter moved to his side and the two men studied the freighter's movements. Manning began to type into the keyboard and McCarter watched the Canadian with a newfound admiration. It appeared he knew a bit more about computer systems than he'd let on.

"Look at you go," James observed.

"I was just thinking that myself," McCarter said over his shoulder. He looked at Manning again. "You been sneaking down to the Annex at nights, mate?"

The Canadian grinned. "The Bear's been giving me extra homework, and I've had a few extra lessons on the side from Carmen and Akira. That last class we had in 3-D cartography kind of piqued my interests some."

"That's our Gary," Hawkins teased, although McCarter detected some pride in his tone. "Always the strategist, he is."

"So, what are you doing now?"

"I'm mapping possible new coordinates based on direction and speed," Manning said. "There's nothing that seems to be a viable target in this area, near as I can tell. Their present direction can only take them one place, and that's into the northern region of the Bay of Biscay."

"What are the ports there?" James asked.

"Concarneau, Lorient and Carnac," McCarter responded, reading from the screen.

"Maybe they figure it's a lost cause," Hawkins suggested. "Maybe they're going to try to abandon the freighter and get lost in France."

"Not likely," Manning said. "I don't see them operating that way. No, whoever planned this operation is bold, real bold. They'll continue with their mission no matter what it costs. I think they'll try to use the area to put heavy shipping traffic between themselves and the blockade."

McCarter nodded his agreement. "Agreed. It's sure as hell what I'd do if I were in their bloody situation."

"The other thing about this strategy is that it still puts them close enough to their target," said Manning. "The northern shoreline of the bay is only 267.2349 nautical miles from Portsmouth, according to the computer, which is well within the range capabilities of that missile."

"They want to make it a sure thing," Encizo remarked.

"They can't afford not to," Hawkins said. "We've already taken out one of them, and chances are better than good that Able Team will hit the second before they have a chance to unload their missile. The way the Qibla probably view it, this is their last chance."

"And we aren't going to give it to them," McCarter said, making the determination evident in his voice. "Gear up. We'll do a flyby and have Jack bring us down at the nearest landing site. I'll contact the Farm and have them make contact with someone who can get us watercraft. We'll make our assault that way."

And the men of Phoenix Force began to prepare for battle once more.

THE FACT STONY MAN had contacts in every nook and crevice of the world wasn't more evident than when the men of Phoenix Force arrived on the French island of Belle-Île. Grimaldi had managed to get them into the Belle-Île en Mer Airfield near Quiberon, and an island resident, a retired American who used to work for the Pentagon, shuttled them to the home of a friend who had a boat-rental company.

The man's house sat on stilts above the waters of the marina, and beneath the house was a makeshift dock. The Frenchman pulled back a massive tarpaulin to reveal two large speedboats. They were sleek and polished, with powerful engines built into the aft sections. The boats were powerful enough to require twin exhaust pipes out the back. At first viewing, the eyes of most of the Phoenix Force warriors popped from their heads.

Hawkins let out a whistle. "Very nice."

"Oh, my American friends, these are the finest boats on the island," the Frenchman bragged. "They are very fast and quite dependable. I think that you will have no problems."

McCarter stared the man in the eye. "Do you have any idea what we want them for?"

"Er..." The man looked uncertainly at Phoenix Force's liaison, an overweight bear of a man named Krabowsky.

"He doesn't know and doesn't need to know," Krabowsky said. "Your people already took care of compensating him well."

"Good," McCarter said. "Because I can't guarantee what sort of condition he'll get them back in."

"Oh, not to worry, sir," the boat dealer said, showing the Phoenix Force crew a mouthful of gold teeth. "My friend Krabowsky is correct. I have been paid more than enough to replace them if they are not returned in good shape."

"They may not be returned at all, pal," James said as

he dropped into the nearest boat and began to study the controls.

"Mr. Smith, you'll pilot this boat," McCarter told James. He turned to Encizo, "Mr. Gomez, you take the other."

Encizo nodded and went to it. McCarter shook hands with the Frenchman and Krabowsky, then dropped into the boat piloted by Encizo. Manning was on board with him, while Hawkins boarded with James. The two boat pilots got their bearings and quickly familiarized themselves with the controls, then Encizo led the way out of the dock with James closely on his tail. As they powered smoothly out of the marina, keeping their speed low to avoid attracting the attention of police patrol boats, McCarter looked over Manning's shoulder as the Canadian continually monitored the progress of the freighter.

"Where is it?" McCarter asked.

"Close," Manning replied. "We almost missed them."

"Well, these boats seem pretty bloody fast to me, mate. We ought to be able to catch up with them quickly."

"It's not catching up with them that has me worried," Manning replied. "It's what we do once we get there."

"What do you mean?"

"Well, it's safe to assume we'll run into the same level of resistance as we did before. There won't be any second chances on this one. And that blockade is getting close, too. We can only hope they'll hold back until we've had a chance to neutralize the threat."

McCarter clapped his friend on the shoulder. "It's like I told you before, mate. We can't worry about the political ramifications. We need to shut this thing down any way we can. It's no rules now. We're going to have to hit them and hit them hard. This one counts like it's never counted before."

As soon as the powerboats had cleared the no-wake zone of the marina, Encizo threw the boat into high gear and opened the throttle full. Sure to the Frenchman's promise, the boats accelerated and began cruising across the water, bouncing through the choppier parts with their noses pointed skyward at nearly a forty-five-degree angle. McCarter felt the rush of sea air against his face and the saltiness stung his eyes, causing them to water.

After about twenty minutes they could make out the freighter's distinct lines on the horizon. They would be within striking range in about five minutes. A quick survey of the area revealed the British blockade was nowhere to be seen, which meant that they were just ahead of the game.

McCarter double-checked the action of his 9 mm Browning Hi-Power pistol secured in shoulder leather beneath his left armpit, then brought the MP-5 into battery. Manning had already turned to a similar procedure, first checking Encizo's weapon for him and passing it to the Cuban with a nod of assurance, then attending to his own weapon. For this encounter, he'd brought an extra bit of firepower packed with the Fabrique Nationale FAL battle rifle. A rugged, dependable weapon, it had long been a popular choice among all the members of Stony Man for various reasons. The Belgium-made assault rifle was chambered to fire the heavy 7.62 mm NATO round, and was probably one of the most successfully designed rifles in small arms manufacturing history. A product of its time with distribution in over fifty-five countries, the FN-FAL was extremely rugged, reliable under the most stringent conditions and could dispense its heavy-caliber slugs at a muzzle velocity exceeding 850 mps. Manning had first developed his tremendous respect for the weapon while serving as an RCMP officer.

"White Lightning to White Four," McCarter called into his radio.

"White Four, here," Hawkins answered.

"You guys pull ahead. Put as much heat on them as you can, mate, until we can find a way aboard."

"Roger, wilco, White Lightning."

"White Lightning out, here." McCarter keyed off and said to Manning, "Get ready."

Before they had even reached the freighter they could see muzzle-flashes winking from the railings. At least ten terrorists were standing at the portside rail, near the bow of the ship, and putting out a heavy firestorm of lead. McCarter and Manning opened up with their assault weapons in reaction, actually knocking a couple of the terrorists out on their first pass. At the last moment before they reached the bow, Encizo cut a hard right and headed for the starboard side while James continued on a straight course.

There was a brief moment of eerie silence from either side, and suddenly a massive ball of flame rolled skyward from the deck, followed a moment later by the thunderclap of an HE M-383 grenade.

McCarter and Manning watched as the starboard side went by at a blinding speed. They both looked to Encizo to try to understand what the Cuban was doing, and why he hadn't chosen to stop, but it didn't look as if he was planning to come to a boarding point on this pass. It took McCarter only a second to deduce what was going through Encizo's mind. He was doing a sweep, checking to make sure that when he found a point on this side for them to board, they wouldn't get cut in two by terrorists just waiting for them to try something like that. McCarter had to admit that the Cuban's savvy was admirable.

Encizo traversed the entire starboard side, then moved past the wake of the freighter before making a hard turn and heading back toward the boat. There were a few ladder rungs built into the side of this particular vessel, which the team could use when they decided to storm the ship. It looked as if Encizo was about to make another complete run when suddenly he stopped the engine and brought the boat clanking roughly against the side of the freighter, the noise just coming to rest below an access ladder.

"Go!" McCarter shouted, but Manning was already in motion.

The Canadian stepped onto the nose of the boat, nearly slipped and fell into the depths, but quickly reached out and caught a handhold on the railing. He fired a harsh look in Encizo's direction.

"Sorry," the Cuban said sheepishly. "I'm trying to keep her steady."

Manning dismissed the irritation and vaulted up the ladder, McCarter right on his heels. Encizo moored the boat against the freighter by tying off a good strong knot against the lowest ladder rung, then put his foot up to climb. The unmistakable clack of a bolt chambering a round drew his attention. Encizo quickly located the source and found himself in the gun sights of a Qibla terrorist on the deck.

In a moment frozen in time Rafael Encizo could see the terrorist smile behind the rifle and his finger begin to tighten on the trigger....

CHAPTER TWENTY-TWO

Caribbean Ocean

Carl Lyons wasn't sure how he did it, but he somehow managed to avoid being cut in two by a swathing blast of terrorist gunfire while preventing a similar fate for his two friends. The Able Team leader yanked on their sleeves and dragged them down as a plethora of assault-rifle fire buzzed over their heads like a swarm of angry hornets. Rounds ricocheted off the walls and ceiling, and a cacophony of deafening reports echoed through the narrow corridor.

Rosario Blancanales seemed to recover from the assault with the reaction of a seasoned pro. Even as Lyons watched with horrific realization, he knew he couldn't do anything to stop his crazy friend. It seemed like he watched Blancanales's finger curve around the trigger of the M-203, but he couldn't do a thing. His legs and arms seemed paralyzed and while his mind screamed out all of the possibilities such a drastic move might bring, he still couldn't seem to do anything but open his mouth and scream the first obscenity that came to his mind.

The plunk of the grenade leaving the launcher could be heard even above the report caused by ignition of the propellant charge. The grenade struck the wall just to the right of the terrorists. A terrific explosion followed as heat and smoke whooshed over the heads of Able Team. The corridor rocked with the blast, dust and gases expanding at a rate much faster than the narrow passageway could handle. The concussion alone burst the eardrums of the terrorists not directly exposed to the blast, which Lyons figured to only number about two. The rest of the group was decimated.

The only thing that didn't die in the hallway was the steady thrumming of the missile launcher and the cargo bay door. Lyons shook his head to clear it, then he and Blancanales helped Schwarz get to his feet, as he'd been the closest to the blast and the one most exposed to its effects. Lyons immediately noted with concern the watery blood leaking from his friend's right ear.

Schwarz noticed his friend looking at him and reached up his hand to come away with the sticky substance. Blancanales stepped over to him and quickly inspected his ear. After about a full minute, he slapped Schwarz on the back.

"Thought maybe you'd ruptured an eardrum," Pol said with a wry grin. "Does it hurt?"

Schwarz shook his head.

"Well, I'd suspect some trauma to the outer ear. I think the eardrum's still intact."

"Good," Lyons interjected. "And while I just hate to be the bearer of bad news, that missile's still intact, too. We need to stop this now."

The three men agreed and turned to start for the cargo hold, but at the last second they realized they wouldn't be able to safely pass through the smoke and flames left by Blancanales's handiwork.

"Well, can't get there that way," Lyons said.

"Now what?" Schwarz asked.

Blancanales's expression appeared to brighten and he patted the M-203. "Hey, if they're opening that top hatch, we could go back the way we came and access it from there. I can put that launch pad out of commission easily with one well-placed grenade."

"Uh-uh," Lyons snapped. "No way, no how. We can't risk exposing ourselves to the chemical loaded in that warhead. Not to mention the fact that the top deck of this freighter is probably crawling with terrorists. We'll have to find another way to the cargo hold."

"Let's go this way, then," Schwarz said, pointing in the opposite direction.

The men set off with Blancanales on point, Schwarz in the center and Lyons on rear guard. The numbers were ticking off, and it wouldn't be long before the missile was in position. Lyons had read up on the effects of the chemical they believed the terrorists were planning to use, and it scared the hell out of him. All three of them were carrying high-dose vials of atropine in their satchels, along with Nuclear, Biological and Chemical—NBC—masks. According to their medical experts, they had to be most concerned with a respiratory exposure since it would take an unusually large quantity of the chemical to be absorbed through the skin enough to prove fatal.

The warriors continued through the bowels of the freighter, keeping their weapons trained on the area ahead, Lyons checking for rear action periodically. Obviously the terrorists were preoccupied with the impending launch and too busy to be searching out Able Team.

With Schwarz guiding their movements, Blancanales led them down the corridors and they descended several flights of steps before eventually reaching the lowest deck. From that point they would enter the cargo area at its base and by that time they would probably have only a few minutes at most to put a stop to the launch. At some point during their trek the thrumming noise ceased. They pressed onward, more determined than ever to make sure the missile didn't get off the ship. As they neared the turn that would take them down the corridor and into the cargo bay, Blancanales halted and the three men took to a knee.

"We're only going to get one shot at this," Blancanales said. "How do you want to do it?"

Lyons considered it a moment, then said, "Gadgets will go for the controls to the pad. He's the one most likely to understand them. They'll probably be well guarded, so you and I are going to have to run interference. We'll go through the door first and clear out the hardforce." He looked at Schwarz. "That should give you enough room to get to the controls and do your magic. Questions?"

There were none.

"All right, boys," Lyons said. "Let's nut up and do it."

Lyons and Blancanales rounded the corner and trotted toward the hatchway. They could only hope it wasn't barred from the inside. Provided they'd created enough of a distraction for the terrorists, the Qibla gunners probably wouldn't have noticed the door being secure or not. All focus would now be on getting the missile launched, and nobody would have likely worried about one little detail like that.

Lyons reached forward and moved the circular hatch lock. It turned freely—their luck had held out. He put a quick spin on the door wheel, then yanked the release handle. The door swung inward, and on a three-count the two Able Team warriors went through the door, weapons held at the ready. Four surprised terrorists to their right were in no position to react to the battle-hardened speed and accuracy of the Able Team pair.

Lyons made a beeline for the left side, triggering his MP-5s on the run. The first series of 9 mm Parabellum rounds ripped holes in one terrorist's stomach and slammed him into a support beam. A second terrorist fell in a similar manner, coughing blood as the round perforated his trachea and lungs. The man dropped to his knees and fell face-first to the deck.

Blancanales took the other pair with a low, sustained burst from the M-16. The 5.56 mm rounds chopped the legs from under both terrorists, ripping out knees and thighs and shattering leg bones. As the sounds of fire died, Lyons heard movement to his right flank. He spun and went low but held off the triggers as he watched Schwarz emerge through the door and dispatch a terrorist with a short burst from his SIG 551. The terrorist had been hiding in the shadows and thought to sneak up on Lyons.

Schwarz tossed his friend a salute, then sprinted for the control panel on the other side of the launch pad. There were no more terrorists visible in the cargo bay, which didn't seem good to Lyons's way of thinking. The rest had been cleared out, with only a small force left behind to guard the missile from sabotage. Steam had already begun to spit from the base of the missile, pouring forth in pressurized bursts.

Schwarz joined his teammates a minute later. "I can't stop it!"

"What do you mean, you can't stop it?" Lyons asked, already knowing what the answer would be and wishing he was anywhere but here at the moment.

"They've locked me out of the system. They must have triggered it from a remote station."

"Or the bridge," Blancanales suggested.

It was better than nothing. "Come on, we'll try that!" Lyons said.

"I don't think it's going to matter now," Schwarz said, looking up at the bottom of the launch pad, which towered above their heads.

As if on cue, the corridor began to rumble and a thunderous noise began building in their ears. The missile was firing, which meant the Able Team trio had all of about ten seconds to get out of the way before the ignition incinerated them.

"We've got about ten seconds before this entire area is filled with superheated gases!" Schwarz said.

"Move!" Lyons ordered.

The three men rushed for the hatch they had come through, what they knew would be their only chance for survival. There was no safe spot anywhere in the chamber. Even if they weren't exposed directly to the accelerant they could sure as hell be scalded to death by the high-pressure carbon dioxide sprayed from high-pressure ports to cool the launch pad and bay.

As the three men dived through the hatch one behind the other, the corridor shook with a frightening force and the noise was deafening in the combined space. Lyons threw his good shoulder against the hatch, spun the wheel to seal it and threw the hatch for good measure.

Schwarz scrambled to his feet, and as he went into motion he warned his partners to get away from the door. He didn't have to tell Lyons twice. Even with the hatch sealed, the pressure was enough that it could still blow the door and turn it into a deadly missile with enough force to crush them. They continued sprinting until they were a safe distance. The three men threw themselves to the deck, sweat soaking their hair and blacksuits.

Schwarz and Blancanales panted with the exertion, but Lyons just sat with his back against the wall in stony silence. As all three of them exchanged glances, they could hear the missile lifting from the pad and the deafening noises in the sealed corridor began to dissipate. They didn't want to say it; nobody needed to say it. The terrorists had succeeded in launching the missile, and Able Team had proved ineffective in stopping them.

"We've got a failsafe," Schwarz finally said when he caught his breath.

Lyons looked at him tiredly. "Send the signal, Wizard."

Schwarz reached to his belt and retrieved a small black box with a hinged door. He snapped a small plastic lock from the box to break the seal, extended an antenna set into the top of it, opened the hinged door and pressed a single orange button inside. The little device was the brainchild of Huntington Wethers. At that moment it was designed to send a special frequency coded only to be receivable by the Stony Man satellite. That signal would then bounce to the Stony Man computers and initiate a sequence to alert Brognola that it was redphone time.

"It's done," Schwarz said, closing the antenna slowly and purposefully.

"Yeah," Lyons murmured. He couldn't help but feel disheartened. "I guess it's in the hands of the Air Force now."

"What's wrong with you, Carl?" Blancanales asked, immediately noticing his friend's demeanor.

Lyons stared blankly at him before replying, "I made a promise to Hal that we'd stop this thing. Now, because I couldn't do my job, a hell of a lot of Americans might die today, all because I failed."

"You didn't fail anything, my friend. If there was any failure, we all contributed to it. Our flyboys there in Florida are the best in the world. They'll put that missile down, you wait and see."

"Snap out of it, Ironman," Schwarz added. "We've got a freighter full of terrorists to stop."

A very hard and very dangerous expression crossed Lyons's face.

"Uh-oh," Blancanales said. "I've seen that look before and it's never good."

"Yeah," Schwarz replied quietly, watching their friend ramp up into berserker mode. "I totally agree with you."

"I don't know about you two, but I've had enough of these bastards," Lyons said so softly that his friends cocked their heads to hear what he was saying. "If a lot of innocent Americans die today, then there'll be an equal number of the enemy going down with them. So, yeah, Gadgets, you're right. We still have a boatload of terrorists to kill and I say we get to it."

With the snap of his wrists, Lyons brought the MP-5s into readiness. His teammates slowly got to their feet. They were instilled by the confidence and fury of their friend and they began to psyche themselves up in the same way. If the Qibla terrorists tried to take their lives, that was one thing; they had signed up for that possibility. But the thousands of Americans they threatened were just ordinary people who went about their ordinary ways. They hadn't done anything to anyone; they were just trying to make it in a hard, cold world.

"I'm with you," Blancanales said, slamming a fresh grenade into the M-203.

"Ditto," Schwarz added, jacking the slide on the SIG 551 following a magazine changeout.

Lyons whirled and went to the door. He touched it to insure it was cool, then spun the handle and opened the hatch. He walked purposefully across the launch pad, obscured by the smoke left in the wake of the missile's departure. He could hear the cheers of the terrorists on the deck above. They were about to pay dearly for that cheering. Lyons hoped they were enjoying themselves, having a good time and patting one another on the back, because he and his two friends were about to send them to hell.

Lyons reached a stairwell that stretched from the bottom of the cargo hold to the lip of the top deck. He took the stairs three at a time, his teammates close on his heels. The terrorists were still shouting and congratulating one another when the Able Team leader emerged from the smoke and steam. A dozen or so gunners stood directly in his path. Lyons raised the pair of machine pistols and squeezed the triggers, crossing his arms over one another as he laid down a barrage of murderous rage in the form of a 9 mm Parabellum hailstorm. Some of the terrorists turned in surprise while others simply dropped to the deck instantly, dead from the lead onslaught. One foolishly charged Lyons and took a swift kick to the groin followed by a controlled SMG burst to the head.

Blancanales and Schwarz emerged from the pit to take flanking positions. Schwarz leveled the Beretta at a group of five terrorists who had watched the missile launch. The SIG 551 spit a vicious fusillade of 5.56 mm NATO rounds, cutting through the bellies and arms of the terror-mongers before even those who were armed could bring their weapons to bear.

Blancanales began his offensive by flipping out the rangefinder sight of the M-203, acquiring the center window of the bridge as his target, and squeezing the trigger. The over-and-under kicked against his shoulder but he didn't appear to feel it. The HE round arced gracefully through the air and landed just below and to the right of the center window frame. The bridge exploded in a fiery orange display of expended RDX and TNT. He slammed home a second round, this one incendiary, and fired it through the gaping crater left in the front of the bridge tower by the first grenade. Screams of pain could be heard as the grenade exploded in a showery spray of bright white molten metal.

On a roll, Blancanales leveled the M-16 to take out two terrorists he spotted charging through the smoke, their rifles up and ready. He discharged the weapon on a full-auto burn and smoked both of them. One danced an odd pirouette before falling into the cargo hold, his body bouncing off the edge of the launch pad before continuing into the blackened abyss below. The other took at least half a dozen 5.56 mm rounds in the chest and was thrown against a railing. His heart exploded from the impact as the rounds turned the better part of his chest cavity into little more than a bloody pulp.

Lyons slung the two machine pistols, then rolled from where he stood in time to avoid being shot through the ribs by a terrorist charging him with an Uzi blazing on full auto. He came out of the roll while simultaneously drawing his .357 Magnum Colt Python from shoulder leather. Lyons drew a bead and squeezed the trigger twice. Both skull-busting slugs smashed through the terrorist's head, blowing it apart like a cantaloupe under the force of a sledgehammer.

A group of screaming fanatics charged their position from the far end of the ship, maybe a dozen with weapons blazing. The three men went prone, Lyons and Gadgets laying out a covering fire while Blancanales popped another round into the launcher. He triggered the M-203 and watched as it did its nasty work. The grenade struck the chest of one of the terrorists who was apparently leading the charge, and the aftereffects were devastating. The explosive force blew him apart, spontaneously separating all four of his appendages, while the blast sent shockwaves through those near his position. Eardrums broke, eyes popped from sockets and a number of the terrorists went down with their clothes on fire.

The few terrorists still alive were thrown to the deck. Lyons and Schwarz made short work of them, both delivering killshots that kept the gunners down permanently.

Silence. Smoke and steam continued to sweep across the deck and the smell of burned human flesh was in the air as small fires consumed the flesh and blood and bone of dead bodies. The Able Team trio waited nearly a full minute for further threats to appear, but none did. They were getting to their feet when a sound somewhere from behind and below them caused all to turn with freshly charged weapons ready for more. The buzz of an outboard engine defied them as it faded, and the trio watched as a boat raced in the direction of Cancun. Someone was escaping from the freighter, most likely the terrorist leader responsible for this atrocity and perhaps even for the launching of the missile.

"Uh-uh!" Lyons turned and sprinted for the motor launch they had left tied at the freighter aft. He called over his shoulder, "There's no way I'm letting anyone get away!"

And before either of his partners could offer any kind of sensible protest, Carl Lyons was diving over the aft railing of the freighter.

CHAPTER TWENTY-THREE

Bay of Biscay, North Atlantic

Rafael Encizo had undergone too many near-death experiences to say that he still saw his life flash before his eyes.

But the flashes he had expected to see milliseconds before the terrorist's bullets smashed through his mortal body never came...at least, not in the way he expected. Instead, the flashes of light he saw were sparks ricocheting off the iron edge of the freighter deck, then shooting upward to punch into the terrorist's form. The terrorist's body went into convulsions as chunks of flesh were ripped away from his torso. The dance ended with his head exploding a gory spray of blood and gray matter.

The roar of a chopper zipping past overhead filled Encizo's ears and the Cuban barely had time to catch a glimpse of the familiar symbol of the British flag before the chopper disappeared from view. He shook his head, not sure what had really happened but glad that it had, and continued to follow his teammates up the exterior ladder rungs set into the freighter's side.

By the time Encizo had reached the lip of the freighter, the battle had already been joined by his colleagues.

McCarter raised his MP-5 and cut a corkscrew burst through a nearby trio of terrorists apparently more intent on cutting him down than on planning for their own survival. Above the din of the hot zone came the unforgettable sound of the FN-FAL as Manning rocked the terrorists' world all along the deck of the freighter.

The Cuban was carrying the latest variant of the FN-FAL known as the FNC. It worked on the same design principles of the FN-FAL battle rifle, but was more compact and durable than its predecessor. It also came with a 3-round burst capacity and because of its size and compactness was occasionally misclassified by some experts as an SMG rather than an assault rifle.

Encizo knelt and helped his teammates clear the deck. He dispatched two hardmen immediately but was then distracted by a round buzzing near his ear. Encizo's eyes roamed across the deck but he didn't see the source of the shooting. He let his gaze move upward and found the targets: two terrorists firing from the catwalk encircling the bridge tower.

Encizo rotated the stock of the FNC into an open and locked position, then lifted the rifle to his shoulder. He aligned target number one in the tritium-painted iron sights and squeezed the trigger. The 5.56 mm NATO round punched through the terrorist's jaw and ripped away the better part of his lower face. His head snapped backward and the impact slammed him against the front of a bridge window.

Encizo swung the muzzle onto number two, took a deep breath and let half out before firing. The round had to have dropped, because it struck the stock of the weapon, then ricocheted and lodged in the gunner's shoulder. The terrorist dropped his rifle to the deck below as he stood and grabbed his shoulder, turning with his back exposed. Encizo triggered the weapon again and put a bullet through the center of the terror-ist's spine. The man stumbled back and tumbled over the railing, landing on the deck and coming to a stop within just inches of his weapon.

Encizo turned to Manning. He gestured in the gen-eral area of where the missile was being kept. "Go! We'll cover you!"

The big Canadian nodded, dropped another terrorist coming at him from the left, then burst from his spot and headed for the nearest hatchway that would lead him be-lowdecks.

As the little Cuban watched him go, the buzzing of chopper blades began to grow louder. Encizo turned and looked until he spotted the chopper. It was a Lynx MK 8, the same kind that had saved his hide less than a minute earlier, and it looked as if the pilot was about to make another pass. Encizo whirled to locate

McCarter and shouted a warning for him to get down, waving in the direction of the chopper.

The fox-faced Briton tossed him a salute before hitting the deck. Encizo joined him and pressed his face tightly against the cold iron plating. The terrorists thought their enemies were surrendering, and they were apparently oblivious to their surroundings. A number of them broke cover and rushed to take their prey, paying no heed that a chopper was bearing down on them. The results were disastrous as the 30 mm chain gun aboard the chopper sounded. Heavy-caliber rounds covered the deck like a plague of locusts and decimated every terrorist in the open and unlucky enough to come under the effective gunnery of Her Majesty's finest rotary wing pilots.

The surface of the deck turned into a wash of reds as terrorist after terrorist fell to the merciless onslaught. As the chopper ceased firing and buzzed by them, Encizo lifted his head in time to see McCarter deliver some kind of special salute. The pilot obviously recognized the gesture and it solidified his place as an ally and not a terrorist in their mind.

The deck was silent, almost as silent as a cemetery, as the chopper departed. Only the lapping of water against the sides of the freighter could be heard above the occasional moan of the dying terrorists. Encizo had never seen anything quite like it before, but he imagined in some ways it might have looked something like this on the decks of the Higgins Boats in the aftermath of the Normandy invasions.

McCarter quickly joined him. "Snap out of it, mate. We need to secure this ship, and quick. Head for the bridge, but wait for me to join you before assaulting it."

"Where are you going?" Encizo asked.

"Well, someone has to make sure Cal and T.J. don't get their bloody heads shot off when coming on board."

IT TOOK NO MORE THAN a few minutes for Manning to find a hatch that would get him to the lower decks. As he proceeded for his target he considered the fact that it didn't seem this boat had been populated by nearly as many terrorists as the other. Not that it mattered. The important thing was that he neutralize the missile, and he'd have to do it quickly.

A noise ahead caused Manning to go into a combat crouch. He kept the stock of the FN-FAL pressed to his shoulder as he inched forward. It had been a scraping sound, like the kind the sole of a boot makes when someone shifts their weight from one leg to the other. There it was again. Manning froze now, not certain of how to proceed. He double-checked his back, but the corridor remained clear. He had two choices. He could wait it out to see if whoever was up ahead exposed themselves, or he could charge like a madman and hope to take any potential enemy by surprise. After waiting another full minute, Manning decided to risk the latter option.

The Canadian came to full height and catfooted to the end of the corridor. After counting to himself, he turned the corner in high gear, the muzzle of the FN-FAL held at the ready. The corridor was empty. It terminated at a hatch-style doorway that was slightly ajar. A bright light spilled through the opening, a light much brighter than that produced by the recessed fixtures in the corridor.

Manning eased himself down the hallway, keeping his back pressed firmly against the smooth iron hull of the freighter. He knew there wasn't time for a diversion like this, but he didn't want to get shot in the back while wiring up the launch controls because he'd failed to clear his six. His mission with the monstrosity in the cargo hold could wait a little longer. Manning stopped at the end of the hallway and peered through the crack. He couldn't see anything from that position other than a metal table in about the center of the room. Manning moved the hatch aside a little more and leaned in farther....

Manning felt pressure suddenly applied to the harness strap of his LBE and was yanked forward. His weapon scraped against the frame of the hatch as his head smacked the heavy iron door. Stars danced in his eyes as the blow nearly knocked him unconscious, and his right eye stung as blood began to pour from a laceration left by the blow.

The Phoenix Force commando acted instinctively, grabbing the fist wrapped around his strap with his left hand and turning inward. He stepped backward and heard the satisfying grunt as he yanked his opponent into the door in much the same fashion as had been done to him. Manning had to consider the fact that his opponent had underestimated him, thinking that the first blow would have knocked him cold. Had it not been for his FN-FAL acting as somewhat of a stop jamb, it might have very well done the trick.

The hold released enough on Manning's LBE strap that he was able to break free, but he lost his balance in the process. The Canadian turned and scrambled farther into the corridor before getting to his feet to face his opponent. He barely got his eyes on the big, lumbering form that rushed him with a speed that certainly was incredible against the size of his opponent. Manning attempted to draw his .357 Desert Eagle, but he didn't quite get it pointed before the giant terrorist smacked it out of his hand with relative ease. Pain rocketed through nerves in Manning's wrist. The Phoenix Force veteran was definitely not dealing with a novice.

Manning stepped back a moment to size up his opponent, and for the first time he got a good look at him. The guy was huge, at least six foot six, with muscles that bulged beneath his tight black clothes. A goatee was the only facial hair, and a white-gray scar ran from his right eye down to his cheekbone, traveled across the prominence of his nose and terminated on his left check at a point just above his jawline. Dark, glaring eyes stared at Manning. The Canadian didn't see the slightest indicator that the eyes were human. Purely animal was the man's look, as though there wasn't a decent shred of humanity left in him. It was like fighting a horrific beast concocted from the imagination of some Greek playwright.

The man charged Manning, who sidestepped the attack and fired a punch to the man's jaw. The blow would have broken most men's jaws, but it only staggered this guy. He quickly recovered and reached down to wrap a meaty hand around Manning's throat. It was a simple maneuver, almost too simple to seem real, but it was effective in that it instantaneously cut off his air supply.

Manning fired a snap kick as his opponent lifted him off the ground, but the man turned sideways. He deflected the kick meant for his groin off his hip. The Phoenix Force commando reached to his belt just behind his left hip and curled his fingers around the Bowie hunting knife he carried with him. He brought the blade free of its sheath and snapped it open, then brought it around in an attempt to slash the hand choking him. The big man grabbed his wrist with his free hand as it came around and effectively neutralized the attack.

Manning was just about out of options. His right hand was pinned, he couldn't breathe and his left hand was occupied in trying to ease the pressure of the iron-like fist closed on his throat. In a few more moments his attacker would strangle him to death.

"Part of what makes a man want to go on living is his spirit," Katz had told the weary Phoenix Force warriors following a particularly grueling day of training. "Whenever you're in a situation and you think your life is about to end, you have to call on something more than brawn or brains. You have to call on the spirit and will to live. Look at it as a secret, as something your enemies don't know about. Don't abuse it. It may only come to serve you once in your life, maybe twice if you're lucky. Bolan's the only man I've ever met who can call it almost at will time and again. But it is there, and you can use it if you learn to harness it."

Manning realized in that moment that he didn't want to die, and that if he had wished to die it wouldn't be at the hands of this maniacal gorilla. No, there were many more days to come of fighting terrorism. Gary Manning was going to live, and he was going to live now!

In a last-ditch effort to save himself, Manning summoned the last of his strength and used his legs to push himself off the thighs of his opponent with enough force to get his back to the hull. He then dropped his left hand, pressed his palm flat against the wall and swung his right leg up and over his opponent's right arm. The terrorist's eyes went wide, puzzled by the Canadian's sudden and bizarre acrobatics, but Manning knew exactly what he was doing. There was no way that even a man of this size had arms stronger than those well-conditioned thighs built from years of mountain-climbing and hiking. He exerted downward pressure and quickly broke the grasp from his throat.

Manning sucked in a deep breath and used it to focus all his power into a low back-kick that smashed his opponent's groin. He then spun onto his backside and executed a leg sweep that knocked the terrorist from his feet and slammed him backward against the hull head-first. Before the terrorist could recover from the vicious reversal, Manning lunged forward and buried the Bowie knife he was somehow still clutching deep into the terrorist's throat. The terrorist let out a scream that died as a bubbling gurgle escaped from around the gaping wound left by the knife.

Manning stood, retrieved his pistol and pumped two rounds through the terrorist's chest. He turned and collected his FN-FAL, then continued toward the cargo hold.

DAVID MCCARTER AND RAFAEL Encizo stood on the bridge and exchanged victory signals when they heard the thumping of charges resound from the cargo hold below.

Gary Manning had completed the job.

McCarter kept the bridge crew at bay while Encizo began to power down the freighter's engines. From that observation point, the Cuban could see James and Hawkins now rounding up the stragglers. The terrorists had thought to put up a fight until they saw the British blockade of ships appear over the horizon on a direct course. A few shots from the heavy guns of one of the advance assault gunships were enough to make the terrorists reconsider their options. One of the destroyers also fired a series of shells from their 114 mm guns that blew massive holes in the aft portion of the ship where they were hiding, killing a number of terrorists.

When McCarter arrived and told them to surrender, his British accent evident, the terrorists figured he was SAS and decided to surrender. That was okay. He had no problem letting the terrorists think they were with the British Special Air Service, one of the most elite fighting teams in the world and Her Majesty's greatest option when a full military response wasn't in order.

McCarter noticed one of the terrorists staring at him, and the Briton had to take a long hard look before he realized he was staring into the eyes of Jabir al-Warraq.

"What's with you, al-Warraq? You have some kind of problem?" McCarter asked him.

"So, you know who I am," he said with a smile that under other circumstances McCarter would have sworn was almost pleasant. "How nice. That must also mean that you cannot believe you have ended this war between us. It is only beginning. Don't you see that? Why, even now, I think you didn't know that our freighter near the United States was able to successfully launch its missile."

McCarter laughed mockingly, not wanting to really believe him but yet somehow knowing deep down that the terrorist leader spoke the truth.

"Oh, yes, you know it's true," al-Warraq said. The man was trying to goad him. "I would say that within approximately ten minutes, there will be widespread death in the city called Dallas. Yes, I would think many people will die."

Manning appeared at the door to the bridge. "What's he talking about?"

"He's claiming that they got the missile off and it's headed toward the Yanks," McCarter said. "He says it's going to hit Dallas."

"I can't believe it," Manning replied. "Ironman wouldn't let that happen."

"Believe it," Encizo said, holding a headset to his ear. "I've just checked a secure channel and it's true. They've scrambled a response team."

CHAPTER TWENTY-FOUR

Gulf of Mexico

A pair of F-117 Stealth fighters cruised above the Gulf of Mexico at fourteen thousand feet.

One of the pilots, Major Janis Brest, considered his craft as he sped to intercept the missile headed toward Dallas. None of the radar systems in the immediate area would be able to track him unless especially equipped to do so. The external skin of the aircraft was predominantly made with aluminum, combined with a special boron-polymer fiber known as Fibaloy, and sheathed with tiles made from radar-absorbing material.

The entire craft was controlled by a central computer brain and digital flight system manufactured by Lear-Siegler. Brest had engaged his heads-up-display—HUD—in preparation for intercepting the missile. Manufactured by Honeywell, the HUD consisted of a Digital

Tactical Display with color CRTs and a full, three-dimensional mapping system.

Despite public opinion, the F-117 wasn't strictly confined to a bombing role, although that was its primary purpose. It was a versatile aircraft, and Brest considered he was one of the lucky few able to pilot such a fantastic aircraft. A low beeping sound alerted him that his target was approaching. He flipped two switches to engage the Sidewinder A-A-Ms. He would have preferred a better missile for this kind of mission, but there hadn't been time. That's why there were two of them. This mission had to be accomplished. The entire country was counting on them.

"Foxtrot Seven to Foxtrot Eight, I have the bogie's signal," came the voice of his wingman, Lieutenant Colonel Frank Maple. "You got the same over there?"

"That's a roger, Seven," Brest replied. "I mark it at a height of 16,700, point drop of 48 degrees, speed as 800 knots."

"That's an awfully sharp angle, Eight," Maple replied. The tone of his voice read his insecurity.

"I copy, Seven, and I agree," Brest said. "Are you sure the computer can target this baby?"

Maple chuckled. "See that bogie, she's in the can…"

"And if Kaiser can't hit her, nobody can!" Brest replied, finishing the old saying in reference to the Kaiser Electronics HUD system on board the F-117.

The two planes accelerated to an attack speed and approach vector that would give them the best opportunity.

The mechanical SPN/GEANS Inertial Navigation System provided a 4D view that ensured accuracy. The system would perform exactly as expected. Now all Brest had to do was to make sure he performed exactly as expected.

"Seven to Eight, engage targeting beacon."

Brest switched over from ready to armed, and then set the HUD to begin a long-distance tracking. Of course, it wasn't really all that far away. Because the Sidewinders were primarily designed for shooting down other planes by locking on an infrared heat signature, they would have to come considerably closer to the target than was normally required. Each one of the missiles was extremely accurate, but they didn't have the same size window to play with this time around.

Brest willed himself to relax. He'd just have to play it by ear and trust the computer would do the job.

"Foxtrot Seven to Foxtrot Eight, I've got tone," Maple said. "Target's locked and…it's away!"

There was silence and Brest kept close to his wingman, his HUD getting closer. They needed confirmation quick, otherwise he wouldn't get a second chance. They could only allot one missile each for the shot, since once the firing mechanism engaged, the pursuing aircraft would lose hold and need at least thirty seconds to reset it. That could mean the difference between the success and failure of the mission.

"Foxtrot Eight to Seven, what's the story?"

"It's a miss!" Maple said. "Lock on target and fire! Repeat, lock on target and fire!"

Brest moved his fighter into position, watching carefully to ensure that Maple pulled back and didn't get caught in his jet-wash. Sweat began to drip from his forehead but he resisted the urge to take one hand from the targeting HUD to wipe at it. The sweat band in the helmet would prevent it from rolling into his eyes. Brest took a deep breath and waited patiently for his signal. The HUD continued to beep, but it didn't seem as if he was ever going to find tone.

Beep…beep…beep…

"Come on, damn it," he whispered. "Just a little more…"

The flashing red light went solid orange, then changed to green.

"I've got tone," he said as he flipped up the firing switch on the trigger next to the throttle. He depressed the button and held the stick steady, fighting any urge to move his eye away from the targeting sight. "It's away," he cried.

The light remained green in his scope, locked solid then a moment later it winked out. Brest pulled his eye away from the targeting HUD and pulled up even as he saw the bright flash light up the night.

"Seven to Eight, you hit it! You hit it!"

Brest let out a sigh of relief. He had saved his country from his enemies and averted a terrorist disaster. There wouldn't be any medals given out for it. At least, nothing they could put in the official records. But as he turned his ship and headed for home, Brest wondered how many others had known about it. And he wondered how many others were out there right at that very moment, sacrificing their lives for the country.

CHAPTER TWENTY-FIVE

Cancun, Mexico

Carl Lyons managed to catch up to the motor launch as it docked at a small marina on the outskirts of the city.

The Able Team warrior felt odd having left his companions behind, but he couldn't worry about that now. This was between Lyons and whoever he was pursuing. Whoever had escaped the freighter was probably responsible for launching the missile, and quite possibly a high-ranking official in the Qibla terror group. Lyons couldn't be certain, but it was possible he was chasing Jabir al-Warraq or Mahmed Temez. If that was true, he would have been negligent not to pursue them.

As he neared the boat, Lyons saw the reflection of light on metal. He turned a sharp right and was nearly thrown from the boat. The maneuver saved his life as a single shot rang out. Somebody was lying prone in the motor launch and trying to gun him down. Obviously it wasn't a skilled sniper he was dealing with because whoever was shooting at him didn't know the first thing about the importance of cover and concealment, or of making sure to hit the target with the first shot.

Lyons started to move the boat away from the motor launch but then thought better of it. He had learned a long time ago that sometimes the most effective move against an enemy was the one they least expected. Lyons kicked the motor into high gear and rushed the motor launch. The sniper was startled, jumping to his knees and shooting at the raft in hopes of deflating it before his opponent could reach him.

The tactic didn't work because Lyons was just too close. Seconds before impact, the blond warrior bailed from the vessel and entered the water. The raft smacked into the motor launch, its bow catching on a sharp edge and deflating almost instantly. The outboard motor continued forward and the rubber raft acted as a slingshot, propelling the heavy engine out of the water. The majority of the weight was built into the top of the engine, which caused it to flip as it rocketed through the air, making the sharp exposed blades the head of the grisly missile.

The terrorist turned to attempt escape but he was too late. Lyons recovered from his jump into the water in time to see the propellers catch the terrorist in the back of the neck and nearly rip his head from his body. The corpse landed prone, half dangling from the motor launch as the engine continued forward, bounced once on the dock and continued over the other side and into the water, and sank to its final resting place.

Lyons swam to the motor launch, pulled himself on board and checked the interior for clues before quickly exiting to the dock area. He looked around and tried to pinpoint his quarry. The subject could have gone in one of three directions. Eliminating one of those as the boardwalk that led to the other boats in the marina left two choices. It wasn't much of a choice as he knew that the remaining routes both led into the heart of the port of Cancun.

Lyons was attempting to decide what his next move should be when a voice sounded behind him. "May I help you, sir?"

Lyons whirled and reached instinctively for his pistol, but he came up short when he saw the inquirer was only about five foot two with long dark hair and brilliant eyes. The cocoa-colored skin of the petite woman shone starkly against the noonday sun. The Able Team warrior wouldn't have guessed her to be a day over nineteen, if she was that. Lyons felt a little self-conscious about his appearance but quickly dismissed it as egocentric.

"Yes, I seem to be lost," he said, changing to a more congenial tone. "I was following my friends in that boat." He pointed to the wrecked launch and hoped she didn't take notice of its condition.

"I see your friends," she said. "I get them a taxi. Can I get you a taxi, too?"

Lyons scratched his head and tried to put on a show of looking like a hapless tourist.

"Well, I suppose, but I'm not sure how to get back to their hotel." He let out a laugh and said, "I think they were playing a trick on me."

The woman just stood and stared at him for the longest time, and Lyons wasn't sure if she was trying to convince herself he was telling the truth or explain what she had done in a former life that would have caused her to have to be exposed to so many stupid people now.

"I do not know, but you wait for Raul to come back and he tell you. You seem to be all wet." She laughed, and Lyons was a little taken aback by how she had just changed the subject so quickly.

"Yeah, I uh…um, I had a little accident. Fell out of the boat."

"Well, I have fresh clothes," she said. "Very cheap. Just down here. You follow me?"

Lyons gave it some thought, then shrugged and gestured for her to lead the way. He watched her backside appreciatively as she led him down to a building constructed with the traditional veranda-style architecture popular at one time in Mexico's history. Lyons followed her through the courtyard and into a small shop. He was surprised to discover the young and attractive woman was a dressmaker.

"You shocked by what you see," she observed.

"A little," Lyons said. "A seamstress. It seems like a funny thing to do out here."

Something bordering between hurt and anger flared in her eyes. "You think I'm funny?"

"No, I don't think you're funny. I said, I think it's funny that someone would need a seamstress in a marina."

"Everyone comes to Consuela," she said with a giggle. "Everyone needs clothes."

Lyons had to assume she was talking about herself, using her name in the third person like that.

"Listen," Lyons said, "I'd love to stick around and chat with you some more, but if you have those clothes ready, I really need to get them and get going. When will this friend of yours that drives the cab be back?"

"You are a policeman, no?" she asked in that deliberate yet innocent way.

"No," he said. "What makes you think that?"

"I saw what you do to that man on the boat," she said. "I saw him shoot gun at you."

"Well, actually he was shooting bullets," Lyons cracked with a grin, but he quickly changed the subject when he saw her blank expression and knew the humor had been lost on her. He cleared his throat to let the moment pass. "Listen, I just need to find my friends."

"Friends not shoot at each other," she said.

"Oh, yeah, well, my friends do," Lyons said. In this case, it was the literal truth.

"Those are bad men that leave here with my Raul."

"Who is this Raul? Is he your husband?"

She giggled at that, and Lyons thought he could see

a slight flush come to her face. "No, Raul is my brother. He is younger. I am oldest in my family." She said it as if there were some pride in that fact.

"How many brothers and sisters do you have?" Lyons asked.

"No other, just Raul," she answered. As she handed him a pair of white shorts and a silk shirt, she asked, "Are those bad men? Will they hurt my Raul?"

"Yes, they're bad men," he said, taking the clothes and nodding gratefully at her. "But I don't think they'll hurt him as long as he doesn't ask them any questions."

"Oh, Raul ask many questions," she said, her eyes widening with fear. "He is very friendly. All tourists like him."

"Well, let's hope he's not feeling so chatty today, for his sake."

"Who is this, Consuela?"

Lyons whirled, going for his pistol the second time in as many minutes. He saw a young man, definitely younger than Consuela, standing there with his hands in his pockets. His hair was combed back, and he had a wide, flat nose and bushy eyebrows. The eyes were dark, a sensual dark like Consuela's, but assuming this was Raul, that's where the family resemblance ended. Lyons relaxed a little and wished to hell people would stop sneaking up on him.

"Who are you?" he asked. "And what you doing with my sister?"

Lyons scowled. "I'm not doing anything with your sister. I'm just buying some clothes from her." He looked in her direction and asked, "How much do I owe you?"

"You keep those," she said. "Come back and buy more later when you clean." She held her nose and waved a hand in his direction.

Lyons didn't take offense. He probably did smell rank as hell. He focused his attention on Raul. "You took some men somewhere just now in your taxi?"

Raul nodded.

"How many," he said.

"There were two," Raul replied.

"Where did you take them?" Lyons asked.

At first Raul didn't answer, and Lyons was about to reach out and throttle him when he realized what the boy was really waiting for. Raul was obviously an opportunist of the highest order, and he saw he had something of value to Lyons. Any way to make a buck off some information was the name of the game around here, and Lyons could understand it. The economy in this area was solely supported by tourism, which the government took a good part of in taxes, to say nothing of additional undeclared sums for bribing public officials and police officers whenever it proved most convenient and expedient.

Lyons reached into his pocket and withdrew a handful of soaked cash. Raul stared at his open palm as if Lyons were handing him Monopoly money, then snatched the cash and counted it before giving the answer.

"They go to downtown," he said. "They were talking in strange language most of time."

Lyons nodded. Arabic.

"Take me to where you dropped them off." When Raul looked expectantly at him, Lyons added, "Listen, kid, you just took at least sixty bucks in American bills off me so I think you've been compensated."

"Okay, I take you," he said. "You want change clothes?"

"I'll change in the cab," Lyons said.

"Oh, no, he not change in cab!" Consuela jumped in. Lyons looked askance at her. She folded her arms and said much more demurely, "Car half mine."

Lyons sighed deeply and then said, "Dressing room?"

Consuela and Raul pointed simultaneously toward a room in the back.

As CARL LYONS EXITED THE cab on one of the main thoroughfares through downtown Cancun, he checked either side of the street. He didn't seem to be under observation and nobody appeared to be watching the door. In one respect, Consuela had done him a favor by offering a change of clothes. He would have stood out like a sore thumb dressed in the skintight blacksuit. Consuela had promised to burn the waterlogged uniform and, given her sensibilities, Lyons had no reason to disbelieve her. He tossed another twenty at Raul, shook the kid's hand and watched him drive away.

Raul had dropped the two terrorists at the Luna Verde

Hacienda, a twenty-story hotel in the downtown area. Without the kind of luck and cooperation he'd had up to this point, Lyons began to wonder if he would have ever caught up to them. Well, sometimes he just had to act on faith and go with his gut. This time it had paid off.

Lyons entered the hotel and gave the lobby a quick inspection. The Luna Verde was a busy place this time of year, especially considering it was the tourist season. Then again, Lyons couldn't think of when it wasn't tourist season in that part of Mexico. The party never really stopped, and people from all over the world visited year-round.

The Able Team leader located one of the public phones and quickly dialed a number he had memorized. There was dead silence on the air for maybe thirty seconds as the call was routed through a series of cutouts, then Aaron Kurtzman's voice sounded over the satellite-encoded connection.

"It's Ironman," Lyons said. He had never trusted the security of the line.

"Well, I am sure as hell glad to hear from you. The whole place is up in arms. We got it, pal. They got the missile!"

Lyons let off a sigh of relief. "I'm glad to hear it. Tell Hal I'm sorry."

"Sorry for what? You guys did a great job!"

"Yeah, well, I appreciate the vote of enthusiasm, Bear, but before we break out the party hats there's still a little unfinished business here."

"Hey, are you okay?" Kurtzman asked. "We got a message from Pol and Gadgets that—"

"Look, I'm sure you did, but never mind that right now," Lyons replied. "I've tracked two of our pals on the freighter to the Luna Verde Hacienda in Cancun. Gadgets said something to me earlier today that made me think that perhaps you can get into their system and check registrations."

"Okay, no sweat, but what are you looking for exactly?" Lyons could hear the clacking of keys already starting on Kurtzman's end. "Do you have a name?"

"No, I need all the names of anyone who checked in from fifteen to thirty minutes ago, but not sooner or later than that window." Lyons had it figured that that would keep the list to a minimum.

"Well, let's see…eh, okay, I'm into their system. Hell, it didn't even put up a fight. All right, uh, looks like mostly Mr. and Mrs. This, Mr. and Mrs. That. Wait! Found something, I think. Party of two checked in, both males, and the name of the guy who signed in was Zemet Dumham."

"Zemet Dumham," Lyons murmured, "is Mahmud Temez spelled backward. What room is he in?"

Kurtzman gave it to him, and said, "Oh, I've just been informed that I'm supposed to give you a message from Barb."

"What's that?"

"When you get done on this little personal vendetta, she wants you to get to the airport and meet up with

Gadgets and Pol. Charlie's ready to fly you guys back here on the double. I think deep down she misses you."

"Yeah, well you can tell her I said this is no vendetta," Lyons replied. "Just some unfinished business with the Qibla."

Lyons dropped the phone into the receiver and then took the elevator to the top floor. He stepped onto the twentieth floor and quickly located the room number Kurtzman had given him. He thought at first about knocking, pretending to be room service or a hotel attendant, but he reconsidered the risks involved. These weren't hoodlums of subaverage intelligence; they were hardened terrorists who had done more than their fair share of deceiving an enemy.

No, the best approach here was the direct approach.

Lyons drew the Colt Python from where he'd concealed it beneath his shirt, stepped back and drove the heel of one of his newly acquired tennis shoes against a point six inches below the lock. The flimsy door gave under the powerful kick and Lyons came through the doorway in a shoulder roll. The hotel suite was anything but, the only separate room being the bathroom. The main area had two double beds, positioned on opposite walls.

Lyons turned to see one of the terrorists sitting on the bed, a cigarette having just dropped from his open mouth. The television was blaring and the smell of cigarette smoke mixed with hashish filled the room. A glance told Lyons it wasn't Temez on the bed, which was too bad because his enemy actually went for a gun beneath his pillow.

Lyons never game him the chance. He aimed point-blank and squeezed the trigger once. The roar from the Colt Python was deafening in the small room. Blood sprayed onto the walls as the bullet went through the man's skull and blew his brains out. Lyons turned from the grisly scene and looked at the television, then toward the closed bathroom door. He stepped over to the body and lifted the remote control off the bedside table. He pressed the Mute button and listened carefully.

It was the sound of running water, a shower going, behind the bathroom door. Lyons marched to the door and stood to one side while turning the handle. It gave easily and the door opened.

The Able Team leader walked over to the shower, which was covered with a curtain, and ripped it aside. Temez was cowering against the wall, and his eyes widened with terror. Lyons grabbed a handful of the man's soaked hair and dragged him out of the shower. He shoved the muzzle of the Colt Python between Temez's shoulder blades, then led him out of the room and down the hallway to the sign that indicated the exit led to a fire escape. He pushed through the inner hallway door and through an outer door that emerged onto the fire-escape landing.

An alarm began to sound, and Lyons knew he had less than a minute before his presence would attract attention. Fortunately, what he had in mind wouldn't take that long.

"Did you do it?" Lyons demanded.

"What—who are you?"

"I'm asking the questions here, pal," Lyons growled. "Answer me. Did you do it?"

"Did I do what?"

"Did you launch the missile against my country?"

"Yes," he said. "It is for all of the missiles that you have launched against my country. It is for the egregious sins and atrocities you have committed against the Iraqi people. It is for the murder of my fellow soldiers."

"In case you haven't noticed," Lyons said, "there's only one murderer in this crowd."

"Yes, and it is you. You have killed my people with your poisonous, Western ways. You have killed the traditions of the Islamic faith. You have killed the very children that would one day carry on the honor and loyalty of the Iraqi people. It is you who are the murderer, and for your sins Allah will punish you. He will send you into the eternal damnation!"

"Then I guess I'll see you there," Lyons gritted before shoving the terrorist over the fire-escape railing.

Lyons had already turned away when Temez's body hit the pavement of the alley twenty stories below.